Advance P

Richard Cumyn has long demonstrated an uncanny ability to transform the familiar and ordinary into not just interesting, but fascinating stories. *This Lark of Stolen Time*, a novel of intertwining lives filled with humour, heartbreak, tragedy and triumph, shows once again that few writers are as adept at making compelling fiction out of the peculiar, maddening, messy particulars of family life.—IAN COLFORD, GUERNICA PRIZE-WINNING AUTHOR OF *THE CONFESSIONS OF JOSEPH BLANCHARD, EVIDENCE, PERFECT WORLD, AND A DARK HOUSE AND OTHER STORIES*

A collection of interconnected novellas just might be fiction's most generous form: so many entrances, so many ways to come *in* to the story. Cumyn wastes no time on neat and far-too-tidy character and narrative arcs. Instead, he dances with characters the way Pollock danced with paint, creating dreamy yet connected–deeply connected–novellas. Connections forged, flubbed, and missed in the characters' lives shine light on our own flaws, failures, and deep needs for love. —MICHELLE BUTLER HALLETT, AUTHOR OF *CONSTANT NOBODY*, WINNER OF THE THOMAS RADDALL AWARD FOR ATLANTIC FICTION, AND *THIS MARLOWE*.

This is sly storytelling at its best. Playing with time and structure, Richard Cumyn's head-hopping novel reads like cunningly connected stories that push the narrative towards a soaring epiphany. Each corresponding voice spreads its wings and brings the reader to the affecting reminder of stolen time.—LEE KVERN, AUTHOR OF *AFTERALL, THE MATTER OF SYLVIE, 7 WAYS TO SUNDAY*, AND THE UPCOMING *CATCH YOU ON THE FLIPSIDE*.

At the centre of this novel about love and belonging, Cumyn gives us a portrait of family and its familiar rhythms: dispersing and coming home again; together and then apart; in and out like breath. In prose that is warm and full of humour, *This Lark of Stolen Time* captures precisely the small moments of transformation that connect and help to define us.—RYAN TURNER, AUTHOR OF *HALF-SISTERS AND OTHER STORIES*

THIS LARK OF STOLEN TIME

This Lark *of* Stolen Time

Richard Cumyn

Enfield & Wizenty (an imprint of Great Plains Publications)
320 Rosedale Ave
Winnipeg, MB R3L 1L8
www.greatplains.mb.ca

Great Plains Publications gratefully acknowledges the financial support provided for its publishing program by the Government of Canada through the Canada Book Fund; the Canada Council for the Arts; the Province of Manitoba through the Book Publishing Tax Credit and the Book Publisher Marketing Assistance Program; and the Manitoba Arts Council.

Design & Typography by Relish New Brand Experience
Printed in Canada by Friesens

Library and Archives Canada Cataloguing in Publication

Title: This lark of stolen time / Richard Cumyn.
Names: Cumyn, Richard, 1957- author.
Identifiers: Canadiana 20240289862 | ISBN 9781773371177 (softcover)
Subjects: LCGFT: Novels.
Classification: LCC PS8555.U4894 T45 2024 | DDC C813/.54—dc23

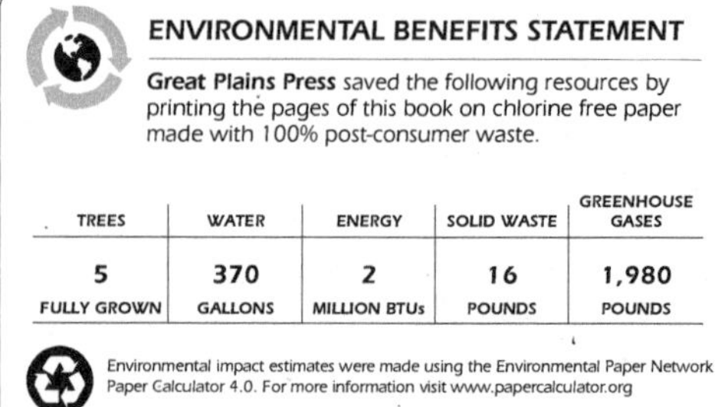

ENVIRONMENTAL BENEFITS STATEMENT

Great Plains Press saved the following resources by printing the pages of this book on chlorine free paper made with 100% post-consumer waste.

TREES	WATER	ENERGY	SOLID WASTE	GREENHOUSE GASES
5	370	2	16	1,980
FULLY GROWN	GALLONS	MILLION BTUs	POUNDS	POUNDS

Environmental impact estimates were made using the Environmental Paper Network Paper Calculator 4.0. For more information visit www.papercalculator.org

Canada

For Sophie and Hugh

Lauder Jones

A Full House

March of that year when they were all back home again was a month to try the patience of a rock. It was no snowier or colder than it had been the month before, but this—this was dispiriting. Freezing rain had painted the sidewalks lethal. The invisible parliament usually heard conspiring in the hawthorn hedge was silent, breathless. Nature brooded over her next move. Annapolis Valley apple growers cursed and prayed. The climate had divorced itself from normalcy. It was a time to turn inward, miserly, protective of one's own.

A convoy of snow ploughs and salt trucks roused the household before four in the morning. Coffee was freshly burred and brewed, cereal bowls charged with flakes of ancient grains and with low-fat milk. Those of the younger generation drifted back upstairs to bed, burrowing, cleaving to their still-warm pillows. Their parents remained seated at the kitchen table. It was after all not that much earlier than they were used to waking in answer to the demands of their ageing bodies.

Having the two eldest home again felt like a lark of stolen time. Children no longer, the four of them managed to avoid conflict while resuming the best traits of their past roles. They picked up after themselves, made their beds, washed and shelved cooking utensils, set and cleared the table at mealtime, and replenished the larder. No one had to be told to pitch in; they did so willingly according to talent and inclination. Merin, who loved the smell of lemon oil, was tall enough to dust the tops of bookshelves and cabinets. John rose from his lovesick funk long enough to vacuum rugs and carpets mid-morning on Saturday when everyone was usually elsewhere. In the evening, Cary placed garbage and recyclable material outside in their respective bins. And Anya, who loved fabric and knew at a glance how a garment should be handled and cleaned, had taken charge of the laundry.

They took turns cooking, having inherited their fearless, catholic relationship to food from their father. When they were small, he would introduce a new taste to their palates every week, his only requirement being that they try one bite. He respected their acute sensitivity enough not to make food a source of anxiety. If they showed interest, he handed them a wooden stirring spoon or a knife, showing them how to hone the latter and not lose a fingertip while chopping vegetables. He took them to the farmers' market, where the seasons finally made sense. They learned what was fresh and how or if to cook it. What they could expect from Swiss chard and kale. What to look for and what to question, in a garden as in the larger world. Their stomachs they treated well; their hearts would require further conditioning.

John was not yet talking about what had gone wrong. The woman, Danica, was nine years older than he was. They had met in his mother's lab while he was there on a summer NSERC grant between third and fourth years of his undergrad. His mother's principal investigator, Dani, as she was called, had inconclusive findings. Her post-doc and work visa would soon expire. She was legally separated from a man named Stanko, a shale-oil geologist working in North Dakota. A fracker, she told John. The word seemed tailormade for him. She had wanted him to shorten his name to Stan or change it to Stephen or Seve, like the Spanish golfer. She took his refusal to do so to be an indication of their incompatibility.

"When we got married, in the little town where we grew up," she said, "I thought we were perfectly suited for each other. I have thought about this a lot, John. When somebody doesn't change in the ways you wish he would, whose fault is it? Is it the problem of one person's selfishness or the other's unrealistic demands? He is a proud man. His Croatian pride—it was what I loved about him back home. Over there he was like every other man: assertive, loud, never wrong. He held his ground, as a man must do in our country. We were children during the war, but still, we knew things, we weren't blind. It was best to leave that place. But as soon as we came here my Stanko, he stood out like a dirty white car. He made me see that love follows no universal law. Your Novalja prince becomes a rough angry bully in Fort McMurray. I don't know what to think about this."

Not having experienced the altering effects of geography on an intimate relationship, John did not know what to think about it, either. Except to say that he could not imagine his love for Dani subverted by anything so arbitrary and external as a change of country. Unlike her husband, she had made a successful transition to North America, her accent now as recognizably Canadian as that of anyone born here. As soon as she found a mailing address for Stanko she was going to write again, she said, and demand he participate in divorce proceedings. After she had written him care of the exploration company he worked for, the letter came back marked undeliverable.

"What does your mother think of us together?" she asked John, feeling she knew the answer.

"She doesn't. All she cares about is her work."

"I'm not so sure about that," said Dani. "I have some experience with mothers and their firstborn sons."

Dani did not ask John if his father approved of her. It was as if she had already met Douglas Lauder Jones through his books. She could tell, from the first story she read of his, that he was a gentle, vulnerable man, an encourager, someone eternally hopeful though saddened by the brutality of modern life.

Douglas used to be able to manage both his writing and the quotidian needs of the household. He would descend from his garret, gauge the scope of the situation, keeping the greater domestic goals at the forefront of his mind, and delegate ancillary decisions to those he knew could make them. That was then. Now, a grapeshot's whiff of worthy prose, a third of a page, adequate not to make him sick to his stomach, was a day's victory. Housekeeping would have to be managed without him.

Before they boomeranged home from their first foray into adulthood, John from the one-bedroom he was sharing with Dani on South Street near the university and Merin from a bachelor apartment on the Danforth in Toronto, the house had been a silent, sometimes lonely place for Douglas Lauder Jones. The dog kept a respectful distance. Anya and Cary occupied the parallel universe that was their adolescence. On a good day Douglas might write until noon, after which would come lunch and the reward of a drink, replenished until weariness took hold, followed by sleep. His wife, Ursula, commanded her own fighting force, and when she was home she had neither the energy nor interest left for mundane matters. "The roof is leaking again? Douglas will handle it." "You say our two eldest are returned to this faulty shelter after having subsisted elsewhere?" Her only response was to ask after their well-being. She had the cures for Alzheimer's and Parkinson's to chase down. Gladly would she talk to any of her progeny about her work, so long as they kept up. It was her only rule. She refused to simplify it for them. She was allowed to be ignorant of their accomplishments, failures, and relationship changes. They, on the other hand, had grown up acutely aware of her all-important work. If her offspring were going to waste her time asking basic questions an elementary survey of the literature could answer, they would have to excuse her, she had only so many remaining heartbeats and so much yet to accomplish. "Talk to your father about what he does. You enjoy that. I know he appreciates the attention."

In the previous decade, Douglas Lauder Jones had published little of note. Although he had not yet, after years of promise and modest accomplishment, secured a publisher for his latest book, and had never earned anything that could remotely be called a living from what he wrote, he refused to complain about it, even when those who loved him did. It was all part of the given mix, the dealt hand, he would say, what they as a family and he as an artist had to work with, and for that reason it did not warrant a fuss.

AFTER THE COMPACTED RESIDUE of the past month's snowfall had been scraped off the streets and carted away, and within an hour of Merin saying she hoped this would be the last of it and that spring would finally poke its cowardly snout up out of its hiding place, heavy snow again filled the sky. She brewed a pot of strong black tea and, with it and some biscuits on a tray, climbed the stairs to the third storey, where her father's office sprawled under the attic's sloping walls. At the far end his desk looked out through a large semicircular window onto a spacious back yard. This was the one place in the world where he was content. Merin and John were old enough to remember a time before they lived in that house on Coburg near Robie. Anya and Cary had known no other home and tended to take its high, ornate ceilings and five spacious bedrooms for granted. Their father the esteemed author would have slept on the hard ground in a lean-to as long as he could climb the steep stairs to his typewriter and books each morning, shut the world away, play soft instrumental music, and continue the slow unwinding of existence on the page, life as it was revealed to him and as he felt it, observed close and from afar. His precious six hours.

Merin was a perceptive reader and a competent editor. She could stand far enough away from her father's writing to see that he was probably never going to garner a large audience for his short-story collections and novellas. She knew each of his ten thin books intimately and was the only one in the family who re-read them every year. Her mother once told her that Douglas Lauder Jones was a wonderful man with many admirable traits, but that his little books of esoteric fiction would subside into oblivion. He would have to look back on his life and face the fact of a largely futile effort.

Merin also knew that Ursula would deny ever having said such a thing. It was not forgetfulness so much as evidence of a mind so full of her work that the way her husband chose to spend his days afforded her only passing consideration. Once upon a time, perhaps, when they were married students living in squalor, with John still a baby, she might have criticized her husband for his impecunious vocation. Institutional and private daycare having been too expensive, he had been the one to stay home with the infant while Ursula completed her doctorate. He wrote the first of his published stories while seated at that kitchen table, the baby asleep nearby in a wheeled bassinet, the erratic sound of his Royal Aristocrat blending with traffic noises arising from three stories below on Spadina.

Merin loved the stories of her parents' early married life together when they had only each other for support. Ursula's family, in Kitchener, Ontario, showed little interest in her academic success and was too poor to supplement her various small bursaries and scholarships. Douglas came from old Toronto money. When he declared that he would rather be a writer than study business administration or the law, his father crimped the financial pipeline. Douglas had been too proud to compromise his convictions. What artist, he would write, relegates his passion to part-time or hobby status? None who hopes one day to garner approval from the defiant face framed in the mirror.

Merin listened for the sound of his manual Olympia, a heavy green office machine. Douglas had made noncommittal stabs at computer use over the years. One summer, after her junior year of high school, Merin transferred his first two collections of short stories to her laptop, the idea being that she would maintain all his writing in electronic form. A publisher who had expressed interest in bringing out the collected works backed out of the deal, for a combination of reasons that included an unsuccessful grant application and a readership survey indicating that interest in the gathered writing of Douglas Lauder Jones lay only slightly above the public's passion for worm composting. Nevertheless she continued, transcribing while sitting cross-legged on her bed, holding the book open with one hand and typing with the other.

Occasionally he would poke his head in her doorway to see how she was getting along. "Don't worry," he would say. "I don't have anything new to add to your labour." Sometimes he would suggest she stop altogether. "The enterprise is doomed. Let's pack it in while we're ahead. The day is calling us, my darling girl." Outside, in sunshine or gloom, it wouldn't matter, off they'd trundle. She couldn't see yet that he had all but given up. The tap of creativity yielded little but sputtering air. "Come away from that now," he would coax. "You are much too young and vital to be wasting your time on my dead words."

"They are no such thing, Dad. Stop saying that. Go away, please, and let me work."

He did pry her away for short periods. There were films to screen, noontime lectures at the university and library to attend, strolls along the water, lunches out. He liked one unpretentious diner on Argyle. Its large plate-glass window was crowded with tall pot-bound plants, which on cold or damp days left a film of condensation obscuring the pane. John was spending long days then working for a house painter. Anya and Cary were away at summer camp. Ursula was immersed in the chromosome-snipping mysteries of amyloid beta-peptide. It dawned on Merin before midsummer that she was less her father's amanuensis than a companion meant to distract him from his inability to write.

Secretly, although she adored him and was proud he was an author recognized by discerning readers, she did not love his writing. His stories all seemed too much alike in tone and situation, and they ended inconclusively. They were about unhappy people, usually unhappy lovers and married couples, good people tortured by their inability to extricate themselves from painful relationships. It made her sad to read stories in which children and young adults were largely absent, as if she and her siblings had made no impact on his imagination. Her sure-fire antidote that summer, the way she washed the dolorous grey of her father's fiction from her mind, was to sit by herself under a shady tree or in a corner of the public library and fall into the fantastic world of wizards and dragon slayers, where actions drew consequences, catastrophes were averted, villains ate the bitter fruit of defeat, and magic was irrefutable.

Douglas asked her if she was interested in writing stories of her own. "Not anymore," she said. "I used to. I wrote a whole novel when I was nine. It wasn't any good. At least that was Mother's assessment."

Where was it? He demanded she produce it. Why had he not been told that his daughter had accomplished such a momentous thing?

"I threw it away," she said. She didn't have the heart to remind him that he had in fact read the typescript, all sixty-eight, printed, triple-spaced pages in 16-point font. All he'd said when he handed it back to her was, "Keep going, don't stop." It was his most endearing and infuriating trait, his inability to criticize anything his children did. But it's finished, she remembered thinking at the time. Had he not read the words, "The End" printed on the last page? She thought she understood his psychology now. Only encourage. Handle young shoots delicately. Let them strengthen, root deeply and clad themselves in tougher bark. At the time, she thought he didn't care enough to tell her what he thought. In contrast, her mother the incisive analyst, directed her attention to the flaws, structural and stylistic, emotional and logical, marring Merin's story. The nine-year-old hears, "You are not clever enough. Give up trying," when the parent asks, innocently enough, "Would your character really be able to hold her breath that long under water?"

Yes. She's a superhero. Breathing under water is one of her powers. You didn't read very closely, did you, Mother? What if you approached your research with the same carelessness? Merin stowed this with all the other comeback zingers she had never voiced except to the panel of stuffed animals listening intently at the head of her bed.

She knocked but didn't wait for a response before opening the study door. The room ran the depth of the house, a long narrow space made narrower by the slope of the walls and by the bookshelves forming an alley leading to his desk. He was not at his typewriter but slumped, eyes closed, head thrown back, mouth agape, on a small, deep, brown-leather two-seater set perpendicular to the window. Whenever she went up there, she had the urge to roll a bowling ball down this central lane. Knock old Da off his pins.

She set his tea on a small low table close to him and shook him gently at the shoulder. Manuscript pages of a piece he had been working on for years, a story about the painter Gwen John, were strewn across the coffee table and on the floor. His breath smelled chemical: Listerine over Canadian Club. He snorted loudly but clung to unconsciousness. She stifled a giggle. Found in hiding: one Mr. Bennett in refuge from female hysteria and courtship mania. Except that romantic love and marriage were at that moment subjects few in the Lauder Jones household wished to discuss or contemplate. John moped, incurably it seemed, over Danica. Cary considered the institution of marriage, when he did give it a thought, all right for old people like his parents and pathetic older brother but antithetical to his self-image. Anya, on the other hand, loved every arcane tradition touching upon the ceremony. Marriage she hadn't much use for—but the dress! And cake decoration, bridesmaid gowns, grooms, flowers, tuxedoes, best men, food catering, the musical band, first dances, going-away outfits, the trousseau. The ever-loving honeymoon!

"Dad," said Merin.

"I'm awake," he sputtered, running a hand through thinning hair a month past needing a trim. "What did I miss?"

"Nothing," she said. "Douglas Lauder Jones misses nothing, even dead to the world." She regretted saying them as soon as the words were out of her mouth.

"I feel like a hibernating bear these days," he said. "I used to believe I couldn't live without true, white, frostbite-cold winter. I could slap my younger self for thinking such a thing, I truly could." He stood and turned to face the window. "I mean, look at it out there." They watched a miniature figure tramp a path, from the rear corner of the house next door through that property's back yard to a tiny trailer that sported an improbably high cap of snow on its roof.

"You just need to get out in it. Nothing's been cleared yet. We could ski all the way to the tip of Point Pleasant and back."

"Ski? I can hardly walk. Never get old, Merin. The indignities of age are demoralizing."

"Sixty-two is not old."

"It is when you feel ancient. It's this paralytic cold. Nobody clears their stretch of sidewalk anymore. Everything tenses up when you're trying not to slip and fall."

"Dad, we need to talk about John. I'm worried about him."

"Oh, he'll get over her. All he needs is time and privacy. The space wherein to mend his broken heart."

"I'm not so sure. He's talking about going with her."

He shook his head. Oh, that kid! Prodigy, master of anything he tried, from Rubik's Cube to chess to the French horn. Why, then, was he forever in need of rescue? If it had been anyone else they were talking about, Douglas would have set them straight with a few well-chosen words. With his firstborn it had always been trickier, partly because he knew John was smarter than he was and partly because he suspected that his son considered him a hollow monarch, someone to tolerate but not take seriously.

"Where? Not North Dakota."

"No, she wants to go home to wherever she's from and then they want to travel for a year. Do development work, something like that. Work on sheep farms, dig irrigation ditches."

"And that is a problem because…?"

"Dad! She doesn't love him. She only wants a travelling companion. She's treating him like crap, calling it off and saying goodbye one day, the next telling him she can't live without him. He hangs on to this stupid hope that everything will solidify, that they'll get married. It's incredible."

"Is it really so?" Where was that other bottle? He sat at his desk and pretended to look for something, a crucial piece of paper amid the controlled chaos there, rifling drawers. "Your mother and I had the deck stacked against us, too, at the beginning, and look how we turned out."

A defeated hermit and a workaholic who's never home, thought Merin. *Perfect. Sign me up.*

"That's just it," she said. "He wants to reproduce you and Mother."

"I repeat my earlier statement, not without a measure of discomfort at the suggestion that there should be anything wrong with his desire to do that."

"Because they are not you. Because John doesn't have a clue what he wants to do with his life, and you always did know. Because Dani is an arranger not a discoverer, and I think—no, I know—that John will ultimately be devastated when he figures that out about her."

He wanted to tell his daughter something reassuring, that her brother would be fine, that he had to live his life and make mistakes, otherwise he couldn't mature, but at that moment he remembered where he'd stashed a sample bottle of Singleton's single malt that he'd tucked into the toe of his Christmas stocking, and all he could think about was Merin leaving him alone so that he could get down on his hands and knees and reach up under the love seat to retrieve his *bouchée d'ambroisie*, his blessed relief, his key to the puzzle of how to keep on breathing.

ANYA HAD NOT SEEN THE MAN in the wheelchair in months, not since the beginning of winter. She worried about him. He fared poorly on the city's steeply sloped, icy sidewalks despite a sophisticated ability to Tom Sawyer people into doing what he wanted. Dabbling his often bedroom-slipper-clad feet along the ground in front of him, an ineffective gesture he nevertheless made whenever someone was pushing him, he looked like a helpless baby too large for its pram. This and speech incomprehensible to most ears made him a benign oddity. Those who knew what he was up to avoided him. Anya imagined him to be someone who had once walked unaided, been employed, perhaps owned a business, had a spouse, and expressed opinions now trapped and irretrievable.

When Anya did see him again, he was trying to enter Merin's theatre. Her big sister, the unlikely entrepreneur. Of all the dumb-luck things to fall into her lap, Merin, at the time a lowly editorial assistant working in Toronto, was bequeathed money in the low six figures, unexpectedly, from the estate of a woman whose papers she had helped compile. Merin had spent two weeks at the woman's house, sifting through boxes of correspondence, manuscripts, playbills from theatrical productions and publicity matter promoting her three books of poetry and dozens of other authors she had helped publish. The woman had been about as welcoming as a riled badger. Anya thought her sister was not telling all there was to know about that time and its consequence. Merin must have done something to win the old heiress's heart. A hundred large and change! She quit her job, moved back home, and used the money to buy a small, struggling, two-screen movie house on the second floor of an office building on Barrington that had been home to many different businesses over the years.

Wheelchair Man had a chin growth like something you would see on a Billy goat, and indeed, she thought, he did look like a pent-up farm beast preparing to take a run at an obstacle in his path. Merin had a small elevator on order. In the meantime, Anya's stair-challenged friend had no way of getting from the street-level entrance up to the screening rooms and he was not happy about it.

A couple well past retirement age looked on, the man suggesting that with enough hands they might carry the chair-bound man up the stairs as though he were riding in a litter. The concerned citizen convinced three others to join him, none of them looking younger than eighty. It was the day seniors got in for half price. A heartier, more robust group might have pulled it off.

Merin hurried down the wide staircase and refunded Anya's friend the price of admission—a do-gooder had purchased a ticket for him—and promised that in no later than one month's time he would have reliable access to her establishment. That she was contravening health-and-safety and accessibility by-laws by not having an elevator did not appear to bother those in attendance. The seniors who frequented Merin's cheap-Tuesday screenings still called the handicapped "shut-ins" and "gimps" and those few young adults waiting to see the next film would rather not have had to look at or think about the poor compromised creature stranded at the bottom of the stairs.

Anya had already seen the movie. Girls she knew were saving a seat for her. She told Merin they were her friends, when really they were a venomous klatch of snobs she had met when they were students at Tower Road School and whom she had hoped to impress by playing up her sister's new venture. They came out into the lobby to buy popcorn and soft drinks, saw Anya, and drew her back into their gravitational field. When Merin stepped out from behind the counter to say hello, they were all sickeningly polite. Anya studied them, four girls whose approval she thought was the most important approbation in the world to her, as silently they evaluated Merin, her oddball fashion sense, her clunky boots, her nerdy good humour. Anya, who loved her sister with fierce loyalty, would have gone for the throat of anyone daring to speak ill of Merin Lauder Jones, but sometimes being in public with her was like being seen riding a donkey when everyone else was astride a thoroughbred.

Looking behind her and down the stairs, seeing him still there, his chair pointed missile-like at the unscalable flight, his upturned face baffled and accusatory, Anya knew she had her means of escape, however temporary and yet permanently damaging to her status, from the demeaning quartet who so complicated her life. She would leave Merin to her business. Was her sister oblivious or merely guarded? If the latter, Anya thought, grant me that ability.

Merin became preoccupied with ticket and refreshment sales. Anya told the Fearsome Foursome she would meet them back inside—she wouldn't be a minute. The concerned council of oldsters had by now abandoned Wheelchair Man to make their own slow ascent into the theatre proper. Merin went down to him again, briefly during a lull. Sorry, she said, there was nothing she could do. In a month's time. Promise.

"I offered him a freebie. I'm not sure he understood," she said. She seemed to be addressing the emptying space more than she was talking to her younger sister.

Oh, he understands plenty, thought Anya.

She couldn't tell if he was angry or not. The squeaks and hisses he made were louder than usual. She had gathered, the few times she had pushed him along the sidewalk, that he did not hear well and that over time this had compromised his ability to make himself understood. Anya liked to think she had developed an ear for his speech. She had always been in love with the idea of learning a new language or at least trying to master it. Where another might have shied away from conversing in Italian with a Tyrolean shepherd, for example, Anya was fearless, reaching into her limited sack of words and phrases, pronunciation be damned, and by a combination of spoken word, exaggerated gesture, and assistance from her phone, she could make herself understood. More or less.

She was thinking of her grade-eleven class trip to Europe. The Fabulously False Four looked glumly bored out the open windows of the chartered bus, which had chosen than moment, in the middle of the most beautiful and remote countryside in the region, to stop running. It was the result of an overwrought engine or radiator, some such greasy clanking thing. How she ended up outside conversing with the shepherd had more to do with her proximity to the front of the bus than with her ability to speak the language. The driver, a Sikh gentleman who spoke German and English, busied himself with what was wrong under the steaming hood of his vehicle, fussing with a rag and a long thin piece of flat metal that he kept inserting into and drawing out of a hole in the engine. This coolly angry man, who was apparently above all this, had not been born to chauffeur the spoiled spawn of *Amreeka* all over Austria, and yet here he was.

The tour's co-chaperone, Ms. Matthews, spoke no more Italian than did Anya. "I took five years of Latin," she offered weakly. Her colleague, Mr. Friedrich, should have been on the bus that day, but he had eaten something that was keeping him confined in acute discomfort to his bed at the hotel. Not that he—math and phys ed—would have been much help communicating with the pleasant rustic who drove his flock ahead of him down the narrow road. The bus appeared to be floating in a pungent sea of wool.

"Anya, you look like you could be from here," someone said. "Go out there and talk to the sheep guy. See if he knows anything about auto mechanics."

Sometimes no finer logic emerges from the mind of a sixteen-year-old. One's apparent ability to pass for a native must by extension include fluency in the language. For what Tyrolean in his right mind would be seen dead talking to somebody who didn't look like him?

MOBILE-MAN-IN-CHAIR lived in an assisted-living facility north of Quinpool. The few times Anya had pushed him home she brought him up the ramp and into the lobby but no farther than that. As they passed through the lobby this time, a large woman who spoke with a Trinidadian accent greeted them from behind the office window. She called him Mr. Saint-Amp, as if acknowledging a resident dignitary in a Michelin-starred hotel. Anya lingered to watch him dabble his way over to the elevator, the woman all the while continuing her play-by-play like a reporter witnessing the arrival of royalty. He pushed the Up button conveniently located low enough that those unable to stand could reach it.

What was his story? Anya wanted to ride with him, make him a cup of tea in his room, discover all there was to know about what had brought him here. She didn't know yet, for example, that his name was not Saint-Amp but Stamp, and that he was gradually but steadily losing control over his muscles. If he was at all sad about the diminishment of his powers, the circle of ability tightening around him, he did not express it in any way that she could discern. He foot-wheeled into the elevator car without looking her way. It wasn't that she needed to be thanked or even acknowledged. To hear something personal from him might have made a bridge, assuring her that she was not merely a convenient servant interchangeable with anyone else who happened to come along to rescue him. How wonderful it would be to hear him say, "Get your grubby hands off me!" or "How I'd love to get my grubby hands on you, pretty Anya of the sultry dark eyes" or "The Dow soared 300 points today and I made a killing. Let's do lunch, just us two! On me!"

WHEN ANYA GOT HOME from delivering Mr. Stamp to his residence, Danica was there in the living room, talking in low but intense tones with John. This was what falling in love did to you. Anya vowed never to let such a stupid thing happen to her. Her big brother, whom she had grown up idolizing, the boy who could do most anything effortlessly, now moped about like a psychiatric out-patient. Perhaps more than anything, more than Merin's risky foray into the business of showing movies on the big screen at a time when people were more apt to stay home to watch, more than Cary's aloofness after having been her closest sibling her entire life, more than her mother's preoccupation with her life's work or her father's immersion in drink and creative paralysis, seeing John so at sea frightened her.

He was sitting in the armchair they all considered their father's, a deep, dark brown, leather-upholstered piece they loved curling up in, into the folds and corners of which they would press their snouts, inhaling the faintly musky, animal scent. John was perched on the seat's forward edge and leaning out over his knees towards his beloved. Anya hated her in that instant because she looked so much more vital than it seemed John would ever be again, and more attractive. Dani's boots were discarded at the door. They were tall, tight-fitting, black-leather, sharply pointed at the toe, with lethal-looking heels. To Anya they looked like some sleek beast's sloughed hide. Danica sat at the farthest end of the loveseat away from John, the two pieces of matching furniture set at right angles to each other. She wore a dark-blue camisole and tight black jeans with a wide belt and ornate silver buckle, her overcoat filling the space beside her. John's beseeching posture seemed to be pushing her into the corner of the little sofa. On the surface she looked poised, her legs crossed at the knees, one hand on the armrest, the other opening and closing gently, unconsciously, on the nap of her wool coat. *Yes,* Anya thought, *it's still there, the way out. Your exit can be swift. Why not do us all a favour and go away now? You're making my brother miserable. He looks terrible beside you. Go back to your husband, go back to the fracking war zone, where you belong.*

"You remember my little sister. Anya, Dani."

She hated the way he had jumped up when she came into the room, the thoughtless, automatic show of manners. Her arrival had saved them from something unsaid or recently said, in either case a source of awkwardness. She recoiled at the falseness of his pretence, as if this were merely a social call. Nobody made social calls anymore. You arranged to meet in public. Somebody picked someone else up. This, this hunched tête-à-tête—no, it wasn't anything as intimate as that. This, she could see, was not a meeting of equals. The love object and the spurned, disconsolate lover. He looked awful: days unshaven, hair unwashed, clothes rumpled and stained. By agreeing to come to his parents' house with him she was being either thoughtlessly insensitive or intentionally cruel. How was it that Anya could see how pathetic this was when John could not? Danica certainly could. *Look at her*, she thought, *the picture of smugness posing as compassion*. She was relishing a younger man's fawning attention. What was he thinking? That when she saw what a gracious, stable home the Lauder Joneses kept she would melt into his arms? *Wait a minute*, she could imagine the object of his ardour thinking, *aren't you all back living under the same roof? Who are you, the fucking Waltons?* What would she be getting herself into? Or maybe she would think it quaint. Or maybe it would remind her of her own home and native land.

ANYA'S PLAN AFTER HIGH SCHOOL was to attend art college in Toronto. Her interest in painting had begun in that city, in her Aunt Marie's kitchen, with watercolours, pastels, oils, acrylics; on good paper, on board, on canvas. What in life is more absorbing, more seriously pressing, than unnumbered childhood hours immersed in rapt expression?

Marie taught her the rudiments of tint, line, form and shadow. Perspective. Balance. Representation melting into abstraction. Anya took to saying, "When I am a famous artist," and no one dared contradict her. "When I am a famous artist, I will buy Aunt Marie a mink coat and a trip to Italy," she vowed, having understood at such a young age, eight years old at most, that her father's sister, like Douglas, was not a beneficiary of the family wealth. To Anya, poverty was merely the temporary absence of certain tangibles that restored happiness. It was like losing a cherished piece of jewellery, marshalling a search team, finding the lost object, and rejoicing for a while, but not for too long a time lest one annoy the jealous gods who alternate between protective love and petulant mischief in their guardianship. She didn't know yet that, for some, poverty could be a life sentence.

Every year or two, usually near summer's end, Douglas would announce that he had to fly to Toronto "to see people." From the first time she begged to accompany him it was assumed, if she was free to do so and the family could afford the expense, that Anya would be his travelling companion. He would check into the Park Hyatt and meet editors, publishers and other writers and poets during the day. Meanwhile Anya stayed at Aunt Marie's small apartment on Carlton Street, where she slept on the fold-out bed, and in the daylight painted, feeling that this was something expansive and adult she alone did.

Marie insisted on mounting and framing much of what her niece created, covering the walls with the artwork. If it was a Saturday morning, they rode the streetcar to the St. Lawrence Market and on Sunday the Bloor Line subway west to High Park. They ate grown-up lunches at little cafes only Marie knew about, visited the ROM and all the galleries, Marie providing expert commentary on everything they studied. It seemed, when Anya thought back on it, that she had spent every free weekend of her childhood there. So can a handful of extraordinarily happy days, spread across the span of a year or two, become definitive, casting the mould of one's character and plotting a life's trajectory, their memory incomparable should one ever be able to relive them.

Anya was accepted to begin her studies at OCAD University in September. Meanwhile it was July, and she still didn't have a summer job.

"There is always work for good people," her mother pronounced, insisting that Anya repeat the sentence until she could state it convincingly. Ursula was not so adamantly strident in her belief in rugged self-determination that she failed to feel sympathy for her daughter. If Anya had shown any interest in science, Ursula might have found her something to do in the lab. It was rebellion, she supposed, not necessarily a bad thing, Nature fostering diversity. If everybody did the same thing, think of all the unfilled holes. But did her youngest daughter's choice have to be such an impractical, chancy pursuit? Ursula thought that had she been more present while they were growing up, she might have steered her children towards interests of greater consequence and leading to the betterment of life. In theory that was what she had done with John, who, being the eldest, did everything he could to win her approval. She didn't ask him if he wanted to be a scientist; it was understood that he did. It was there in his childhood fascination with the natural world, its components examined close-up, the universe in microcosm. Hunkering in short pants, he brought shed skins and vacated beach-shells to his squinting eye, trapped livid wasps under glass. All through school he took home prizes in math and chemistry. Surely this was evidence of a natural talent and not one hammered on the anvil of formal inculcation.

"You like to see yourself reflected in him," Douglas would chide. "Can you separate your pride in his success from the boy's own needs?"

"Needs? He needs to learn; he needs to achieve. He's still too young to know what he wants. There is nothing wrong with a firm push from our end. Less cheerleading, more direction, that's what he needs from us."

Like many who enjoy remarkable and remarkably effortless academic success early in life, John was less certain at twenty-six of what he wanted than he had been at thirteen, despite knowing so much more about so many things. He could say one thing for sure, however, and that was that he no longer wanted to be a scientist.

THAT THEIR FATHER had not ventured up to his office on the third floor in days bothered the Lauder Jones children less than did his newfound interest in their lives. Such transparency was not the paternalistic approach he normally took, the veiled advice, the caution dressed as anecdote. It might begin, "I was reading in *The Guardian* the other day," and they would be alerted to the imminent arrival of a Pertinent Fact, one impinging, at least in his mind, on their current affairs. John's early-morning runs, for example, taken before anyone else in the household had arisen for the day, might be overly taxing on the young man's heart, given that one's coronary arteries are stiffer than usual so soon after waking. Douglas would never say this directly to his son, of course, but take a tangential approach, introducing the subject by way of an apparently unrelated memory.

"You know, I've often wondered about the circumstances surrounding your grandfather's death. Mother said he died while shaving. He suffered a heart attack and cracked his skull against the edge of the toilet bowl. Now I know for a fact, John, that my father, if he were going to shave his face at all that day, never did so before midmorning and always at the office or his club. He was a late-day warrior, often working until well after your Aunt Marie and I had gone to bed for the night. So, my question is this: What was he doing shaving his face at home and hours earlier than he was used to doing, and did that change in his routine somehow contribute to his demise?"

"I'm careful to warm up before I run, Dad,"

"That's very good, son. Excellent. Of course, I have no worry when it comes to you, my boy, none whatsoever," and he began his long climb to his aerie and his halting pursuit of literary expression, his step having gained a barely perceptible, youthful bounce.

Lately his incidental association with his offspring had taken on the scrutiny of an investigative journalist. He was remaining in their midst longer, not always speaking but listening with apparent concentration while he pretended to read the newspaper, as if immersed in a culture and language he was learning for the first time. Merin was the first to suspect that he was harvesting their conversations and experiences for use in his writing. She didn't share her perception right away, even after Cary came right out to ask, "What's with Dad lately?"

"He's enjoying our company," Merin replied. "He's allowed to do that. It has been a while since we've all been together like this, after all."

"Yes, but it's creepy. He hardly says anything. Do you think he's all right? It's not early onset, is it? Can he, like, tell time using an analog clock sort of thing?"

They looked at John, who was staring at his phone, willing it to buzz. "How should I know?" he said. "I study protein strands."

Studied. He had not been to the lab in weeks. He didn't know what it was he did anymore. The woman he loved was leaving, he could not say where, possibly home to Croatia, possibly to North Dakota to find her husband and either patch their tattered marriage or tell him she wanted out. John was under the naïve impression that the latter of these possibilities was the one she leaned towards, and that Eastern Europeans were more open to the painless dissolution of their intimate affairs than were North Americans. He assumed these were people who made monumental changes in their lives as casually as they might stub out a cigarette. He should have known that the opposite was true, especially in the past few days, the hours of empanelled talk, the endless circuits through alternatives to her leaving, his pleading, which, ever since she had decided to travel on her own, became in retrospect pathetic and intensely embarrassing, to both of which effects he was oblivious at the time. They resolved nothing. She could not promise him a thing except to say that she loved him and had no right to expect him to wait for her.

"I don't understand why we can't do this together. What about the plan? What about Africa?"

"We could meet there," she said unconvincingly.

He vowed to spend the rest of his life waiting for her. He would find her, they would be together again, and he would never let her out of his sight. She was his Rosaline; defiantly he dared any Juliet distract him from his exquisite anguish. He told her that he would harden his heart against any other woman. That he should have chosen that image, at a time when his father was warning him about the dangers of early-morning exertion, red-meat consumption, and unrelieved stress, was a spot of irony that at any other time he would have acknowledged with enjoyment.

During that brief period of reunion, the Lauder Jones children were never together at the house more than an hour or two on any given day. When they woke and came downstairs for breakfast, their mother had usually left for work or might be on her way out the door, waving adieu while instructing someone on the phone. Ursula was pleased to have all her chickens home to roost. A stranger looking in on the scene would have been mistaken thinking that she was fleeing her brood. She had time-sensitive work to attend to. This apparent coolness towards her children was not new in her but merely the philosophy she had believed in from the beginning. You gave birth to them, you made sure their vaccinations were up to date, you paid attention to their nascent interests, bents, and talents, making them aware of these if they weren't already so, but you avoided smothering them with praise, and tried above all to instill in them the drive and stamina to work hard at something and stay with it even when it became difficult. You shooed them outside to play, told them at what time they should return, and trained them to avoid evident danger. Otherwise, they were on their own. Fuelled, independent, happy.

That being the theory.

It did bother her to see her eldest neglecting a promising research career, and all because of a girl. If Ursula could be said to have a spongy spot of indulgence in the rigour of her parenting philosophy, it resided in the person of her eldest. Her other children had thriven on neglect, she saw that now. Perhaps she had pushed John too hard towards her own field of study. Perhaps she was that stereotype, the mother in love with her firstborn son. The rest of them had not felt the same compulsion to excel and thus to please their mother, and so had done well enough at whatever toil or intrigue disturbed the moment to please themselves, apparently all the happier for it. John, on the other hand, had been an anxious child, prone to depressive bouts from before adolescence, a brooder, a boy she once found practising his smile in a hallway mirror.

"I can't get it to look right," he complained. "Whenever we take pictures, my face looks weird."

She knew enough not to agree with him, though what he suspected about himself was true: he could become almost paralyzed in self-consciousness. She had a hidden corner of her mind devoted to memories of John from when he didn't know he was being observed. They were usually times when he was engrossed in a book or game, his face relaxed, beautiful for it, his hair hanging down over his eyes.

The day he appeared in her office doorway, his was not the look of serenity she had so lovingly archived. She knew at once that he had spent some time working on his smile. He should have been using the time to accomplish something worthwhile, she thought. He should have been writing his sections of the paper they were submitting for publication, for example, the one in which he was going to be primary author. Danica, to her credit, had made sure her usable findings were in order, comprehensible, and in John's possession before she left. Ursula had liked that about the young woman. It was the trait that had led her to Dani in the first place. She had interviewed smarter, more accomplished postdocs. It hadn't been flash she was after but doggedness, a primary investigator who could maintain scrupulous records, allowing nothing to slip, every measurement, every observation replicable. Now she was gone. Ursula swivelled in her chair to look up at her son and thought, *But apparently not forgotten.*

"Before you say anything, Siddhartha has all my results on SNCA transgenes and he's up to speed on everything still in progress, including the norepinephrine trial. I have every confidence in him."

"You should. I trained him. Why does hearing this make me less than assured, John?"

"I'm taking some time."

"How much time?"

"I'm not sure. It feels like it could be all the time. The rest of my life?"

"Danica is gone. Try to forget her. I know it doesn't feel like it now, but believe me, you're going to recover."

"If it were only that," he began, breaking off and gazing down at one corner of the room, which was unruly with texts and thick binders and an obsolete hard-drive and terminal he had been unable to persuade her to abandon.

"You don't want to do this type of research anymore. Well sure, gosh, who can blame you? It's the world's largest haystack and smallest needle. Every time we think we've found something it morphs into something different. Stable funding would be nice. So much is pitted against our success. John, believe me, I understand completely. Me, I'm immersed in it, this infuriatingly large yet elusive cloud. I've come to define myself by it. But you, you're still young. You have everything ahead of you. Someone of your ability..."

"Mother."

"Hush, let me finish. I only want to say, I only want to let you know how proud I've been of you. I don't imagine it's been a picnic working for your tyrannical mother. You need to find your own problems to solve. And you will, of course you will. I should have kicked you out of here long ago, made you find your own way."

"That's not it. I don't think I want to do science anymore."

"Nonsense! Of course you do. You're ABD. Once you submit and defend, you will officially be a neuroscientist. One does not stop being a neuroscientist."

"I do. Am going to."

"What are you saying? I won't allow it. You're talking about throwing away your education, all that specialized knowledge. Have you been talking to Douglas about this? I suppose he put you up to it. Of course he would encourage you in this."

"No, I haven't told Dad. Or anyone else, for that matter. I don't see this the way you do. I don't consider it a loss. I believe nothing we do and learn is ever lost."

"Oh, you do, do you? Nothing ever gets lost? What a delightful notion. I'll be sure to tell that to the next Alzheimer's patients I see.

Not that it will do any good, because they won't know what the hell I'm referring to. You know, having lost their minds and all!"

A young woman in a white lab coat appeared in the doorway. Ursula barked at her, "What?"

"I'm sorry, Ursula, I can come back later."

"It's all right. What is it, Wei?"

"So, Dani has this note in the supplies folder, something about alpha-syn E46K no longer being available because the company that we get it from doesn't make it any longer. We're pretty close to running out of it completely."

"Define 'pretty close.'"

"Our last two vials."

It was suddenly as though John were no longer sitting on his mother's utilitarian couch that was taken up for the most part by bankers' boxes stacked four high at one end, file folders at capacity and held closed with large, brittle, elastic bands, and spiralbound reports, some of which had slid onto the bare tile floor. He knew not to move a crumb, location being essential to retrieval.

Ursula peered at her screen, the new P.I., Chen Wei, looking on at her shoulder. It appeared that no other pharmaceutical company they dealt with supplied the substance, crucial to many of their experiments. Science was a single-minded, voracious animal. It consumed whatever and whomever it needed. In an instant Ursula had changed, from someone expressing shock over her son's decision to alter the direction of his life, into a detective, her natural mode, bent on solving a logistical problem threatening to derail her work. The sacrosanct research. If she was concerned about her son in that moment, she was keeping it to herself.

John stood, said goodbye, and quietly walked out. His mother, if she did reply, did so out of earshot.

Civic Improvement

Soon after Irma and Dick arrived at Mountcastle Framing to ready the shop, a woman, sporty in cross-trainers and all-weather jacket hanging mid-thigh over black tights, burst in, mid-utterance.

"…and in no uncertain terms. You have to stand firm. These people must be scaring half your business away, Richard."

"Five-eighths, actually," he said. "Pleasure to see you so early on a Monday, Laurel. We're not officially open for another thirty."

"If you weren't open, you wouldn't have left your door unlocked, now would you," she said, her tone a maddening concoction of flirtatiousness and pretension. Laurel Gaudry was married to the QE's chief of cardiology, a superb surgeon. It was the first thing she told newcomers about herself. The second was that however proud she was of her husband, she was not going to sit at home waiting for the great man to show his face. The third usually entailed a lengthy description of her service as a member of city council, long enough ago that most could no longer remember what her impact had been on municipal affairs, although in her mind it was recent enough that her tenure as an elected official continued to show, like a tropical tan or a chic suit from Paris. Now it seemed her raison d'être was the unflagging surveillance of the port city's downtown core, the preservation of its economic health her guardian philosophy.

"I keep telling those homeless folk they have no right to live and be so vital and free," said Dick. "Really, don't they realize that their very existence makes a mockery of everything you and I hold dear, dear?"

"You, Mr. Smarty Pants Vance, can keep your marvellous sense of humour to yourself and provide me with a quote."

"Very well. How's about a little Pope? 'Nor public flame, nor private, dares to shine; / Nor human spark is left, nor glimpse divine!'"

"Ha-ha-ha. I mean, excuse me for watching out for your bottom line. If Lionel is going to allow obstacles to commerce to establish themselves on his very doorstep, who am I to criticize?"

"No one's ever referred to my trousers as fancy before," said Dick, whose wardrobe tended towards work-clothing styles for men of generous girth. "I do believe I'm flattered." He smoothed the front of his flannel shirt, the hem of which hung like an awning over his belt, and looked down to see if the cuffs of his trousers were presentable. "Donnalee won't be at all pleased, but it's so much better to be truthful about these things, don't you agree, Mrs. Gaudry?"

She rolled her eyes at him as she might a child in her care, one for whom there was little hope of rehabilitation. She was after all a woman who understood what was funny in this life and what wasn't. Such silliness as Dick Vance displayed only distracted a serious person from her life's purpose, and the precocious, fractious pets he had spent a first career in the classroom encouraging only grew into problem adults, as far as she was concerned. They lacked motivation, led unhealthily alternative lifestyles, abused their bodies with chemicals, became the chronic cases her saintly husband inevitably had to try to cure, and, perhaps the most unforgivable sin, they had no respect for money.

With a sigh she let her head flop chin-to-chest and shook out the tension in her neck, shoulders, arms, and fingers. The restorative tremor gradually took over the rest of her trim, fit body, driving all negativity from her corporeal shrine. Raising her head, she smiled inwardly, aware of the impression her great strength and resilience must have been making on the late-career store clerk, for Mr. Vance was three decades too old to be doing this sort of menial work. It was criminal. Why did Lionel Mountcastle not do the responsible thing and replace him with an attractive, bright, peppy, high-school senior, someone like her son Bradford, who was already smart enough to keep his inside thoughts where they belonged. Pity sake, it was a disgrace. The only redeeming truth to Vance's employment here was that he was no longer turning young, vulnerable, malleable minds towards his deviant notions. His shop mate, Irma Zlotsky, was no better.

"My Rahim, as you know, is a frightening talent with a camera. We are going to have to build another room in the house just for his trophies and plaques. You must wonder, as I do, where he finds the time and zeal to pursue his vocation, after the gruelling long hours he spends in the operating theatre. And that does not include his teaching, speaking engagements and radio spot Saturday morning, I'm sure you've caught it, I mean who with half a brain would pass up the chance to hear a physician of Rahim's stature impart free medical advice?"

"Not I," said Dick, from behind the counter, where he placed cardboard corners gently on a newly framed painting. He cut a large piece of brown paper with which to wrap it. "Not knowingly."

"Some mornings I lie in bed long after he has left for rounds. I'm telling you, unable to move, it overwhelms me so, Dick, to think how lucky I am to be married to this paragon, this... *Übermensch*. Who, bringing me to the point of my preamble, is turning the big five-oh this year, in just over a month, as a matter of fact, watch this space for announcements, invitations, et cetera, et cetera. Well. It occurs to me that his photography—his oeuvre—deserves a proper showing. Enlargement, enhancement, blocking, framing, and hanging. In a real gallery," she said, turning her head to pan the walls of the little shop and sniffing dismissively. "Where we all get dressed to within a hair's breadth of our lives, sip Champagne, and drift from still to still, gushing over the finest renderings from the eye of my celebrated..."

"Shutterbug?" offered Vance, winking at Irma, who had been working in the back room and who normally was able to ignore conversation emanating from the front of the shop. Laurel Gaudry made for an irresistible spectacle, on this slow, cool morning when all Irma wanted to think about was her sunroom at the back of the house, a cozy afghan, a mug of strong coffee, the novel she was reading, and the achievement of a state of perfect suspension, like chimney smoke standing motionless against the coldest bluest sky.

"I was going to use a different word, but you would only wrap your sick mind around it and ruin the sense," complained the Missus Doctor Gaudry. "My husband's visual discernment is without peer, is the point I am labouring to make."

Irma stifled a snicker. Any woman who spoke so worshipfully about her man was compensating for something, Irma bet, something she could not admit to herself or others. Still, as Laurel burbled on, peppering Dick with questions and instructions about the process and cost of preparing her husband's photographs for public viewing, Irma though about her Desh. Was it disloyal of her not to consider him a paragon of male virtue, as Laurel Gaudry did her illustrious spouse? It bent the nail the wrong way to draw such unabashed attention, nobody's business but theirs really, to what two people were to each other in private.

Desh was more demonstrative with affection than she was. Eight years her junior, a teacher, composer and musician who had had some of his songs recorded by well-known artists, he was liable to plan surprise attacks involving flowers, cakes and, once, a memorized speech instead of his usual song. Irma loved him, could not love any man more, but for her these were just short of excruciating. That one time of "The Speech," his dramatic tribute to her in daMaurizio with two other couples, Desh had downed two gin-and-tonics at the bar while they waited for their table, and having finally been seated, their orders taken, stomachs beginning to protest, bread baskets emptied, he stood on his chair, from which he delivered an encomium to Irma that even her best students, the ones she had predicted would go on to a career on the stage or in film, could not have matched. Not once did he stumble, forget a word, or step out of character. Irma squirmed, praying for it to be over. She could not hear what he was saying anymore, because of the pounding in her ears. Everybody in the restaurant was looking at them. Strangers called out encouragement, applauding before he had finished. She didn't want him to stop, not because she was enjoying the attention but because she was afraid of what might be expected of her after the performance was over. Once home she told him never to do that to her again. Then she made him repeat the speech.

"I almost stood up and kissed you to make you stop. Does that make any sense?"

"Yes," he said, unbuttoning her blouse, "it does."

He could have, should have, been an actor. Dick agreed with her. So many years ago, when Desh had been their student at St. Pat's, Dick had tried to "get through" to the kid, who at the time was failing math and science and was borderline in everything else except for music. All he wanted to do was hang out in the band room playing keyboard and jamming with whomever else had a free period. Desh took art with Mr. Vance and drama with Ms. Zlotsky, continuing in neither subject after that one year in tenth grade. Music was all he needed to fulfill the fine-arts credit requirement.

The next year, Irma switched to Guidance, and that was when she really got to know Desh Patel, not that he was especially troubled or a troublemaker. Music was all he wanted to practise and study, to the neglect of his other courses. The principal and vice principal got to a point with him where they couldn't do anything. Detention and brief periods of suspension had no curative effect and so they referred the boy to Irma. Big mistake. Sixteen-year-old boy with long black hair all in his eyes. Pretty, almond-coloured eyes when he showed them. And Irma, twenty-four, fresh out of teacher's college, brainy and talented but too shy to act professionally or teach drama particularly well, and unaware of how attractive she was. Back then she didn't have the time to stop and look around, let alone look in the mirror. She carried a theory of education around in her head and it was going to address all the deficiencies in schooling. It was going to turn the entire enterprise on its head so that learners took control of the experience, coming away owners of their education and not mere survivors of it. Well, she would tell people, you can imagine what kind of trouble ensues when theory collides with hormone-laced reality.

AS USUAL, Dick and Irma were there to greet him, having opened the shop an hour before his arrival. Dick Vance and Irma Zlotsky, friends and colleagues from their teaching days—someone had used the term "work spouse" to characterize their relationship—were even better picture framers than Lionel Mountcastle was. Lionel spent most of his time now drumming up new business, meeting his banker, his accountant, and his art scout slash agent, as well as hosting a variety of charity events. People were known to walk into his narrow store on Spring Garden and within the first minute of being there forget the reason why they had come in. Mountcastle might have a stunning new landscape painter on prominent display. Or he could very well have laid out one of his popular silent auctions to benefit art classes for homeless teens like the young man and his dog who were sitting on the steps leading to the store's entrance, just up off the sidewalk, when Lionel arrived. He looked kindly on them, these nonconformists set on leading authentic lives in a hard world that valued only wealth and fleeting pleasure.

What made this day different was that he had woken up seriously thinking about selling the business. Nothing untoward had happened to precipitate the decision. He wasn't being pushed out. It was more a feeling that the time was right for a change. After thirty years of building the business from something begun in his garage to one to which people travelled a great distance, to benefit from his expert sense of colour, composition, and textural balance, it was probably time to quit while he was still making money. The attraction, to continue a year or two longer while revenue was still relatively high—no one could accuse him of bowing out a wealthy man—remained like a gambler's roll of good luck, a streak, but he knew it couldn't last forever. A disruption was coming, new sewage pipes for the downtown core. Customers would stay away until after the work was completed. His wasn't an enterprise people thought of as essential, not like groceries or medicine. They would shelve their picture framing until everything else was back to normal. And then? Higher property taxes and rents to pay for the roadwork and drains. Get out while you still have a shirt on your back, Lionel, he could hear his father telling him. Know when to walk away, as the gambling song says.

Laurel Gaudry, one of Lionel's oldest and dearest friends, had Dick and Irma by the lapels, he could see looking in from out on the sidewalk. The woman needed a vocation—development work in Botswana, car counting for Transportation and Infrastructure, Brownie-pack leader—instead of talking all day to shopkeepers, distracting them from their business. He loved her, but some days she was hard to like. To delay his entrance, Lionel chatted a moment with the boy panhandling near the door.

"Okay if I pet him?" he asked, admiringly, about the white and grey Siberian that lay beside the young man where he sat cross-legged with his money bowl and cardboard sign. The dog had the spookiest ice-blue eyes. Lionel wanted to keep looking deep into them even though he knew that to do so was to risk spooking the animal.

"Go ahead," said the youth, "but let him smell the back of your hand first."

Lionel squatted gingerly, keeping his paper cup of coffee well clear, and allowed the animal to make up his own mind about the store owner, who thought he detected a glance from dog to boy: *Is it safe?*

"He likes people," said the kid. "More than I do. I aspire to his simple acceptance of all things. He's teaching me more than I could ever teach him."

When Lionel offered to fetch the boy a coffee, he said, "Food is the more pressing need right now, sir," and so Mountcastle went to the coffee shop three doors away, returning a few minutes later with a toasted bagel with cream cheese and a box of doughnut holes, both of which the boy shared with his dog, whose name was Zephyr.

Lionel handed over a bottle of orange juice.

"How long you plan to be in town?"

"Rest of my life, probably. I live here." He said his name was Zachary. He'd grown up in the South End, gone to school there, and was in fact still registered as a student at Citadel High. "I do this because people need to see the poor amongst them."

"Are you poor? You don't look it."

"I can still be their representative. Life isn't always what it appears to be."

"That's an interesting way to put it," said Mountcastle. He gave Zephyr a deep dig of his fingers all along the dog's back. He whined for more when Lionel stood to go inside the shop. The door opened and Laurel emerged.

"Don't go away," he said to Zachary. "Hi Laurel, nice to see you. Did you find everything you needed?"

"I did indeed, sir," she said, stepping wide around Zephyr, almost onto the street. "Your staff provided me with particularly valuable service, Lionel. I am planning a project, something—how should I put it? Something monumental. Ta-ta, must run," she tittered as she walked backwards, "but I'll come back when you and I can have a proper conflab about it. In the minutest detail. Promise!"

ANYA DIDN'T GET TO MEET the owner, Mr. Mountcastle, until she had worked in the shop for almost a week. Mr. Vance—"Please, call me Dick," he'd insisted, "I'd just as soon bury my classroom incarnation for good!"—had been the one to hire her. He was a nice man, not at all like a teacher or what she imagined a boss would be like, and for the first two days she assumed that he was the owner. She liked Irma, too, Ms. Zlotsky, who spent most of her time in the back room—and liked her even more when Dick was around. They spoke in a kind of shorthand and bickered affectionately in a way she had never experienced before. Her parents checked in with each other periodically, less so now that Merin and John were back living at home. It was as though Douglas and Ursula Lauder Jones were workplace colleagues and this couple, Dick-and-Irma, Irma-and-Dick, had taken vows of love and loyalty in some long-forgotten past and had merged into a single entity. Which, she learned, was not exactly the case: each was married to someone else, people they referred to during the workday and talked with on the phone. Once, Dick's wife Donalee came by to deliver his lunch. Anya was often too busy learning where everything was kept in the shop or dealing with customers to pay close attention to the dynamic between Ms. Zlotsky and Mr. Vance, but it made an impression on her. Somewhere in the back of her mind she tucked a few salient details pertaining to Irma-and-Dick.

Before long she figured out why she had been hired. It wasn't that they were overwhelmed with work. Two people could easily have handled everything there was to do. Her interest in art had certainly made her an attractive prospect when she showed up one morning, résumé in hand. As for the bulk of the work, anyone with adequate dexterity and a pleasant demeanour could do it. It helped that she knew something about tone, texture, proportion, and balance when helping customers choose pieces to hang on their walls or frames and mattes for their prints. The real reason why Anya had been hired for the summer was to give Irma and Dick a reprieve from the regulars who considered Mountcastle Framing their second home. It didn't bother these customers that Lionel was rarely there. They knew that Mr. Mountcastle was not always the best one to attend to their needs. Usually, Anya learned, those needs had little to do with the actual commerce that went on in the shop and everything to do with tolerance. Mountcastle Framing was somewhere they could go, Venti latte in hand, and feel if not welcomed unconditionally then tolerated above a minimum grade. It was a gallery, after all, and if the pieces displayed on the walls did not change more regularly than once or twice a month, depending on sales, these habitués of the visual aesthetic were not ones to be told they couldn't gaze at the same painting more than once. Mrs. Gaudry, wife of the hospital's chief of surgery, was the only customer Anya had difficulty pleasing. The woman came in daily as soon as the shop opened its doors, with a new grievance, not only against the store, which apparently in her mind existed solely to fulfil the demands of her latest crusade, but against the downtown business association, the city, the province, and whatever unfair power complicated her life.

On her fourth day of work, Anya found herself directly in the line of fire. That is, she should have been helping Mrs. Gaudry, not that Laurel needed help from a mere child. Being a conscientious person, Anya wanted to be seen to be doing her duty to its utmost, a desire complicated by this customer's lack of candour: Laurel wanted attention and, if necessary, affirmation, but what she wanted more than anything else that day was to bring the regular functioning of the store to a standstill. It was evident that the woman could not abide the commonplace. Anya was uncommon only in so far as she was not someone Laurel recognized; one glance affirmed her suspicion that the girl had lost her way trying to find the lip-gloss and glitter store at the Mic Mac Mall. The situation became sticky when Anya presumed that, being frontline, she should intercept this visitor and attend to her needs.

"You'll have to excuse me," insisted Laurel. She directed her statement not to Anya but in a loud arc lobbed over Anya's shoulder towards the back of the room, where Mrs. Dr. Gaudry knew that Dick and Irma and possibly Lionel Mountcastle himself were hiding. At the same time, she moved to squeeze past Anya through a narrow defile between the young woman and the poster racks ranged along the wall.

"Whatever you're looking for, I'm sure I can help you find it," said Anya brightly, innocently.

"I'm certain you could not. I don't remember seeing you at my Rahim's show."

At a loss as to the identity of Rahim and the nature of his show, Anya tried to redirect. "Please let me know if there's anything you can't find."

"There is nothing I could not find in this store, dear. My concern is that you don't seem to know your way around."

"Well, I am still learning. I haven't been working here all that long."

"That is supremely evident."

Anya sighed something under her breath.

"I beg your pardon?"

"I didn't…that wasn't," Anya stammered.

"Wasn't meant to be heard? You're going to have to learn how to whisper your slurs a whole lot softer, missy."

"I'm so sorry. Please forget you heard anything. Go about your…."

"Go about my what? My business? That's hard to do now, don't you think? You're going to have to tell me."

"I'd rather not," said Anya, her voice cracking.

"Let me make it easy for you. Either you tell me what you said or I report you to your employer. A moment's discomfort or your inevitable dismissal. Are you a gambler at heart?"

"What if it wasn't about you?"

"I find that hard to believe."

Anya had meant to hold her tongue. She had met people like Laurel though never anyone this tenaciously disagreeable. What she intended to say was that the utterance made under her breath had been just this: "I wish I was painting right now." She wished she were home or at Aunt Marie's, with no one making demands of her, no distraction, no external thought, nothing that could be expressed in words, nothing but colour, light, depth, stillness, and energy. Had she been confident in her ability to do so convincingly, Anya might have communicated that notion to this woman. Less than a year ago she would have been so flustered that nothing she tried to say would have done any good. Those few crucial months had given her some armour. She couldn't put it down to a defining event. She hadn't even gone away to school yet. It was simply a feeling of clarity about herself, what she believed so far and what she knew to be her ability. It was like the difference between the way her mind worked when she was fourteen and now.

Back then, studying her schoolwork had been a mystery composed of hours of concentration on the material but done in a state of blurred faith. That is, if she stared at something long enough, all its pertinence would somehow enter through her eyes and pores as if through cosmic absorption, arranging itself in the proper compartments of her brain. Now, she refused to move a step further in the process of learning something new until she could say that she truly understood what it was about. If she couldn't ask herself the right questions about recombinant molecules or Planck's Constant or the conditions leading to the outbreak of World War One and answer them in a meaningful way—meaningful to her, that is—she kept working until she could.

She remembered one of her teachers saying that the difference between a child and an adult is that an adult will suppress a desire for no better reason than that it should be deemed right, and that this rightness might have nothing to do with the person exercising self-abnegation. It was not an axiom: some children are able to resist temptation even if they perceive no consequential benefit, and many adults live entire lives unable to suppress their urges. But when she played her encounter with Laurel Gaudry over in her mind later that day, she understood that her decision not to tell the woman the particulars of her whispered utterance had nothing to do with suppression—establishing truth in this instance would have given her little satisfaction in light of what she perceived to be Mrs. Gaudry's gargantuan ego—and everything to do with hitting back. This childishness surprised her, more so after the fact than in the moment, because she saw herself to be if not a mature then a kind person. Aggression in others usually made her feel ill; in herself it was unprecedented. For this reason, she was repulsed and fascinated, in equal and alternating waves, at what she said in reply to the woman's challenge: "You're right, it was about you. I said to myself, 'My God, please don't let me turn into this much of a royal pain in the ass.'"

BEFORE HE LEFT TO GO OUT WEST, John woke most mornings unable to recall his dreams except as extraordinary sensations, memory without detail. He thought of it as having been captive of an experience unlike any in his waking hours, though hardly seeming at all odd while it unfolded. One day, after weeks of inertia and depression, he woke himself shouting. He thought it had been, "Put your back into it! Sleep when you're dead!" repeated, each time at greater volume. When he asked about it, no one in the house could remember having heard it. That didn't matter, he decided, because he knew what it meant: he needed to go away and do something intensely physical for an extended period. It had to be a considerable distance from home, somewhere he was unknown and where nobody cared about neuroscience, or at least not with the unquestioning fervour he was used to. He needed once more to leave home, despite the comfort it had given him these past few months to be surrounded by his family again. You can go home again, he saw, but only for short stretches.

John had a friend from his undergrad years, Samuel Chu, whose father was a bureaucrat in the federal department that oversaw the operation of the coast guard. After a chance encounter and during their ensuing conversation over a beer, John revealed his status: former researcher no longer enamoured of science and unsure what it was he wanted to do with his life. "I'm truly at sea," he confessed, unconscious of the significance of the phrase to his immediate future.

"There's your answer," said his friend, with a wink. "Shove off for distant shores. A time-honoured option for those who yearn to escape their troubles."

Having never been out of sight of land while on a boat, John predicted that he would become seasick aboard a real ship. He based this on his memory of throwing up in the car while on the ferry to Prince Edward Island. It had been doubly embarrassing because he was the eldest and because Merin, seated beside him at the time, had kept her lunch in her stomach, where it belonged.

"You might be okay."

"You're talking like I'm shipping out tomorrow," said John.

Chu made it seem as though all John had to do was say the word and an interview would be speedily arranged. "A formality," he added. The Canadian Coast Guard happened to need deckhands that summer, aboard its supply ships servicing the waters off the coast of British Columbia.

Sam took out his phone. "I'm texting Dad right now. He loves ships, spent most of his working life on board them as an engineer. You should hear him go on about the old days. He'd trade his desk for that time again in a heartbeat. I'm telling you he would absolutely love to set you up. Confidentially, I think one of his greatest disappointments was that I never signed on as crew. It would be like a fulfillment, John, a father's romantic dream of watching his son follow in his footsteps. In a way you'd be getting me off the hook!"

"I do like the idea of doing something adventurous," John admitted.

DOUGLAS MADE A RARE APPEARANCE in the doorway of his son's room while John was packing to leave. The room looked as though no one had occupied it during the six months of his stay. The same posters covered the walls, the same plaques and trophies were displayed on shelves, and those were the same curtains that had been on the windows since the boy was in the seventh grade. It had an unsettling, time altering sense to it, as though the intervening years had never happened. *John is leaving,* he thought. *John is always leaving*. The anomaly had been this capsule of time, these precious months of his and his siblings' reoccupation of the familial abode. It made Douglas think of those slide shows people put together to commemorate birthdays, weddings, and retirement parties. It took coordination, people coming together to find and pool photographs, home movies, anecdotes, memorabilia, and the like. This was what the presence of his adult children again resident in the house felt like. It was as though they had planned just such an elaborate presentation, made the event happen in fitting tribute and then stayed on to continue the performance. Now the living sound-and-light show was ending. Anya would be moving to Toronto in a few weeks. Merin had mentioned getting an apartment with the young man she was involved with, Aubrey, the shy one with the lumberjack beard. Before long Cary would follow them. In a way, it would have been easier had John and Merin not moved back home after Christmas. Easier to loosen the heart strings, learn to see them at a distance, their autonomous selves blossoming, solidifying, becoming harder to envelope completely.

"Extraordinary part of the world, the Queen Charlottes," said Douglas. "Unique flora and fauna. Or so I've been told."

"It's called Haida Gwaii now," said John.

"Ah, yes, as it should. You'll encounter some Haida fishing boats, I imagine, in the course of your duties."

"I have no idea, Dad. It could well be." John upended a duffel bag, its contents spilling onto the bare floor. He began refolding the clothes and packing them into the canvas bag again, tighter together this time. He wished his father would leave and let him accomplish this alone.

"I wanted to wish you luck, son, not that you'll need it. The work—I have no idea what it will be, what you'll be doing to pass the days, but I hope you'll write us regularly. I'd be very interested to know. The details, that is. It all seems quite remarkable to me."

"What does?" said John.

"The work, I mean, shipboard life, the setting out and charting a course and returning to port after the mission has been accomplished. I take it you will be sailing during the week and returning to Prince Rupert on weekends. That regularity appeals to me. It will be like having a Monday-to-Friday job except that you'll be living in your office."

"That's one way to look at it," said John. "When you said you thought it was remarkable, I thought you meant something else. That you couldn't believe I would be doing something so…"

"So?"

"Different. Otherworldly. Not what I was trained to do."

"I'm not judging you, son. I'm the last person justified in criticizing your choices. Now your mother, on the other hand…"

"Yes, she has expressed her feelings on the matter," said John.

"Just…be careful. Let us know how it's going. Send back stories; I'm dying for material!"

They laughed together. He assumed that Douglas Lauder Jones's first motivation in any experience, his own or another's he might have heard about, was to gather the stuff of his fiction. It had been so long since he'd read anything new from his father that John had stopped thinking about him in that way. The young man felt a cloak of cruelty settle across his shoulders, and he looked at his father in a pitying way under cover of the laughter that had pricked the bubble of tension between them. Douglas looked suddenly old. John hadn't noticed until now just how aged and diminished he appeared. The young man hadn't been paying attention. He'd been preoccupied, with love, with love's disappearance, with his decision to leave science to others, and with the resulting guilt he felt having made that change in his life. Now compounding that guilt was the belief that he had been taking his father for granted. Not only had he assumed thoughtlessly that the author would always be there in that big old house on Coburg Road, but that the man would never change.

"I THINK YOU ARE VERY LUCKY, Anya Lauder Jones," said Irma one afternoon. The shop was quiet. Lionel was in Boston for a few days, at a liquidation sale of an art-supply company, and he'd brought Dick with him. Irma suspected that a double-header at Fenway Park was also on the itinerary. The road work on Spring Garden Road had moved up to engulf the area around Mountcastle Framing, bringing walk-in traffic to virtually nil. The sewer system being replaced, from the look of some of the blackened wooden remnants exposed by the deep excavation, was a century or two old. From one day to the next, pedestrian pathways changed according to which side of the street was receiving the most violent attention and which stretches of concrete sidewalk were either no longer there or too dangerous to walk on. Idle men of a certain vintage watched the work with the sort of expression usually reserved for construction foremen or project engineers.

What was this fascination with the exposed guts of the urban world? Irma wondered. She would never understand this compunction to open a wound and peer down into Stygian darkness. She was grateful to those who maintained such necessary infrastructure, but she would rather they exerted their labours at night while she and other sensitive Haligonians were far away, home, and asleep in their beds.

"Lucky? Why do you say that?" said Anya. Even in this back room, where she and Irma were sitting near a cooling electric fan, they had to raise their voices above the din of the street work.

"Why, growing up with such a talented father, I suppose. Surrounded by books. Told the most wonderful bedtime stories, I imagine."

"My father," Anya began to say before stopping. The question was how to complete the utterance without disappointing the woman, who was evidently a devotee—Irma was the first person not a friend or family member Anya had ever heard praise the writing of Douglas Lauder Jones in specific terms—and deflating her father's reputation in the mind of this thoughtful reader. "Dad has always been guarded about his work. While he was writing he was...elsewhere? Does that make sense? And when he wasn't he was like any normal dad, I guess. Who was it that told me bedtime stories? If anyone it was Merin. Occasionally John."

"Then you were lucky to have such loving siblings," said Irma, who was not about to let Anya away with not having something to be thankful for. It was her guiding belief that everyone, regardless of what difficulties they might have had to face, could find a reason to be grateful. In her case she was blessed to have met Desh, the love of her life. She sometimes thought, *Lord, what if I hadn't been a classroom teacher? And what if I hadn't felt so stale, on the verge of burning out? I might not have switched to Guidance.*

It made her shiver to imagine the final decade of her career unravelling in the art room. She and Desh would have followed divergent paths. Not only that, her love of fine art would also surely have been extinguished.

Irma had propped the back door open to encourage whatever airflow she could. Her ankles were swollen and the veins on her right leg looked like puffy purple worms. It was too hot to wear the compression stockings she was supposed to have on to enhance circulation and prevent further varicosity. The best she could do during these strange long days of oppressive humidity, so unlike the usual breezy Maritime climate, was to wear outfits with long, loose skirts. She could bear it while she was at work and occupied, but at home with Desh, still-young, vital, immortal Desh, she would catch him looking at her, a look that to her seemed to teeter on the edge of disgust, and she felt as though the floor under her had given way.

She read somewhere that we should always try to be the age we are and not younger or older. That could mean many things. She could think of benefits gained from youthful thinking, although she understood what the caution meant or thought she did. It meant be who you are when you are. Otherwise, you are either trying to dredge a version of yourself probably buried under the deep silt of false memory and forgetfulness or approximating what you might guess is a more mature and hence more worthy self not yet in existence. In both cases it was not recommended. That was the reason why, sitting there coaxing a cooling breeze in the back room of Lionel Mountcastle's most un-busy business, she avoided offering advice and peer-to-peer connectedness in equal measure to Miss Anya Lauder Jones, artist in embryo.

Irma was about to ask the girl about her living arrangements in Toronto for September—would she have a room in residence, where it was always a gamble given that you risked spending eight months yoked to someone so disagreeable you ended up throttling her?—when they heard the front doorbell sound followed by the loud thump of something hitting the floor. Anya got there first. The door had been pushed fully open, held in place by warped, uneven floorboards so old and smooth and wide they were probably priceless.

A figure was sprawled beside a toppled wheelchair, the large back wheel closest to the ceiling spinning. A large Husky, the young panhandler's dog, licked sympathetically at the bald pate of the man on the floor, the animal whining, *Do something, do something, can't you see this guy can't get up on his own?*

The youth, the dog's companion if not owner, slowly entered the space as if he were a stop-action figure. He was in no hurry to do anything. His dog could speak for him. Lending a hand was going to mean relinquishing his large, paper coffee cup and he looked loath to do any such thing. Which struck Irma as odd, later, when she thought about that bathetic tumbling in. Given the two steps leading up from the sidewalk, which was now because of the roadwork a springy, unpredictable expanse of plywood, to the front entrance of Mountcastle Framing, someone would have had to help this wheelchair-confined unfortunate to negotiate the obstacle. It explained the upending: if one helpful hand was otherwise occupied cradling an iced cappuccino, then the force applied to the vehicle would have been uneven. But wait, Irma thought, recreating the scene; simple mechanics in that case would have demanded earlier disaster, outside the store. Oh, how Desh would love to Sherlock this one out. It meant that Mr. Do Gooder here had to have put his beverage cup down and with both hands reversed the chair, tipped it back so that only the large wheels touched the ground, and bumped the man in the wheelchair up the steps and through the door. Was the door already open? There were too many parameters! Maybe the canine had been instrumental in sending paracustomer sprawling?

"Oh, my goodness, are you all right, Mr. Stamp? I'm so sorry!" Anya righted the wheelchair as she spoke, getting between the man and the dog, the tail of which was whacking the prostrate man in the face, lending him an air that might have been one of alarm or delight. He appeared to have facial expressions unique to him. Anya knew him, evidently. Irma watched her move the chair so that it faced the man, who was now seated on the floor, his legs stretched in front of him and towards the footrests. These Anya flipped up and out of the way before applying each large wheel's brake. She got behind him, crouched so that she might encircle his chest with her arms and, lifting as much with her legs as with her arms and back, tried to help him to stand. For all the commendable precision of her technique, she was unable to lift him and so he resumed his position on the bare wood floor.

"I know your legs work," she said to him, familiarly, the way she might address an uncooperative baby brother. "I've seen you. They are your paddles, aren't they, and don't deny it. So, let's try this again. And please, Mr. Stamp, this time if you wouldn't mind, try to get your legs under you? Okay?"

Irma came around in front this time, taking hold of his hands and pulling while Anya hoisted from the rear. He became tentatively upright, despite the agitated dog's apparent resolve to trip him, and together the women helped him dance a silly pirouette until all he had to do was let himself be settled, like a heavy sack positioned atop a similar sack, into his chariot. Anya reinstated the footrests, lifted first one and then the other of his feet onto them, and checked all around his head for signs of trauma the fall might have caused.

Dust and noise blew in from the street. Together Irma and Zachary, the dog's person, jimmied the jammed door closed. She was now used to seeing the young man sitting outside on their front steps. Some days he busked with a ukulele or harmonica; he could use music lessons, she thought. Standing now, out of the daylight, pungent and grimy from the street, seeming unsure of himself indoors—trapped? caged animal?—he reminded her of Desh, the way he kept his jaw set and tilted up, wary, defying them to place upon him an unreasonable demand. He stood for something. It was the way Desh had used that same defiance to define his identity, his otherness, his place in the school. He had a story, this weather-browned, not-so-talented minstrel. I won't be your mother, she thought, looking stern.

"He was insistent," he said, indicating Mr. Stamp, who, aside from an egg growing above one eyebrow and a moue indicating impatience with the pace of recovery in the confined space, appeared unharmed. "He was like, ramming into the bottom step, backing up and going at it again full tilt. I'm surprised he didn't break his front wheels right off. 'Here,' I said, 'hold up, Cap'n, I'll tip you up at the right angle.' You know, you can get these ramps, small ones like? In fact, I think it might be a by-law says businesses got to have them now. Otherwise, you're discriminating against the stair challenged."

"Thank you," said Irma, her tone suggesting the opposite of gratitude, "for bringing that to our attention. And for helping Mr. … this man, our customer…" turning to Mr. Stamp, "and yes, now that you are here and settled, how may we be of assistance, sir?"

Levelling

It was the way Cary wanted to live the rest of his life: in endless Saturday mornings warmed by a tentative April sun, lungs cleansed by bellows full of antiseptic air. He was worried that if he thought too much about the pleasure, the promise of the day ahead, he might lose it completely.

The air was warmer than the ground. Any snow there had been, except for shaded corners of the back yard, was finally gone. He was standing in the driveway of his family's house on Coburg. All he had on, besides winter boots with leather uppers and rubber soles, were jeans and a thin shirt. He slid his hands into his back pockets, leaned back and looked up into the sky's infinite membrane until his eyes began to water.

The next-door neighbour, Hank Hislop, followed his shadow out from behind the little trailer that was his bedroom. He had eczema covering the backs of his hands, the insides of his wrists, and his forearms to the elbow. It looked as though he had plunged his arms into boiling water or a vat of weak acid. Hank's brother and sister lived in the house. Cary wiped his eyes with the back of his hand. He considered the Hislop siblings to be hideous, ancient, and best avoided. He wondered if Hank was in exile. Or was it his preference to live in the tiny trailer in the back yard, even in winter?

Hank had hands as strong as vice-grips and a drinking problem. Cary's father sometimes paid Hank with a bottle for working on their car, a used Oldsmobile that Douglas said he had won in a poker game. Did such transactions still happen? Cary listened to the question, its sentiment and tone, voiced in his head as if not he but his mother were thinking it, and it didn't bother him to know that he could sound so mature. Fifteen, he would have done almost anything to be twice that age.

He leaned forward so that the front of his body draped the hood of the car, his father's winnings, its caramel-coloured body radiating the sun's warmth. His father never backed the car into the driveway the way Hank Hislop and his brother did. It would never have occurred to him to do so, to think ahead to the next time he would have to pull out into traffic. Cary had no desire to learn how to drive, unlike many of his friends.

Hank Hislop was two days unshaven. His hair, thick and bluntly cut, stood up in spiky disarray. He yawned while scratching his chest, armpits and pubic area, his hand disappearing beneath the waistband of a shapeless pair of faded, soiled, blue work trousers held up by black suspenders. His torso was covered by a grimy red Union suit. Cary caught a glimpse of the black holes and jagged gaps of the man's ruined teeth.

Hank's brother Robert dressed in a suit and tie every day and drove to work at an electronics assembly plant in Dartmouth. Robert complained that Douglas parked his car across the invisible line bisecting the driveway shared by the two houses. He also complained that the Lauder Jones dog was making a disaster of the Hislops' front lawn and flowerbeds, doing his business there and digging holes whenever he broke loose from the back yard. The dog liked to squeeze under the fence and take off on a grand tear around the neighbourhood. "On a grand tear," the phrase Douglas liked to use to describe an exceptionally good time. Cary preferred to think that McCoy, a collie-German Shepherd cross, was out surveying his realm, out on a grand tour rather than a tear. The animal was supposed to pass the time tethered to the clothesline. Sometimes, when Ursula came home and looked out the dining-room window at the muddy track McCoy had worn in the grass and weeds, she shook her head and laughed in a way that sounded like a moan.

Hank Hislop had a soft spot in his heart for McCoy, whom Merin had named for the doctor on the starship *Enterprise.* He got his sister Amelia to save thick beef bones for the dog. Enthusiastic McCoy, in temperament the opposite of his namesake, dug under the fence to get closer to the source, and in doing so repeatedly pulled the clothesline down. Once, he went so far as to separate the line at its joint, dragging the leash and the heavy line, with one metal reel still attached, behind him down the street. When he became snagged on a sewer grate, McCoy was saved by a passerby who unhooked him, found out where he lived, and brought him home. McCoy was crazy but happy. Cary liked to think that the dog trusted in the goodness of all his loyal subjects.

"Come on over. I need a hand with the back end," said Hank, leaving it unspecified to whose or which posterior he was referring. Cary followed him around to the far corner of the trailer, where Hislop had positioned a manual jack. The device held the little trailer a few inches up off its support, one of four large cinder blocks. The man inserted a flat piece of wood between the block and the underside of the trailer, then lowered the jack so that the two-wheeled abode was again resting on its now-adjusted pedestal. The boy wondered why he'd been asked to help.

"How's that look to you?"

"I don't know. Fine?"

"Level, would you say?"

"Sure. I guess."

"Take a good gander. Go on back a couple yards."

He did so, walking to about the midpoint of the litter-filled yard, turning, crouching as if lining up a golf putt, and squinting as he concentrated on the line formed by the trailer's undercarriage relative to the thawing ground, which was more or less flat though soggily so after winter's restless heave.

"It looks good there," said Cary, trying to sound decisive the way he'd heard workmen in the street and on construction sites speak to each other, with confident force and volume.

Hank Hislop seemed pleased with his levelling job. He mumbled something about objects sliding and rolling off his little kitchen table. Now that wouldn't happen anymore. When he told Cary this, Hislop seemed embarrassed. His neck and face flushed, becoming almost as raw looking as his arms.

"Come inside and I'll show you," he said.

"That's okay, I don't need to, I'll take your word for it." Besides, he thought, now that the trailer was level, a pencil would stay where it was supposed to, wouldn't it? What would there be to see?

Hislop jerked his head dismissively to one side, a kind of ear-to-shoulder motion as if he were trying to scratch an itch. It was fine, he had things to do. "Off you go, then. Mornings like this was never meant to be wasted. Imagine you got your own battles to fight. Away to you. Give my regards to your father. Tell him I read that there book he give me. Tell him Hank is willing and able, any time, any job. Man like me gets thirsty to work, you tell him that. A man needs to wrap his hand around something worthwhile."

Cary kept watching him while he pretended to investigate something in his own back yard before going inside. Hislop hiked up his trousers, wiped saliva, thick and dried, from the corner of his mouth, and walked up the driveway to the side door of his siblings' house. He patted the pockets of his trousers, pulled a folded envelope out, looked at it an instant and returned it to the pocket without opening it. He raised a fist as if preparing to knock on the door, caught himself, opened the aluminum storm-door, turned the handle of the sturdy wooden inner door, leaned his shoulder into it, paused to listen for sounds inside, and waited like that, in a stance anyone viewing from the street might have construed to be that of a housebreaker working the lock, but which was merely that of a man trying to gather the strength needed to face trial by his peers.

ROBERT HISLOP was the kind of man who didn't know what to do with himself when he wasn't at work. Saturday mornings for that reason were a penance. He helped Amelia with the household chores, carrying the full laundry basket to the machines in the basement, emptying the dryer, folding the warm clothes, and bringing them back upstairs. If Hank wasn't about, Robert might putter around outside the house. Hank had his odd jobs he did for money, mostly for neighbours: automotive work, if it wasn't too complicated; such electrical appliances as toasters and beaters rewired; fences mended—he was getting used to repairing the damage done by the mutt next door.

Given that Hank depended on these commissions to keep him semi-solvent, Robert was hesitant to ask him to fix eavestroughs and window frames or replace roof shingles and the like. Robert did it himself, after a fashion; he could figure out how to repair most things, usually after doing it wrong first. The result often made Hank shake his head and redo the job when Robert was away at the plant.

Hank thought that his brother should stick to managing accounts there, a factory where Hank had worked for a while and where he had for a few weeks become a knowledgeable, skilful, valued employee, until he came to work drunk one day and broke an expensive piece of equipment. Robert could hardly show his face on the production floor after that, he was so ashamed. He had pulled strings to get his brother hired, and this was the way he'd been repaid. That all happened three years ago. Was it that long ago now? Hank marked his termination of employment by disappearing for a week, not telling Robert or Amelia where he was going except to say that he would be back, and they weren't to worry about him.

When he returned, he looked as if he had spent time living in the forest without adequate shelter. Leaves and twigs were woven into the thatch of his hair, the knees and elbows of his trousers and shirt were dyed with mud, and his breath stank. While he'd been away, Amelia kept saying, "Leave him do what he must. He let you down, Robert. Don't make him feel worse by going after him, dragging him home or calling the police to do it. Allow him his dignity, what shred of it he has left. He is our big brother. He will come back to himself, he always does."

Robert was sorting the laundered clothing into three piles at the kitchen table when Hank came in. Robert was dressed the way he always was, in dark slacks, a pressed white shirt and regimental tie, RCR, the only one he had ever worn. When he retired from the armed forces, he was a master warrant officer, having served in Logistics in Germany before coming home and completing his tour on military bases across the country. He had married a woman from Lahr, but when the time came for them to leave for Canada she didn't want to go. She was convinced that people would hate her because she was German. She was having a difficult time with English. Besides, she said, how could she leave her mother, who was lame and going blind? Robert had to follow orders and accept his posting back in Canada. Nothing he said convinced the woman to accompany him, although they had lived together almost seven years. It was as if she had been play-acting. So long as he learned her language, became acclimated to her culture, discovered through her that Germans were naturally tolerant, civilized, and intelligent, not the monsters the world had portrayed them to be, she was content. "See?" she kept saying. "We're really very good. I can't remember the last time I ate a baby." It broke his heart that she refused to come home with him. He wrote to her in a steady flow of weekly letters for two years until he gave up hope of ever seeing her again.

The brothers stood silently in each other's presence. Robert knew that Hank was embarrassed to have come upon him while he was folding their sister's undergarments, and that Hank's rare appearance inside the house meant one of a few possibilities: he had injured himself and needed medical attention; he had to use the telephone, a device he tried to avoid; or he needed money.

When he saw the letter Hank was holding, he had a feeling this wasn't going to be a straightforward problem to solve.

Their mother had written not to Robert or Amelia, who were literate, but to Hank. Having handed over the folded pages, the letter's tiny, precise script laid out shakily on unlined blue airmail paper, he stood before his brother, waiting for the message to be deciphered. The old woman had to be all right to have written so much. She had recently celebrated her eighty-third birthday and, except for a litany of low-grade physical ailments common to those her age, enjoyed a feisty vigour. Had a barnacle been given gloating voice loud enough to trumpet its triumph over all the living things it had managed to choke, and imagining a peripatetic barnacle who never missed an episode of *Coronation Street* or her weekly game of bingo down to the Legion Hall, it might have sounded like Mrs. Gertrude Hislop, Gert to her friends and acquaintances who had not yet predeceased her but who expected to do so soon enough, according to her crowing predictions.

Why she had chosen to communicate her present state of desperation, for once a predicament requiring immediate attention, to Hank rather than to his more able siblings in matters such as these, spoke to the woman's enduring fondness for her firstborn and to the fact that she remembered more about the time when he was a boy of twelve than she did about his present deficiencies and trials, those suffered by a grown man in his fifties. Robert read the first few sentences to himself and knew immediately what images were running though their mother's mind as she wrote: Hank, old before he deserved to be, forced into early maturity by the sudden death of their father; Hank, leaving school before he had completed the eighth grade, having to work to replace some of their father's income, first as a pot scrubber in a restaurant kitchen, then a berry picker, farm labourer, garbage man, auto-mechanic's helper, ship's oiler, night watchman, parking-lot attendant, soldier, construction worker, assembly-plant employee and newspaper deliverer, none of which he occupied for longer than a few months at a time, some as repeated stints but most ending with the stipulation that he never return.

After her children grew up and left home, travelled, and explored the worlds of employment and love or, as in Amelia's case, apparently neither, Gertrude went to live with her sister, Mary-Louise Stephenson, recently widowed, and Gertrude's niece, Holly, and Holly's husband, Lloyd Banks, near Canning, Nova Scotia. Holly and Lloyd had two children, a girl and a boy, who grew to love their Great-Aunt Gert as much as they had their Granny, Mary-Louise, who died barely two years after Gertrude's arrival. At that sad moment Gert might have gone to live with one of her own children, eventually and not right away, though, because Hank was a recently demoted private soldier living in barracks on CFB Petawawa, Robert was still serving in Germany, and Amelia was living with a woman in an apartment on O'Connor Street in Ottawa, keeping house while her companion, a friend from high-school days, worked as an administrator in Indian and Northern Affairs on Parliament Hill. Gertrude gave up asking her daughter about prospective love interests, gentleman callers, as it were, men with whom she might be inclined to make a life.

After Holly's mother died, Holly and Lloyd built Great-Aunt Gert a small apartment attached to the house. They figured the old woman wouldn't live much longer than her sister had, and when she was gone Lloyd could use the granny flat as an office. Their children were growing up so quickly and spent as little time as possible at home that Gert often confused them with her own children, calling the boy Hank and the girl Amelia. She never called him Robert, her husband's name, the memory of his passing still a painful one, all these years past. Of the two Hislop men, Hank most resembled his father; Robert, steady, reliable, unremarkable, took after Gertrude's father, a farmer from Holland who lost everything when his Holsteins were wiped out by Foot-and-Mouth Disease and who worked himself to death in a gold mine near Cobalt, Ontario.

Robert read the letter aloud to Hank:

My dear boy,

Your father would have wanted me to call you Henry at a time like this. I don't even know how to tell you this. He was always so much better than I was when it came to bad news, dealing with it and telling it, both. If you believe he's close, his spirit I mean, and I do, then you know that his hand is helping me to write this.

Your cousin Holly, I'm telling you almost not believing it myself, has done a regrettable thing. I won't say it's the most terrible thing she could have done, because I know what the flesh and its associated desires are capable of. No, this first part is more pitiful than condemnable. You know that she was working for the farmers' co-operative as its bookkeeper these past eleven or so years and everything there seemed as fine as fine could be, with no reason for anyone to complain. Then one day, a week before Christmas, she came home earlier than usual and said she could no longer work for those people. She said something to the effect that they did not appreciate all she did for them, that with all the unpaid overtime she worked leading up to tax-return time and the deals that Lloyd bent over backwards to offer on machinery, those ungrateful farmers didn't know a good thing from a hole in the ground. Without the tractors Lloyd provided them and without Holly's ability to make everything add up the way it should, they'd all be scratching around in the dirt with sticks and not even two pennies to rub together for feed. Actually, Henry, and I know this to be the God's honest truth, your cousins got along well with almost everyone they knew and had dealings with. There was only one man who made life difficult for them and that was their neighbour up the Third Line Road, Mr. Kronkheimer. I don't suppose I have to tell you who it is who just happens to be the chairman of the co-op's board of directors as well as municipal councillor and lord knows what else. Nothing poor Holly could do under that tyrant's scrutiny was ever good enough. She would come home late at night after a meeting of the finance committee, lugging those heavy black ledgers and laying them open on the kitchen table with their so many pages and columns and writing small enough to make a person squint close to blindness, and we could be sure that something Mr. Kronkheimer said was making her pull out her scratch pad and pore over those impossible numbers well into the tired hours of the early morning. You children know so much more than I do about accounting and credit and finance and the like. All I knew was that when dear Holly told us she was never going back to work at that dreadful place I wasn't surprised in the least. One can be momentarily thrown off-balance by something and still not be surprised that it happened, not after engaging in a few minutes of contemplation and prayer.

We drew her into our embrace, Lloyd and I did, and we told the child that it was not the end of the world. A woman with her experience and skill, I mean, you have to be something of a diplomat to get these cheesemakers working together, as in sharing the wealth and helping each other out when times are bad. Somebody with all she had going for her was sure to land a good job, something even better than the one she left. Well, my good Henry, you would think that we had told her she better say her prayers and put her affairs in order, in preparation for meeting her Maker. Didn't she up and storm off to the bedroom, where she locked herself inside for I don't know how many hours. Oh, the crying and sobbing we heard through that closed door, it was like unto a Tribulation, it surely was. I truly thought that slip of a girl was drawing her last breath. Of course, she's no girl, petite as she is, but a woman in her middle years very close in age to our Amelia, as you know, and my first thought was that she must be experiencing the first stirrings of the change of life we women must necessarily suffer as we leave behind our ability to bear children. She would grow quiet for a spell and then it was like an ocean crashing over her once again.

I'm sorry to say I directed the most hateful thoughts towards those men and to one in particular—you can guess whom without much difficulty now. Though she is not my own daughter, I think of her as such now that she is an orphan, and it was a real struggle during Holly's crying jag for me not to go over to the Association Hall and give that man a piece of my mind.

How wrong we can be about a person, even about our own flesh and blood, and how duped into thinking they are one exemplary thing when the contrary holds all the truth. I have been worried, these three months since learning what was so and what wasn't, that if I wrote it down it would somehow make what Holly did actual and irrevocable, because, believe me, it still feels like I'm trapped in a bad dream, an old woman's nightmare from which I have yet to wake. But lo, there it was, the bleak fact of the matter, it might as well have been carved into the stone of the memorial to the war dead: on January 27 of this year, Holly Frances Banks, wife of Lloyd Banks of Canning, Nova Scotia, was charged with theft in the amount of $26,377 over the course of what the authorities think was a two-year period.

Oh, my son, my honest Hank, if I could look you in the eye I would know how to continue and what to say, the right words. You have lived a full life, perhaps fuller already than my own, and you have had more than your share of hardship, some of which was of your own making, some not. I know that conventional book learning was neither your strength nor your inclination, whereas I feel I've spent most of my life inside the pages of other people's writing. I suppose I thought that of all people I could turn to, you would be the one most likely to understand what your cousin did and what was done to her and how she and her husband have chosen to treat me in the interim. Perhaps "chosen" is not the most appropriate word in this instance. Two souls at peace with themselves and with God do not in all good conscience choose to treat the weak and the vulnerable the way they have recently treated me. I can think about it for only short stretches of time without crying. What comes over good people? Why does innocence fly and where? If I had answers to these two questions, I could die contented.

The facts are these, they were printed in the *Chronicle-Herald*, which I missed reading at the time, as you and your brother and sister must have, too, since none of you ventured to investigate or called to find out what was what and whether or not your old mother was in any way worse for wear, given what her niece allegedly went and did, which was to write herself a whole passel of cheques on the Growers' account, some 280 of them when all was discovered, made out to "Cash." I do believe her when she says that she started out meaning to pay the money back, and thought of each one, usually for less than $100, as a loan. She hasn't admitted as much, but I think they eventually stopped being loans, and in her mind turned into her own secret attack on Kronkheimer and his cronies, the gang who made her working life so miserable. What did she use the money for? Your guess is as valid as any, although it does appear to be the case that her children have not been asking her for money of late, not the way they used to. The upshot is that Holly might have to go to jail for her crime, and Lloyd, innocent as a newborn, owes all that money plus court costs and the lawyer's fee. I call him innocent only because I don't believe he had anything to do with Holly and her forgeries. But the manner in which he has treated me since his wife's arraignment is another matter altogether, and in that regard, no, I cannot say that he has acted at all like an innocent and certainly not a gentleman.

Just as my niece lost her way when she took that money, I think that Lloyd is distraught over the prospect of losing his wife to prison for a year—it might be less or more time, but the lawyer assigned to the case gave her to understand that her sentence if she is convicted would be about twelve months—and he is not thinking clearly. Lord knows I'm not as cogent as I should be, and I am neither perpetrator nor victim, and spouse of none. You know that I am an able woman still in possession of her faculties. I would not have been able to compose this missive to you, as difficult as it has been, were I not more or less compos mentis. Nevertheless, I find myself frightened for my well-being here, and unsure, truly doubtful, in fact, that I can stay in the bosom of this family and retain my health. When Holly confessed her crime to me, she listed blameworthy names responsible more than she for her predicament, and mine, I shudder to recall, was high on that list. Mine! Apparently, the amount of money I have been contributing to the monthly upkeep of this household has not been adequate. I will tell you that I gave my niece and her husband, bless their petty, inveigling souls ("inadequate"!), more each month of the year than anyone would expect someone in my position to have to pay. Not in a hundred years would they ever find a tenant to occupy my tiny bedroom (it fully suits my needs, I'm not complaining, I require no more than it to contain my small thin bed and a few unfashionable clothes) and cough up the $1200 a month that I pay for shelter and what minuscule portion of food I am able to keep down. A weak beef-consommé and a few saltine crackers and there, my son, is a fit repast for your aged parent. Inadequate! I could move into a small palace of an apartment in Wolfville for that price. I didn't want to do that. I wanted to live in the bosom of a family and feel that I was contributing to the commonweal. I made myself useful. I rocked colicky babies, prepared meals, packed school lunches, mopped floors and laundered and ironed that man's shirts the way he expected, a way, mind you, that his hapless thief of a wife was never able to achieve.

Did I bill them back for my time? Did I deduct my labour from the rent I paid each month? You can bet that I did not. That is not what members of the same family do. Some truths are inalienable. Families help each other out. Introducing price tags in this regard does nothing but pour salt in the wound, and that is the reason why I never kept up a balance sheet of my own and never expected my own kin to hold me to the same accounting. You talk about choice: I chose to contribute to the well-being of my sister's daughter, her husband, and her children. And this, dear boy, is the nature of the thanks I received: I am virtually under house arrest, unable to leave unaccompanied and made to feel that I am supremely annoying and unreasonable when I do ask to be driven to the bank or the department store, which occurrence can be as rare as once a month, and there have been entire months when I have forgone that luxury. My grand-niece and grand-nephew, meanwhile, are banned from communicating with me, for the astounding reason that I refused to hand over my life's savings to Lloyd to help him satisfy the demands of his wife's restitution. Most of my money is tied up in an annuity, he knows this, being on intimate terms with his drinking companion, the bank manager. You know I would have to pay a considerable penalty to withdraw the principal. What alternative does someone like me have? Am I to give it all away and trust that I will be cared for? An old crone like me has no choice but to guard her livelihood with all due care. Were I Lear himself I would feel no less valued, no less honoured and respected, no more vulnerable to his ravening daughters and their scheming, murderous men than I do today. Whatever am I to do? They look at and speak to me as though I and not my wayward niece were the criminal. It has moved me so far beyond the realm of belief as to be almost comic. If only I could bring myself to laugh.

Please come, son, and take me away from these horrid creatures. I pity them their shame and the burden they carry, but I fear more for myself, and you know I am not a selfish person.

THE DAY HE FIRST SAW old Mrs. Hislop, Cary stepped outside holding McCoy's leash. As soon as the dog saw it, he became animated, whining and barking excitedly. It took the boy a moment to extricate him from the rope attached to the clothesline, because it was wrapped around one of the dog's back legs and snagged on the fence between their yard and the Hislops'. After getting the animal disentangled and hooked to his leash, Cary looked up and saw Hank Hislop's head and shoulders rise above the top of his trailer. The man was climbing a long ladder that leaned against the back wall of the house. A woman's bare leg was thrust through and hanging outside the closest of two upstairs windows, her foot at the height of three or four rungs above the top of the ladder.

"Just hold on, Ma," said Hank. "No, bring your leg back in. You can't—no, dear, not that way."

McCoy stood intrigued for a considerably shorter time than Cary did and was soon grabbing the leash in his teeth, pulling on it and dancing side to side. Cary commanded he sit. The dog continued to pull.

Similarly, the woman—an ancient being, it was evident now from the wrinkles on her face and the clots of purple vein marbling her exposed thigh—was not about to stay put. Cary could hear only the occasional word now. By the time Hank reached the top of the ladder, she had gotten both of her legs beyond the sill and was sitting there, the upper half of her still inside, her face turned to one side and pressed against the glass, one fisheye trained on Hank. Cary heard her say, "Fire," and her son reply, "No, Ma, you only think that because you smelled Robert's soldering iron in the basement. Now could you please go back inside and unlock your door?"

Cary assumed that her answer was in the negative. The leg fluttered the way a panicked child's might, and her dressing gown lay open, revealing a night dress hiked much too high.

"I don't much know how I'm going to do this safely," said Hank. "I'm going to need a spotter."

The boy and his dog came out of their yard, across the driveway and around the trailer. Cary tied the dog's leash to the trailer hitch, much to McCoy's displeasure, and planted himself at the ladder's base. He took hold of it with both hands at about the height of his shoulders.

Feeling the tremor in the ladder, Hank looked down. "Not that way," he instructed. "You'd never be able to keep it from going over. You gotta use all your weight. Get around underneath 'er so's you're looking up at us through the rungs." Cary shifted position. "There, you got 'er now."

He felt momentarily dizzy as he looked up at Hank Hislop carrying his mother down the ladder. The man's boots, caked with dried mud, untied, worn to the colour of dry slate, looked too heavy for the rungs of the ladder, which sagged inward towards the house with each descending step. Cary couldn't tell how Hank was carrying the old lady, who had arrived sometime during the past week. When he caught sight of her bare crotch, he turned his head away. By the time he'd looked up, hoping to see it again, dreading he might, the pair had made it to the ground.

Hank said nothing as he trudged with Mrs. Hislop in his arms up the driveway to the side door. She kept saying that she was fine, perfectly fine, and that he should put her down, that he was risking avoidable injury, and what, really, did he expect to accomplish by making such a spectacle of himself? She was not a damsel in distress, she said, no eloping bride. Didn't he have better things to do with his time? He should put her down this very instant. She demanded to see the top man. This was intolerable, Kafkaesque. Cary had heard the word before. It sounded like stiff fabric being torn.

"You're in bare feet, Ma. Can you not hang tight till we get inside?"

"Really, son, through the upstairs window, of all things! Have you forgotten that every house has at least one door? I think you had better call Lloyd and Holly. They will be wondering where I've gotten to."

"You know, Ma, Robert had a chat with them when he drove out to pick you up. They said they didn't know about any stealing. He said Holly looked some hurt to be accused of such a thing."

"What such thing are you on about, son?"

"I'm talking about what you said in your letter. That she wrote all them cheques to cash that weren't her money to do with in the first place. Robert looked into it. He said there weren't no story about it in the papers."

"Oh, Henry, what an imagination you have! Where in the world would you get that idea about dear little Holly? Why, she would no sooner resort to theft than I would swallow a live eel. Of course she would be hurt! Who wouldn't? Good Lord! From whom was she supposed to have stolen money?"

Hank paused with her in his arms a second or two. He didn't look down at his burden, only stared straight ahead. "No matter, Ma. Forget about it now. Let's get you back inside."

WHILE CARY WAS UNHOOKING McCoy's leash from the trailer, the window through which Hank's mother had made her inglorious exit closed and its shade was lowered. He waited to see what would happen next, whether the old bat would try another escape and through what aperture, but no one emerged. The ladder leaned motionless against the blue shake siding of the house. McCoy insisted, desperately, on progress, and so they set off to follow their regular route.

Ambreen

Cary liked to walk McCoy past the house of a certain girl in his class, Ambreen Aswari. If it was after school, Ambreen would be home but not yet buckled into schoolwork. She might be sitting, legs folded under her on the living-room couch, her attention now on the game show she liked, now out beyond the sheer curtains to her street. To get to Ambreen's street he had to lead McCoy along Robie toward a neighbourhood near Saint Mary's University. The dog ran like a bolting jackrabbit after the balls and stones the boy threw for him, and so by the time he was leashed again, the nutcase was panting so hard that he no longer thought about biting the leather strap and orbiting Cary in a silly, backwards hopping dance.

By then Cary didn't fantasize about Ambreen so much as sift through the details he had accumulated: she liked cats; she had an older brother, Sajid, who liked to draw; she was Muslim but did not cover her hair as her mother did; she went to the back of the classroom often to drink water. The teacher had installed a water cooler and a dispenser of cone-shaped paper cups for that purpose, and Cary wondered if the girl had a medical problem that required her to drink so much, the possibility that Ambreen might be ill only intensifying his ardour. What might it be? Diabetes, he decided, but Ambreen had no injection dimples on her arms or thighs that he could see. Perhaps she took her needles in a hidden part of the body. He imagined Ambreen dying in a hospital bed and asking to see him, and when he arrived everyone else would leave the room so that the two of them could be alone. One day he looked behind him to see Ambreen standing by the dispenser and holding the cone cup but not drinking, simply watching the teacher as she marked tests and the rest of the class as they sat bent over their notebooks, and he knew then that this was not someone who was ailing.

Ambreen got the highest marks in science and math, spoke fluent French, Urdu, and Arabic, had a high forehead, jet black hair, sharp high cheekbones, and a strong, arched nose unlike Cary's, which was broad and flat and twisted to the left. Ambreen was the most popular girl in the class. She decided who was in and who was out, and her orders, usually lacerating missives of denunciation, were delivered by her faithful sidekick, Gillian, a brash loud hoyden who played the trumpet and had a way of smiling at Cary that made him want to run away.

He tried to muster the courage to ask Ambreen if he could walk her home. The more he thought about it the greater became his fear that she would say no. Or, worse, that she and Gillian would laugh at him. Cary worked the clock at school basketball games, kept the statistics, and knew the exact date and time in the sixth grade when he had first fallen in love with Ambreen Aswari. Four years later, sensing that his moment of infatuation was ending, he noted the instant his love began to wane. The long hours he used to devote to adoration were dwindling, and when he walked past Ambreen's house, he would put on a distracted air that bordered on dejection. Ambreen would never look out, she would never notice him there, not that it mattered anymore. What was the use? The anticipation of the stroll, the part he used to love the most, was now too soon undone by the act. It was over too quickly, and McCoy, sensing the boy's anxiety, often did something foolish on the lawn in front of Ambreen's house. He would resume gnawing on the leash, or, haunches quivering, squat to deposit a steaming stool. Mortified, Cary would haul him down the street and out of sight. To stop to ring the doorbell now, even without the mutt, was out of the question. And so, his timekeeping gig after school became a sour purposeless thing and his love began to twist in memory's grip without his having exchanged a single private word with Ambreen Aswari.

While other girls were becoming curvy, Ambreen stayed coltish. At the very moment in her life when she was beginning to be interested in boys and wanted their attention, her body was doing the opposite of what it was supposed to, which was to bloom into a garden of soft bows and firm full pillows. Instead, she had long, equine legs with feet that were too big, knobbly knees, bad skin, and the chest of a chicken-ribbed boy. What fate, what spiteful god had relegated her to this? Because of her gawky appearance she was deposed as leader of the posse. For the first time an outcast, she became lonely, the isolation incomprehensible. Even Gillian, who had suddenly become prettily feminine, exchanging overalls and painter's pants for short skirts, abandoned her. Gillian, ever forward-looking, a sexual explorer, became the first of them to snag a real boyfriend. Ambreen, meanwhile, took up running for exercise, alone, through her neighbourhood, because she could—she had won the right after a lengthy battle for the freedom to do so, her parents tired out from argument but still wary—and because she didn't have to stop to talk to anyone or abide by anyone else's rules or expectations. She went for longer runs, after dark when no one would recognize her. Her wind improved. She was able to run for twenty minutes without stopping, then thirty, forty, a full hour. All the tensions, the undefined anxiety, the dark hurt that could without warning turn into self-loathing, faded when she ran. In winter on the snow-packed sidewalk her waffle-soled running shoes squeaked, a sound that delighted her. She ran with loose arms, hands flopping slightly, no tension in her wrists.

The day Cary saw Ambreen running, the old infatuation returned, a more intense, complex feeling than before, because now, with clearer eyes and a confidence he had been missing, he saw that the object of his affection was strong, an athlete, no longer a potential invalid and no longer a tyrant. Ambreen demanded nothing except that she be seen running. Because they had shared long hours in the classroom, and a tacit understanding of what it was to be a solitary person, they now stopped when they saw each other.

"How much more of Monsieur Borque can you stand?"

"I'm thinking of dropping."

"Don't you need it?"

"I speak the language, don't I?"

"I guess."

"You guess, do you?" The way she said it made him uneasy because of its familiarity and the mock annoyance in her tone, one that he never imagined Ambreen using with him despite her reputation for ruthlessness. His dream of the two of them together had never included this unsavoury play-fight bickering. It surprised him that she would want to tussle with him this way. He could love her, he discovered a second time, but not in the way he used to think he would.

"Why don't we go running together some time? I've seen you jogging with that crazy dog of yours. You have that red tracksuit. I didn't think they made those anymore. Does it even breathe?"

It didn't. Nylon, it made the sweat course down the inside of his t-shirt and down his back. Once, on the coldest day of winter, Cary had gone out for a run, alone with McCoy, and gotten dehydrated and exhausted too far from home. It had been a long walk back; he'd been too tired to run any farther. He'd known by the way his legs wobbled unresponsively that he was in trouble. Go running with Ambreen? It could happen again; he could run out of fuel and then where would he be? Humiliated.

"That's okay," said Ambreen, meaning, *You don't want to have anything to do with me now that I'm a freak. That's fine. I understand,* when it wasn't fine at all. *Even this boy we used to tease in the schoolyard, because he was sweet and sensitive and always on his own, finds me repulsive.* He didn't. He was so much more than merely interested. He was forgetting having been so secretly worshipful. He wanted to be able to call her on the phone, not for a date, a date would scare her off, but just to talk. He wanted to ask her what a girl thought about when a boy was trying to ask her out.

"Sure. I mean, yes, I would."

"When?"

"When do you usually go?"

"In the evening, around nine. If I had somebody to run with, my father wouldn't be such a pain about it. He thinks girls should go outside only for school or groceries. If Sajid was here, my father would send him out to run with me, and Sajid hates running almost as much as he hates the cold." Cary asked her where he was now. "Saudi Arabia. Working for some oil company, making tons of money. It's sickening."

"How about tonight?"

"Tonight what?"

"To run. Didn't you…?"

"Is this like a date?"

"No, of course not!" How did she know?

"A running date, silly." She was treating him the way she would a real boyfriend or some boy she was flirting with. Cary felt dizzy from it. Was she teasing him? Was she playing with his feelings, having detected his renewed ardour? This was too complicated. It was making him queasy.

"Call me first," she said. She told him the number. He had nothing to write with.

"What about in your backpack? With your books?"

Flustered, Cary fished out a pen and a scrap of paper and wrote his telephone number on it before remembering that Ambreen was giving him hers. He had to ask her to repeat it.

"Don't be so nervous, silly. It's just a running date. I'm not going to kiss you or anything."

He watched her walk away. His heart beat crazily. *Oh, do*, he thought. *Or anything.*

THEY BEGAN TO RUN TOGETHER, figuratively, in Cary's now reactivated imagination, as he saw himself and Ambreen merging, becoming a unit the way two people might eventually become better, more sharply defined together than apart, and literally, he looking like a sheepdog trotting beside a greyhound. They fell into an easy, fluid pace with equal strides, and though his body was not ideally suited to distance running, and though he tended to land too heavily on his heels, it felt like he was flying.

Ambreen could talk while she ran and so she filled the time with monologue: her father's benevolent tyranny, her favourite music, the hairstyle she was thinking of trying, the teacher who most annoyed her and the one she thought was dreamy. She couldn't talk about the musicians she liked in her parents' presence and any new hairdo had to involve long hair, since she didn't have the nerve or the permission to cut it. Mrs. Connell, the Spanish teacher with the Scottish accent, made her want to scream, and Mr. Turner, her math teacher, was growing a beard and letting his silver-flecked hair grow out to match it.

Cary couldn't talk and run at the same time. It wasn't that his cardiovascular fitness was poor. Instead, it was like trying to read the newspaper and listen to people speaking on the radio at the same time. His sisters could do it. As soon as they left the breakfast table, he would switch to the classical-music station.

On their fourth running date, Ambreen took them on a different route, one that was shorter and easier than the one they'd followed before, and they ended up, not even breathing hard, at a little all-night coffee shop. She confessed that if her father ever found out, she would be in "deep shit." He loved the way she let the mild obscenity hiss and snap casually from her wide mouth with those plump lips he longed to kiss. It was getting to the point where it hurt to be so close to her and not be able to tell her.

She ran the tip of her finger around the rim of her mug, picking up chocolaty froth the way a plough gathers snow off the street.

"Ambreen."

"What?"

"Why...why are...?"

"Yes?"

"Why do you like me?"

"I don't know. You make me laugh. You don't want anything from me."

"How do you know that? What if...what if I told you..."

"Yes? What? Are you having a stroke? Are you going senile like my granny? Are you a narcoleptic? Hello! Wakey-wakey!"

"What if I said I loved you?"

"Well, I'd say of course you do. Who wouldn't fall in love with this?" She vamped, striking a pose with pursed lips, concave cheeks, and palms framing her face.

"I'm being serious."

She downed what remained of her hot chocolate and stood. "We better get back. Don't want our muscles getting cold. That's when you can get injured."

"Say something."

"I just did."

"Do you know how hard that was for me to say?"

"You're sweet. I liked hearing it."

"You did? Do you...?"

"Let's go," she said. "I promise I won't talk while we run. You'll like that. I won't be a blabbermouth. I promise not to say anything else until we get home."

"Okay," he said, flushed, his skin tingling.

"I..."

"What?"

"Nothing. I'm breaking my own rule. No more running off at the mouth."

"Tell me what you were going to say."

"Only if you beat me home!"

She loped ahead of him, looking back over her shoulder, slowing on the last long hill until he caught her, and then sprinting ahead laughing. How could she laugh after what he'd just said to her? How could she tease like this, the way she used to in the playground?

Unless this wasn't rejection. Unless it held the promise that she felt the same about him.

COMMENCEMENT CEREMONY, October of their senior year. Cary and Ambreen were part of a cohort marshalled in the cafeteria of the high school, waiting to troop across the auditorium stage to receive the previous year's subject prizes.

"Mr. Murayama is looking for you, Cary," she said, and the surprise that registered on his face made her think it had to do with the teacher, who was also his academic advisor. She'd lowered her voice when she said, "Cary," making it intimate and sultry without irony. She so rarely used his name.

Tall but weedy, with a bookish air and a mop of straw-coloured hair, Cary was generally liked. He said what he meant and tried not to say anything deliberately hurtful. He got along with everybody except for those who couldn't understand why he preferred to be a loner who didn't engage in team sports. Someone once told him he dressed as if he were blind and, until declaring himself to Ambreen, he didn't much care about how he looked. Eventually he gave up running, gladly, as exercise when he saw that she wanted to spend time with him, whether or not he imitated an athlete.

Ambreen continued to run for fitness until she developed lower back pain, at which point she switched to yoga. This time she didn't try to interest him in learning to assume the various asanas. He was content to come over and watch her go through her routine.

The only rule was that he couldn't talk and so he took to bringing a sketchbook and drawing pictures of her, the girl he loved. You tell a person you love her and sometimes that's the end of it, but when Cary told Ambreen that he loved her and she saw what it was and didn't reject him, but also didn't let it become anything physical, he adopted his newest and, he believed, most attractive trait, one he figured had been latent in him but which needed this trigger for release, and that was patience. He accepted that this was the way they were going to be together. Compared with the alternative—being apart from her—it was a consummation devoutly to be wished, as Mr. Murayama would have quoted.

Mr. Murayama was the only teacher Cary admired and the only one the boy was afraid of, because he was convinced he knew what Cary was thinking. He always wore a suit and tie to class, and when he smiled at you, you knew that it was a smile of great expectation. *Now*, it seemed to say, *what have you been up to? What have you accomplished?* One of only a few teachers in the school to hold a PhD, Mr. Murayama made literature accessible and challenging regardless of the students he faced, their interest or ability. You would kill to please him. You wanted to squeeze everything out of a text, because you knew that he had already done so and was on the other side waiting for you, arm outstretched, beckoning. *Come, you can do it, you can make the leap*. At least that was the way Cary saw him. Not to idealize the man or suggest that his classes were ideal lectures during which ideas flowed like heady wine. There were, as there are in any classroom, the dullards who resisted Mr. Murayama's charms. They didn't read and they didn't listen to his BBC accent—he had gone to Cambridge University, someone said, but no one could verify it because he refused to talk about himself when someone got cheeky and asked him directly. The ones who sat at the back of the room and slept or threw spitballs or fell when their chairs tipped too far backwards didn't stay in the class very long. Mr. Murayama, for all that he was passionate about literature and scholarship and eloquent expression, had no patience for behaviour that some would excuse as socially determined, not the child's fault, corrigible, a challenge for today's educator, as important—nay, more important than the content of the curriculum. To these, Murayama sent icy responses. "I would prefer they learned elsewhere." He always got what he wanted; losing such an outstanding teacher would have been unthinkable.

Murayama was a Shakespeare specialist and, though relatively young, early forties, he could recite long passages from every major play and knew many of the sonnets by heart. Cary preferred Hemingway and had chosen to study and write about the American Nobel laureate's African stories as his yearlong project. He "got" Shakespeare. He understood that the man was a genius and that the astounding range of human experience was present in the plays, that nothing was left out and little was superfluous, but Hemingway spoke directly to him. Reading "The Snows of Kilimanjaro" or "The Short Unhappy Life of Francis Macomber," Cary heard that voice in his head. It had a steady, consistent timbre that rarely wavered. He knew that some dismissed it as telegraphic, lacking poetry, the literary equivalent of a series of grunts, a drunk trying deliberately to sound sober, but for Cary, Hemingway was The Man. He admired William Shakespeare but was in love with old Ernest the way you fall in love with someone you want to be. Oh, he wanted the complete package: the travel, the big-game hunting, the khaki clothes, the drinks under the cold stars in front of a tent in Kenya, the airy Key West house with its six-toed cats and the portable Royal typewriter on the desk.

Although Mr. Murayama said he appreciated Cary's passion for Hemingway, he gave the boy an Incomplete on his first essay. He wrote that Cary had not done enough outside critical reading. Cary assumed that this was the reason why his teacher wanted to talk to him again.

"But all I needed were the stories," Cary had said. "I didn't want anything getting in the way of them, someone else's words and ideas."

"Evidently you are your father's son. Nevertheless, Master Lauder Jones, the criteria for the assignment were set out clearly. You needed to show that you had read and incorporated ideas from at least three critical sources, properly identified."

"I couldn't do that to him."

"Do what to whom?"

"Hemingway. Pick over his bones with a flock of other vultures. I wanted to write something that would honour his memory as a novelist. He didn't think much of academia."

"No," said Mr. Murayama, "not many of them did. It still fails to address the problem of this assignment."

"Fail me, I don't care."

"Yes, you do."

"Fine, I do. But he wouldn't have caved. He wouldn't have sold out his principles."

"Hemingway."

"Yes. Ernest Hemingway," said Cary, as if incanting the name of a saint. The author's narrative voice was water in a swift clear stream overflowing smooth bright round rocks. He told his teacher this.

"You're confusing the man with the books. He wasn't a particularly good person."

"That's what you say."

Mr. Murayama brought the discussion back to the paper Cary had written. He reminded him that universities would not tolerate sloppy imprecise scholarship.

"Then I'll give college a pass."

"No, you won't." He was right.

The reason Mr. Murayama wanted to speak with Cary on awards night had less to do with his student's first essay—after consideration, he decided to grant the paper an A-minus—and more to do with its subject. He had learned that the University of Nebraska was hosting a Hemingway symposium during the coming summer and was sponsoring an essay contest. The top papers submitted to the contest, which was open to high school students in the U.S. and Canada, would get a trip to the conference, all expenses paid. He said that he thought Cary should enter. The deadline was two months away.

"I'll help you. Your paper is well written."

"I guess that's why you gave me an Incomplete?"

"Reassessed. Are you now disputing your A?"

"A-minus."

"Shift with me, Cary. Different context. They are looking for personal essays. Your reasons why this author should continue to be read, his relevance to you, his impact on your life."

"Me versus everybody in North America. Sketchy odds. I don't think so, all due respect, sir."

"Just think it over. Will you do that, please?"

Later in the evening, at the reception in the gymnasium, Ambreen asked, "What did Murmur want?"

"He wants me to enter some lame essay contest. First prize, a trip to...wait for it. Omaha, Nebraska."

"That's the breadbasket of America. I remember that from grade-ten geography. It's the only thing I remember. You should do it."

"Would you?"

She took a sip of punch and gave him a look he'd never seen before. Her pupils were large and shimmery. "Darn tootin' I would!"

"Don't you want to know what the essay's supposed to be on?"

"Let me guess. Your idol." Ambreen thought Hemingway hopelessly male. She saw nothing but machismo covering profound insecurity. She wanted her man, when she found him, not to have to hide behind all the things men did to avoid their feelings: deep-sea fishing, lion hunting, running with the bulls. How infantile, she said. Cary was deflated; the thought of each of these pursuits thrilled him. Secretly he wanted to do everything his hero and Hemingway's heroes had. When it came time to die, he wanted it to happen on a mountaintop in Africa.

That night, Ambreen won prizes in French and history and another for the highest average in their year. Cary took the award for English literature. As he stood there, trying not to spill the little glass cup of sweet pink fluid, he thought about Murayama's essay contest. His teacher *had* said that he was willing to help. He must have seen something impressive in the writing, felt Cary's enthusiasm for the author. And a trip, anywhere, even to Omaha, Nebraska, was away from Halifax, at least for a few days. Maybe he'd be asked to read from his essay. He'd worked hard on it. But it would mean being apart from Ambreen. He wanted to spend every possible second with her. He yearned to be alone with an Ambreen who was completely open, who held out, if not her present feelings for him, then the possibility of love, for a time when they could truly be a couple.

Cary had come to recognize the type of boy Ambreen got crushes on. They were members of the student council and the basketball and volleyball teams. He tolerated them because they treated him with puzzled respect, as if they knew he understood them without revealing how he did. To them he was a lanky, shaggy haired, non-threatening oddity. They all wanted to be around Ambreen, who by twelfth grade had become cheekily confident again, and they knew that Cary was her friend, making him a de facto member of the club.

This group, a bunch of confident, athletic boys who did all right academically but preferred having a good time to working hard and probably didn't have the best judgment about the limits of recreation and pleasure, had adopted a boating club on Lake Banook, a large wooden pavilion that had once seen a more prosperous clientele and which now accepted into membership those just barely old enough to drink, which was almost the case with these boys: tall, handsome, too-healthy gods who trod the earth with ease and drove their own cars. They knew they were talented and didn't have to work hard, coming from money or having enough to have a good time. Their lives stretched ahead of them like a shiny new highway with precise lines painted on it. The girls who adhered to them were just as fair and flawless as they were. Pairings took place, but few lasted so long as to suggest monogamy or permanence, so that you could be going out with this person at Christmas and someone new by Valentine's Day and maybe back together with Santa's little helper in time for track and field season. The group was greater than the sum of its trysts and it knew it. These were almost still children, after all, they were so fresh and apple bright, giddy with late spring's warmth amid timbers dry from age like a Norse longhouse, except that the air was clean, and the music spoke of love not war.

Cary stopped asking Ambreen, "What are we?" and replaced the question with, "Are we, still?" and the answer, to his heart's joy and ease was, "Of course, you silly boy. I can't be expected to get on without you."

That year, Ambreen's parents moved to Lahore for the winter months, which they thought of as September to June in Canada, leaving her living with her father's elderly aunt in a Dartmouth condo near the ferry terminal. Her needs were taken care of; she had food and new clothes and ample spending money, but she missed the bustle and warmth of her family. She took a taxi to her old school rather than transfer to the one closer to where she lived and became dependent on Cary and the rest of the boathouse gang for emotional support. Some would say this was a poor substitute for family, but she did not, and she seemed especially to need his loyal, steady demeanour to help her through difficulty. Academics, sports, the obstacle course of social life in the corridors between classes—these were easy for her. What made her soar and dive, slip and crash, was love, which changed as often as the moon. The latest boy was one Theodore McNamee, red haired, freckled, with Chiclet teeth and green eyes. He was a bigger version of the boy on that old 1960s show, *Family Affair*. The day she saw her first episode on the rerun channel, she fell in love with the whole idea of being with a boy with red hair, and the next day, as if she had never seen him before, there was Teddy McNamee, not the tallest player on the volleyball team but one of the best defensive blockers because he could jump so high.

Cary knew that Teddy was seeing a girl who went to a high school in Bedford. When he tried to warn Ambreen, she said, "Oh, her? She's just a friend of the family. He's spending time with her to placate his parents. Her father and his are in business together. Teddy told me all about it."

Though Teddy was supposed to take Ambreen to the Valentine's dinner dance that year, he took this other girl instead. At first Ambreen refused to go. It took much cajoling and soft persuasion by everybody. Finally, she got dressed up and joined Cary at the table of friends without dates. They were stuck at the back of the hall near the entrance to the kitchen. Though they found it difficult to hear the band and the after-dinner speakers, it was of little consequence and added to their feeling of splendid isolation. Ambreen watched Teddy and his date, the little hussy all daisy delicate in pastels with a honking big floral cancer attached to her wrist and too much makeup and her hair done up so tight it seemed to be pulling her eyes wide open so that she might never be able to sleep. Ambreen whispered these things to Cary as a means of coping and releasing her negativity, but also having some fun on this disastrous night. He didn't know exactly how to react, because he wanted nothing more than for Teddy and this other chickadee, this Cheryl or Cherry or Sugar Plum, to be hap-hap-happy together ever after so that Ambreen could see that and get over Teddy already and just enjoy being part of the group, with—it went without saying—her faithful Cary Lauder Jones by her side.

A WEEK AFTER GRADUATION, Cary took a phone call at home from Mr. Murayama. Could he meet him that day at the school? He had something important to discuss. Having no other commitments, Cary walked to the building which for the past nine months had been the center of his life, that combination of prison, community hall and cathedral of possibility. Unpopulated but for the occasional shadowy figure of a teacher moving lightly with the tread of a happy sprite, it was a foreign place now. A custodial worker was buffing the newly waxed floor of the foyer, and Cary had to scoot around the edge by the trophy cases to get past him.

Mr. Murayama's room was on the second floor, way down at the end of the hall, and walking along its unlit length made the young man anxious, as if this were not a week after the end of his high school career but a day before his first in a new place. The empty lockers stood open. In some, soiled paper and old ballpoint pens littered the bottom. Abandoned posters, balls of brown paper, a three-ring binder torn in half. Being there and seeing these ruins and not feeling the usual hum of the place made him uneasy.

Mr. Murayama looked the way he always had during the school year, except that on this day he wasn't wearing his suit jacket. A filing cabinet near his desk at the front of the room was open and a stack of full manila folders lay on a chair. When he saw Cary, he smiled and bade him sit in a desk at the front of a row. The teacher crossed his arms and leaned back against his desk.

"I have some news that I think will make you happy, Cary. I hope it makes you happy."

"What is it?"

"Do you recall your Hemingway essay from the fall, the one I urged you to submit to the symposium?"

"Yes."

"You never did submit it, did you?"

Cary shrugged, looking away as if to say, *It was my decision not to*, while also feeling guilty about it.

"It needed very little," said Mr. Murayama.

"Very little what?"

"In the way of changes. Of course, it required proper bibliographic citations. Luckily, I found some excellent sources that supported your argument."

"But I didn't use any. I didn't read anybody else. And anyway, you said they were looking for personal essays."

"Yes, I know. But what you wrote, those ideas, they have been articulated by others, you must know that. Reputable scholars. It was simply a matter of inserting some quotations, providing footnotes."

"You did that?"

"Yes. I know that this is highly unorthodox. However, I feel strongly that what I did with your paper was what you would have done had you followed my initial direction."

"You rewrote my essay?"

"And submitted it to the contest. I had to use a courier to get it there on time. Don't worry about the cost."

"The cost? You rewrote my paper and sent it off without asking me. I don't believe this!"

"But Cary, you're not getting it. Why do you think I called you here today? Do you think I would have roused you out of your bed on a morning when you didn't have to be up had you not…?" Only his eyes, slivered, catlike, betrayed his glee.

"Not what?"

"Been chosen as a finalist. You're going to Nebraska."

Cary stared open-mouthed at him. They were going to pay for him and his teacher advisor, Mr. Murayama, to travel to the university, stay three nights in a hotel and attend the conference, where they would each present a paper. Murayama's was on Hemingway's use of Shakespearean tropes in *The Sun Also Rises*. Murayama wasn't even interested in "Earnest" Hemingway, he remembered thinking. At least the man had never given that indication before.

THAT NIGHT a bunch of them from the boathouse took in the late show at the Barrington. Afterwards, as sleep resistant as two-year-olds, they wandered west along Spring Garden and up Robie to Quinpool, that fine, wide, unpretentious street, in the general direction of home. Not much of interest lay beyond the Dragon's Tail, a restaurant that served thin soup, tough egg rolls, morsels of anaemic pork edged with a suspect pink dye, and soggy noodles, unless you were after the staid romance of a stroll through the exclusive neighbourhood where the rich resided, tucked into the pit of the Northwest Arm. Walking there in moonlight was something their parents might do, and so beyond contemplation.

Next to the Chinese restaurant was the Parnassus, which closed its doors in the early evening, well before late-night hunters after almond guy ding and sweet and sour chicken balls were becoming restless and hungry. Some slacker skater-boys were abrading the concrete step leading up to the Greek restaurant. The owner, Stavros Karetonakis, was known to drive by at night to catch these miscreants and confiscate their boards, threatening to haul the boys into the courthouse up on Spring Garden if he ever caught them at it again. The threats did no good. They knew where Mr. K. pawned their wheels, which was at his cousin's shop, and the owner, a former skater himself, was sympathetic to the boys and charged them a scant margin, barely enough to cover his costs, over what he paid Karetonakis for them. "A man has to live," he would complain. "Food itself, the necessities of life, are becoming so expensive as to be luxuries. Where will it end!"

And so they tumbled into the Dragon's Tail, where the buckling pressboard walls were decorated with gaudy plastic masks and the booths had ripped red-vinyl seats. With them that night was Ergo, a skater whose real name was Horst. They called him Ergo because he used the word incorrectly in place of "however." Ambreen was with someone new, Jordan Fitzhugh, the school's best debater. Jordan built homemade synthesizers à la Moog and was the only boy they knew who deliberately shaved his head. He had the right head for it, tapered slightly like a missile's nose, and eyes so blue you expected his skin to be cold to the touch. Instead, he was always hot, sweaty damp even in winter, and when he smiled it hit you like a spotlight plugged into an insanely strong power source. It was as if Teddy McNamee, the freckle-faced two-timer, had never existed.

Jordan said he was writing software for a proposed game millions of people could play at once, with each player controlling thousands of different avatars, an entire planet's worth of characters and resources. Though such games were legion online, the programs were wholly inadequate to his vision. Ambreen teased him, saying that he must have time-travelled from the twenty-third century and brought all his kooky-ass ideas back with him.

When the soup came, Cary thought, *Here we are, white dumplings suspended in thin broth. We float, going nowhere. Inside us is a bit of something, maybe a flavourful morsel, but if we let someone open us with his teeth we're done for.* He thought about Murayama and the contest and the trip to Nebraska. He felt like backing out, despite the chance to get away from soggy Halifax for a few days.

Ergo was sitting jittery beside him in the booth. His pupils were huge. He was some relation to Mr. Karetonakis. That was the reason why he never got his skateboard taken away. Cary felt it with his toe and when it rolled, he was reassured but couldn't say why.

Ambreen said, "You'll never guess what my father wants—no, what he has decided unilaterally without my consent. He just dropped this on me this afternoon in an email. He has found a husband for me. If I didn't believe it could happen, I'd be on the floor laughing. I'd laugh so hard I'd fall off my chair, and Mr. Hong would ask me to leave, and you know things have to get pretty ugly in here for Mr. Hong to throw anybody out."

Ergo, straightening in his seat, said, "But you and Jordan are a couple. You two should be the ones getting married." Cary's stomach lurched.

Jordan said something about finding a compromise solution, seeking a middle way through this, as if he had been handed a prompt and given a minute to respond. Resolved: Sometimes the best rebellion is capitulation. He could be such a prig. Didn't he know what this was doing to Ambreen? Couldn't he see how much she loved him? Or how much Cary loved her? It was going to be August before long. The summer was disappearing. He heard himself say, "You should run away together." It was out before he could take it back. He loved her that much. He wanted to say, 'Go and be with Jordan if that will keep you in my life.' In that moment he hated Mr. Aswari, his love's jailer. Ambreen might just as well have been branded stock. It made Cary so angry he felt like punching Ergo. But Ergo was suddenly sweet, a kid with a sexless prettiness anyone would have warmed to. Ergo would have to be part of this, Cary decided, because the boy had been there when it all got laid out. Ergo knew the street, how to procure valuable things. What if the four of them took off for Vancouver, the other side of the world? Ergo could do his thing, maybe snowboard at Whistler, turn pro, he was supposed to be that good up at Wentworth. Jordan could invent stuff, Cary could write and paint, and Ambreen—what did he see Ambreen doing? Running, doing her yoga, going to shows and galleries. Shopping. Being a mother eventually. He didn't know. He'd never thought about Ambreen being anything but Ambreen. She'd never had to do anything. A-plusses, loads of close friends, the admiration of her teachers, all had come effortlessly in high school. As she would say, "I am who I am and I am where I'm from," and that identity was fully formed in Cary's mind. They had had this discussion a few times: What will the beautiful Ambreen be when she grows up? Boys flitted close to her flame. She loved the attention, liked to flirt and make people jealous. In Cary's eyes she would never change, though like anyone she was becoming a different person. She'd mentioned medicine a few times. Dr. Ambreen Aswari.

"What kind of doctor?"

"Witch doctor," she said.

"No," he countered, "more like bitch doctor. I can see you now: Well, Mr. Patient, I can try to remove your gallstones the usual way, but what would be the fun in that? I think you should have the full experience of passing them through that tiny urethra of yours, don't you?"

"Teddy McNamee!" she exclaimed gleefully.

"Indubitably!"

"Irreversibly!"

Bitch doctor? He laughed at the notion, partly because it no longer fit. She was spending more time and thought in yoga practice. She'd given up meat shortly after having to dissect a foetal pig, and her smooth olive skin glowed as if from an inner light. She spoke quietly unless provoked. Gone were the traces of the former she-wolf of the elementary-school playground. Through her flowed a peaceful healing energy.

He had no doubt she would make a fine doctor. The thought made him proud and uneasy. He was losing her, not necessarily to Jordan alone but to a larger force. She could live without people if she had to. She didn't need Cary as much as she used to. Now infrequent were their chats late into the evening, the long text exchanges that were like a monologue shared by two voices, the ones he wanted never to end.

MR. MURAYAMA flew to Omaha before Cary did, because the teacher presented his paper two days before Cary was due to give his. Murayama had made all the arrangements, booking their flights and rooms in the conference hotel, the downtown Marriott, before Cary had even confirmed that he was going. His father had tried to stay out of it and let Cary make up his own mind, but the look on Douglas's face whenever Cary ventured downstairs and the little comments that burst from him like popped corn were persuasive: "Your mother keeps asking me if you've decided yet. I think she's more impressed than anyone." "You were an early reader, earlier than any of your siblings." "Not to influence you or anything, son, but this would look so good on your *curriculum vitae*."

Mr. Murayama hadn't altered much at all in Cary's paper. The three references he'd inserted supported what Cary had written about Papa Hemingway's style as though the student had found them himself. Murayama had given it a new title: "Universal Truths Behind the Masque of the Masculine in Ernest Hemingway's African Stories." The more Cary repeated it the more he liked its three-beat rhythm and suggestion of erudition. Was he being seduced? He supposed he was.

Murayama picked him up in a rental car when Cary's plane

landed at Eppley Airfield. They drove the three miles into the city, the car's four windows open to the hot dry air. Murayama wore a white linen shirt unbuttoned at the neck and sleeves rolled to the elbows. Cary had never seen him looking so relaxed, left elbow extending beyond the edge of the window, right hand leisurely, almost lazily working the power steering. They might have been friends driving to the beach. They drove beside the Missouri River for a stretch.

Later, in his hotel room, Cary found nearby Manawa State Park on a map. The park was in Council Bluffs, Iowa, across the state line. The student conference was supposed to culminate with a barbecue and swim at Lake Manawa. He had forgotten to pack a swimsuit. He wished Ambreen were there. Telepathically he asked her, "What if nobody talks to me?" Telepathically she answered, "They will. Go up to them and say hello. Everybody will be as freaked out as you." He felt confident about reading his paper and answering questions about it. It was the standing around and trying to talk with strangers afterwards that made his stomach flip.

He changed out of jeans and hoodie into a pair of dark-blue chinos, brown-leather loafers, and a lighter blue long-sleeved shirt with a button-down-collar. Mr. Murayama knocked on his door at 5:30 p.m., as he had said he would, and they rode the elevator down to the hotel restaurant, which he told Cary had better-than-average fare.

"They serve an excellent steak tartare here, though I will never get used to being poured a cup of coffee as soon as I sit down at the table," he said, "whether I ask for one or not."

Cary looked at him, amused: as in the car, Mr. Murayama hadn't stopped talking the entire time they were together. Cary thought, *Fine, thanks for asking. My flights? Well, we sat forever on the tarmac at O'Hare and there was some turbulence over Nowheresville, Indiana, but aside from that… Yes, the mattress is to my liking. I don't know, a little groggy, I guess. Is this what jet lag feels like? It's my first long plane trip…*

"…not that I harbour regrets, mind you, Cary. I suppose what I am realizing, being here in this scholarly milieu—Oh! Oh! Necessary digression. Forgive me, this is too delightful. I must, must, MUST tell you about one of my fellow panellists, I believe he hails from Purdue. Contributing editor to the *Norton Western Anthology*, no less. Not once, not thrice, no, I'm sure it was half a dozen times he pronounced the word, "scarlarly." SCARLARLY! Not a word of a lie! Sorry. It's beneath me, beneath any of us, I know, to draw attention to a "scarlar's" linguistic quirks. I fall on the mercy of such kinder hearts as yours. A-hem." He shifted, still on the verge of giggling, in his seat as though righting a skewed potted plant in its saucer.

"What was I saying? Ah, yes, I realize, being here among these learned minds, that, to draw upon Frost's now hackneyed dichotomy, I chose the road many deem less desirable. It is certainly considered lesser social coin, the work I do. The dedicated teacher must find satisfaction in the less obvious, harder-to-reach places, in a student's intellectual ignition, as it were, someone's such as yours, for example. For every one of you who distinguishes himself, a hundred pass in and out of my classroom door without my knowing, really, what change I have made in their minds. Have I helped them harness their imagination? What do they think about when they think about literature, assuming they do at all?" To the tune of "Que Será, Será," he sang, "Will they be readers, will they be dolts? What does it mean to me?"

Cary's stomach gurgled. He tried to peek down at the menu without drawing his dinner companion's attention.

"Cary, you must be ravenous. And here I've been blathering away like a flapping jib-sail."

A strange feeling washed over him. He looked at the man sitting across from him, a now familiar face, his English Literature instructor clad in natty blazer, crisp shirt, and silk tie. He was speaking to Cary as though they were decades-long colleagues, about matters he assumed the young man cared about as intensely as he did. The man Cary had ached to impress for so long had turned into a species of talking mannequin. Murayama seemed almost nervous, allowing no silence longer than a brief pause to chew his food or sip from his water glass. Cary was there at that prestigious conference because of this man's ministrations. It struck him that what Mr. Murayama had done in editing Cary's paper, if it ever became known, could get them both disqualified and sent home in disgrace. Had that possibility even crossed his mind? He seemed suddenly pitiable. Cary wondered if there was anyone waiting for the man back home or if he lived alone. Why was he so excited to be in godforsaken Omaha with one of his students, when all Cary felt was homesick and sorry for him?

He didn't want to study the greats, he wanted to be one. That was the difference.

His teacher was shrinking before him. Murayama had helped Cary learn because Cary had wanted to. Did he inspire him? The answer was increasingly, no, he no longer did. Were Cary to fight in a war for a just cause and be wounded, or fly a rescue plane into a remote and dangerous wilderness, or write the novel that made the world re-examine its priorities, would he say, "Well done you, Cary Lauder Jones," or would he think that a potential scholar, someone meant to toil humbly as an interpreter in the vast lush lea of literature, had been lost to posterity?

MR. MURAYAMA'S suggestion after dinner that they retire to his room for a brief go-over of Cary's presentation felt strange, presumptuously intimate. The teacher had been engagingly funny in the hotel restaurant, going so far as to draw their waitress into a discussion of Nebraska's literary greats. Pretty in an early Janet Jackson way, she looked young enough to still be in high school. It was such an unusual question that she froze for an instant. Nebraska's literary greats? "I think a famous actor was born over in Laurel," she said. "He played bad guys in westerns and stuff." Her eyes opened wider. "But you mean books, right? Authors and writers? The only one of those I had to read was Willa Cather. I don't think she was born here, though."

Mr. Murayama put her immediately at ease, letting her know that she knew more about the arts and letters of her fine state than he did. "It would be like you meeting me for the first time and, solely on the basis of the way I looked, expecting me to be able to speak Japanese."

"Oh, you're from Japan? I was wondering, you know, because you don't sound like you're from there. I had this friend from Russia, she was on an exchange here for a year, but everybody knew where she was from by the way she talked."

Murayama asked her what she knew about Willa Cather. Had she ever read *O Pioneers!* or *My Ántonia*? The second one, she said, although he shouldn't ask her any hard questions about the book, as she didn't remember much about it. "There's like a museum over in Red Cloud you can visit. We went there on a school trip once. I grew up in Lincoln, so it wasn't too bad of a journey. I guess it was long enough. Are you here to find out about Willa Cather?"

He told her about the Hemingway symposium and asked her more questions about what it was like growing up in this part of the world. It must have been hard being part of such a small minority. Oh, no, she said. She had never been made to feel less than equal there.

"Really?" he probed. "Not even a little?"

"Well, maybe a little. But there's lots of us around and I got white cousins and in-laws all over the place, so it's not much of an issue." She grew quiet as she gathered their used plates and utensils.

"I hope I haven't offended you," he said. "It was never my intention. Sometimes my curiosity gets the better of me."

"Offended? You'll have to do a lot more than that to offend me, mister."

"Oh?" said the teacher suggestively, "such as?"

Cary thought, *He's flirting. This is how an older man flirts with a younger woman.* Thinking of it in those terms brought an anthropological detachment to the situation. He wondered if this was the kind of exchange he could ever initiate. The restaurant wasn't busy, allowing the waitress to linger at their table longer than usual. No one came over to demand she resume her serving duties. Her name tag said "Shaylean." Cary studied her responses: the way she paused before replying, smiling slightly, not at them but at something across the room, perhaps, nobody in particular or no one visible. It was the question itself she was smiling at, the notion that an intelligent, exotic-looking man was paying her the compliment of his attention. Did she see it that way or was this a product of Cary's imagination? Maybe she spoke to all her customers this way. At the same time, laughing, playing with her hair, and moistening her lips, she barbed her utterances with an ironic edge. It was as though she were saying, "Did you really actually ask me that?" And, "Aren't you a little on the old side for somebody like me?" And, "So let me get this straight. You look like George Takei, but you sound like Anthony Hopkins. What gives?"

And what was this for? For whose benefit? Mr. Murayama telling her she was clearly too smart to spend the rest of her life waiting tables and, "Tell me, Shaylean, what are your aspirations, what do you see yourself doing a year from now? Have you read, "Hills Like White Elephants"? You should. You must travel to Africa, go to the Far East, it will nourish your soul." And she replying, "Oh, it will, will it? Are you coming along as my tour guide?" And he saying, "That could be arranged. What do you think, Cary? Should I open lovely Shaylean's eyes to the natural wonders of the globe?"

Shaylean was enjoying Mr. Murayama's suggestive attention. Cary couldn't recall Ambreen ever being this way with him, even when she teased him for his all-too-obvious ardour. It always seemed possible that Ambreen never meant anything she said. "Come on," he wanted to say, "no more joking. My love for you is serious, adult. This is me, your steadfast Cary." Trying, becoming exasperated, and being boring according to Ambreen, who was forever dancing one step out of his reach. What was going on between Miss Nebraska and Mr. Murayama, on the other hand, seemed like it could easily lead somewhere, become something intimate. Could Cary ever learn to talk to a girl this way? He was going to have to learn some moves: how to attract a woman and let himself be lured at the same time. Was it expected or was this all moot if he already knew who he wanted to spend his life with? Why learn how to be a player if he was never going to play?

The meal ended, the waitress brought the bill and received her modest tip, Mr. Murayama being evidently as careful with money as he was with words. What had been a few buoyantly entertaining minutes heavy on suggestiveness though light on substance and consequence ended with a return to cool propriety. Cary felt the arrival of this ending more acutely than did his teacher, apparently. In the elevator up to their floor, Cary said, after thanking him for the meal, "I liked her. I hope we get her again for breakfast."

"Really? She was diverting, I suppose. But rather uninspired. Uninspiring, wouldn't you say? I would not hoist a flag in her honour, if you catch my drift. Prettiness and a musical laugh will take a woman only so far. For me, at least, she must possess something more, some unique quality. Wit or a naïve genius for the mandolin or the grace of a Karen Kain."

Cary had had teachers who had unsheathed their cruelty over the years, and while Mr. Murayama had been strict, he had not, even about those he had ejected from his classroom, disparaged anyone's character. Identified in sharp specifics their transgressions, yes, but to Cary's knowledge the man was ever the consummate educator, one for whom each student deserved an equal opportunity to learn unhampered by Mr. Murayama's opinion of them, if indeed he had ever formed an opinion about them aside from their effort and achievement.

At the door to Mr. Murayama's room, Cary demurred when the man ushered him inside. "I'm fine, really, I don't need to practise my talk. I feel pretty good about it."

"Of course you need to rehearse, don't be silly. Humour me. I have as much riding on this as you do, Cary."

"I don't know. It feels weird."

"Oh, come now. Don't insult me. We shall leave the door open if you'd like."

"No, that's okay," Cary said, uneasily, preceding his teacher inside.

"Make yourself comfortable, my boy," said Murayama, removing his suit jacket and necktie and rolling his sleeves past the elbow. Cary recalled his bare arm resting on the sill of the open window of the car earlier that day, the smooth, hairless skin a different hue but the same flawless quality as Ambreen's. Murayama was standing, bent at the waist, while he perused the contents of the hotel room's mini bar. He chose two small bottles of chilled Chablis, saying, "No brandy, I'm afraid. This will have to suffice. Normally I forego adding such exorbitantly priced items to my bill. Do you condemn me for being frivolous, Cary? Go ahead, I deserve it. I was thinking only that we should mark this occasion somehow. Your achievement, however it goes tomorrow. A toast to Cary Lauder Jones, author of an outstanding student essay!"

While Murayama was filling the only drinking vessels available, plastic water-cups from the room's washroom, Cary almost added, "Your achievement, too, sir." He would not have been able to say it without sounding less than celebratory and so let it pass. It did feel special to be recognized in this way, in a place so removed from his milieu. He really didn't need to practise reading his paper, and though Murayama didn't know how well prepared his student was, Cary wanted him to feel that he was still an important tutor in that regard. Murayama had an investment in Cary's success, after all, having polished the paper to its present lustre. Let him have his moment, Cary decided. After tomorrow this would all be over and soon after that he'd probably see the man only in passing. That was fine. As much as Cary was indebted to him for reinforcing his love of literature, which to the young man was the same as dreaming possible worlds, Mr. Murayama was not a man

Cary saw himself emulating or becoming lifelong friends with. That feeling had gelled after dinner, with Murayama's unconscious imitation of an old-time movie star, that bit of canned flirtation that was as exotic to Cary as were the courtship rituals of a remote society. Had it been a lesson? Was he meant to observe, learn, and eventually follow the man's lead, as though he sensed Cary's shyness and was helpfully showing him how it should begin and proceed, this mating dance? *No thank you, sir,* he remembered thinking. *I will sit here and sip my cold wine and exercise my newfound powers of forbearance.*

"Do you find it cold in here?" Murayama asked. It wasn't cold, it was comfortable.

"I don't know. Maybe a little."

Murayama rose from his chair, one of two in a nook set apart from the bedroom proper and went to look at the temperature control. He caused the air conditioner to stop running by raising the setting to 80 degrees F. Immediately the room became stuffy, the air warm, stale smelling and close. He sat on the edge of the bed, wineglass in his right hand, the other pressing the small of his back. "I must have done something while I was leaning over," he said. "Stupid. I should know better. You wouldn't think that a man with my slight build would experience back trouble, would you? It's an inherited condition, exacerbated by the occasional wrong turn or loss of tone brought on by laziness. I didn't do my stretching this morning." He described in detail his back exercises, which he did as soon as he woke and before having anything to eat, not even tea or coffee. As he spoke, he moved his body in abbreviated ways to suggest the postures. In one of them he lay on his back with one leg bent at the knee and that foot flat on the floor close to his buttock. He brought the opposite foot up and across so that it rested on the bent knee. Reaching his arms forward so that he was grasping the thigh of the bent leg, he completed the move by raising the ensemble off the floor to the count of ten. "Here, let me show you," he said.

He lay back on the bed to demonstrate the movement, only to declare the mattress too soft and his back too painful. "I could use the floor," he said, "but I would most likely seize and then you would have to either carry me out the door to the nearest hospital or call for an ambulance." When he tried to sit up, he gave a yelp of pain. It was high-pitched like a pug's bark. He lay back and curled on his side into a foetal position.

"What can I do?" Cary asked.

"Ice. It's the only thing that works. A bag of ice or a freezer pack," he said through clenched teeth.

Cary filled a bucket with ice from a dispenser at the end of the hallway. The bucket, being insulated, would not have provided much relief. The small waste can beside the ice machine was lined with an empty white plastic bag. He transferred the ice to the bag, tying it closed and hoping it had no holes.

When Cary offered to wrap the ice-filled bag in a hand towel, Murayama insisted the cold plastic be held directly against the skin at the small of his back. He instructed Cary to time it: ten minutes on, followed by ten minutes off, alternating, fifty minutes in all. He lay on his left side at the edge of the bed, the expanse of which struck Cary as wasteful. A family of four adults could sleep there and never encounter each other. He rolled the chair he had been sitting on to the side of the bed closest to the patient so that he could sit while holding the ice bag in place.

Murayama kept thanking Cary, saying, "You have no idea how good that feels, my boy," and apologizing for inconveniencing him.

"Not a problem," Cary insisted. "Glad to help. Are you sure we shouldn't call someone?"

"Oh no," he said. "Experience has taught me that this gives the only reliable relief. It has to do with a narrowing of the spine. When my core muscles become lax and I bend the wrong way, this inevitably happens."

The bright, engaging man-in-charge from dinner was now a sadly supine figure, if not someone in defeat, then a man forced to regroup, be patient, and replenish his arsenal. He looked childlike turned away from Cary, the ridges of his spine forming a delicately bowed archipelago, the sock-covered soles of his feet marking apparently truncated legs. He looked vulnerable. Cary's urge was more to protect than to nurse. If he could have manipulated the man's spine to alleviate the pain with a single decisive pop, Cary would have done so. Suffering and the time consumed by recovery always struck him as just plain dumb. He could never be a nurse or a doctor, he recognized about himself.

At the ten-minute mark Murayama got off the bed gingerly and took a few steps around the room. Holding on to the TV stand for support, he lowered himself onto the floor, bent his legs and pressed the small of his back into the carpet. He breathed in through his nose and out through his mouth. The plastic bag wasn't leaking, but the ice was half melted. Cary repeated his excursion to the dispenser.

When he returned, he was surprised to hear the shower running. The bathroom door was wide open. He placed the bag of ice in the little fridge, unsure whether he should announce his return or leave to give the man privacy. The clothes Murayama had been wearing lay neatly folded on the chair Cary had been sitting on. Of these Cary noted the socks, which were rolled and tucked, the top of one folded back over the ball formed by the pair, so that it looked like an eyeless face smiling up at him.

Cary decided to alert him, saying in a raised voice through the bathroom door that the new ice was being kept cold and that he would see him in the morning.

He heard him say, "Cary, don't go," his voice clear but plaintive. "I need you, please. I still can't get my night clothes back on by myself." The warm shower, he explained, was a needed contrast to the ice application. Alternating heat and cold stimulated blood flow to the afflicted area. "You would have learned that in Mrs. Calhoun's biology class. Don't worry, I will be the model of bashful decorum. It's just that I can't lift my legs high enough to put my pyjamas on by myself. It's not half embarrassing."

"You shouldn't be," Cary said. "I won't look." He tried to sound offhand; it came out sickly, tentative, as though everything he did and said were shrouded in doubt.

Mr. Murayama told him where to find his pyjamas, which Cary retrieved from the top drawer of the dresser while the man dried with a towel what parts of himself he could. He emerged with the white plush bath towel wrapped around his waist. It surprised Cary to see how leanly muscled he was. He looked like a less intense Bruce Lee, at least from the waist up.

Cary knelt on both knees, having rolled the pyjama bottoms in preparation for Murayama to insert his first foot into the leg hole. He could lift his foot only a hand's span up off the floor. Cary had to work quickly because Mr. Murayama was trembling with the effort, his hands placed on top of Cary's head for balance. He got first one then the other foot into place so that Cary could raise the waistband high enough that the teacher could grab the garment and bring it the rest of the way up. Cary thought, just shoot me before I ever reach this state of decrepitude.

"Thank you, my boy. I think I can take it from here."

"Are you sure?"

"Yes. You've been a godsend. I'm just sorry you have had to see me this way."

Me, too, he thought. "Please call me if you need help."

"I will indeed. Off you go, then. Tomorrow's a big day."

"You're sure you're going to be okay?"

"It's feeling better already," he said, trying to suppress a wince of pain. "Thank you, Cary. Sleep well."

Cary left the room before Murayama got into bed. To have witnessed that, to have been there to help him, tuck in his sheets, add a soothing word, would have been too much. For both of them, he sensed.

THE STUDENT DAY of the Hemingway symposium was at once less than Cary had expected and more. He had been anticipating an air of excitement to inform the presentations, a dramatically lit stage with a vibrantly coloured backdrop, perhaps, a large audience filling an auditorium, even television cameras. The event did take place in a large lecture theatre, which had steeply banked rows of seats. He and his fellow finalists, twenty in all, were led in and told to sit in the front row, nearest the slightly elevated platform from which they would deliver their papers. A cursory scan of the hall as they took their places revealed a sparse, scattered audience, slightly more people than numbered the student group.

By the time Cary stood to read his essay, at about the mid-point of the roster, the audience had dwindled. The bright houselights were left on throughout. Attention on him was less than rapt as he began to speak. A young woman sitting two rows behind the finalists was writing by hand in a stenographer's notebook. Mr. Murayama, who was sitting stiffly a few seats away from her in the same row, said he thought she was covering the event for one of the university newspapers. A pair Cary took to be professors were whispering audibly to each other; he tried to block them out as he enumerated the reasons why his favourite author's stories were so important. Somehow what had felt so convincing on the page seemed thin as he heard himself talk about the hammer-forged beauty of Hemingway's sentences. To Cary, the author and adventurer was saying that life is the opposite of fleeting, that it is heavy, consequential. The weight of living is something no one can avoid. The opposite of unbearable, however, that weight, rather than a burden, is precious; it's what keeps us from flying off the earth and becoming lost, insubstantial, mere dust circling the planet. Hemingway pulls us back, time and again, to life's clean hard edges, its vivid surfaces: the obscenely naked head of a vulture; brandy sloshing out of a glass into a nearby saucer; underarm sweat staining a dress; the carved, polished wood of a Swiss wall-clock in a train station waiting room.

Afterwards Cary answered two sets of questions from the audience. The first was from the young woman Mr. Murayama thought was a student reporter: "Given the instances of sexism and racism in Ernest Hemingway's writing, what do you think will be his legacy? Will he still be read in a hundred years, and should he be?"

Cary stood, longer than felt comfortable, for him and for those waiting for him to answer, without speaking. He imagined their waitress Shaylean sitting in the audience, listening for his answer. Her challenging voice in his ear: *Oh, this better be good.* Finally, he assembled a choppy response that began with the admission that he didn't feel he'd studied the author extensively enough to judge his deficiencies and ended with a reiteration of praise for Hemingway's prose style, which in Cary's mind was what the writer would be remembered for. During his halting reply, he began, stopped, and changed tacks often enough that he lost his thread. Somewhere in there he thought he said that Hemingway was both an innovator and a product of his time.

"What did you think of the stream of consciousness passage in which Harry riffs on snow?" asked one of the whispering profs.

"I'm sorry? I don't..."

"It's in 'The Snows of Kilimanjaro.' The couple is talking about his gangrenous leg and what carbolic acid did to his blood vessels and she's begging him not to drink alcohol while they wait for him to be transported to a hospital in time and, suddenly, he's remembering or imagining all these vivid scenes involving snow."

"Yes," said Cary, "I remember now. It's one of my favourite parts. I think he's escaping, in a way, temporarily, from the tension of his situation. It's what the mind does without meaning to. Maybe trying to save itself while the rest of the body is dying?"

The man nodded without a follow-up question. Cary couldn't be sure, but he thought he detected a rewarding smile.

WHILE THEY WAITED in the airport for their flight to Chicago the next morning, Mr. Murayama said he thought Cary deserved at least an honourable mention in the competition. "You handled yourself admirably, given the circumstances."

Cary asked him how his back was feeling.

"Better, thank you for asking. And thank you for your assistance, Cary." He could tell that his teacher was still embarrassed that Cary had seen him so incapacitated.

They sat quietly for a few minutes. Cary scrolled through his phone while Mr. Murayama read a book. It was approaching the time when they should have been lining up to board. Just as Mr. Murayama sighed and placed his book facedown and open on his lap, it was announced that their flight was delayed at least an hour. Connecting with their plane to Toronto, and from there home to Halifax, was going to be tight. Cary expected "Murmur" to become angry or anxious. Instead, the man grew more serene.

"That fellow who asked you the question about snow—do you know who he is?" Cary shook his head no.

"He teaches creative writing at the Iowa Writers' Workshop. I believe he is also director of the program." Seeing that Cary did not know what that was, Mr. Murayama gave him a brief history and list of some of the more well-known writers who were graduates of the school. As he described its approach and format, and watched Cary's eyes grow wider, he became increasingly animated. His grin was the same expression he would get in class when the keeners, that small group of devotees who cared about stories and plays and poems, were with him and nowhere else, not daydreaming about girls or dead leopards or snow so smooth it looked like meringue, but there, rooted, hooked on every word he was saying. The Iowa Writers' Workshop. How was it that Cary had never heard of this place? He decided in that moment that this was where he had to go to school.

It took him three years to get there. He was late applying the first year and his application was thin. Then there was what happened to John and their father. That threw them all into a black hole for longer than a year. Anya started her program at art school in Toronto, dropped out, came home, took up with the boy who used to panhandle in front of the frame shop where she used to work. She moved in with his family for a while. He and she went on to work with troubled youth in Timmins, Ontario. The Barrington movie theatre continued to thrive, proving that nothing can kill our urge to sit in the dark with a bunch of strangers and be transported to other worlds, occupy other lives for two hours. There was the whole business with Ambreen running away from her fiancé. Cary drove out to Vancouver with her. She had a baby, Jordan's, but Jordan bowed out of the scene soon after. Somehow, she and Cary found their footing. They moved into a dry basement apartment with adequate light, just off Commercial Drive. Cary stayed home and wrote while taking care of Elliot, who had Down Syndrome. Elliot would make it to age 36 before he died of multiple organ failure. Ambreen got into medical school at UBC. She and Cary were each other's essential bolster until they no longer needed the support, the human crutch one might call it. Cary went away to Iowa City, learned that thinking and dreaming and reading about writing is not the same as writing. And so he began his long apprenticeship. Not a day passed that he did not wish his father were still alive, to talk to, to read his drafts and bestow upon him his experience and wisdom. Even more than that, Cary wished that Douglas Lauder Jones were there to let him inside, even for a moment, to see what it was that had been haunting him. Maybe there was nothing. Maybe it was just who he was, a private man who loved to drink more than he loved to write. A man who needed someone to tell him, now and again, well done, sir, well done.

While they were airport captives that day travelling home from Nebraska, Mr. Murayama told Cary an odd tale about taking his elderly mother to her accountant to consult about her taxes. That story led to another about a Caribbean cruise he took over the Christmas holiday one year. Perhaps because he had been talking about the Iowa Writers' Workshop, Mr. Murayama said that he wished he had the knack for writing fiction. He thought it might make an interesting short story. Academic writing came naturally to him, he said, but fiction, whenever he had tried to create it, inevitably turned into a lecture. Cary remembered every detail of both anecdotes. Although Mr. Murayama hadn't explicitly given him permission to turn them into a piece of fiction, Cary felt in a way that he was suggesting he do just that. "Run with it, Master Lauder Jones," Cary imagined him saying. "See what you can make of it."

Flu, Flue, Leif, Life

As soon as they walked through the door from the parking lot outside, they were startled by a large dog in the ground-floor office immediately off the entrance. They flinched at the menace in her bark and the looming underside of her, seen and heard through the barrier of the glass door of the office. On her hind legs she was taller than Mrs. Murayama. A man appeared and restrained the animal, holding her though not yanking on the thick leather collar. The man was tidily bearded, white haired, and muscular in a tight, short-sleeved golf shirt. To Mr. Murayama he seemed the kind of man who preferred having his dog with him to leaving the animal at home, despite the detrimental effect she might have on business. Mr. Murayama did not notice what that business was. He imagined that the dog owner was someone who had worked at various jobs demanding physical strength as well as an interest in and knowledge of matters mechanical. Now here he was, retirement age as was Mr. Murayama, passing his days in a low-rent office in a business park, not letting his hound outside often enough, hating the solitude and relative inactivity, waiting for the phone to ring, for custom, for orders, worried that too few people were booking appointments for whatever it was he did, what service he paid so handsomely to advertise. They climbed the stairs to the office Mrs. Murayama thought was her accountant's, only to be told by a young woman holding a plasterer's trowel that, no, sorry, there was no such business there, as they could see by the space, which was emptied of furniture and under renovation.

"You might try the other building," she offered.

"What other building?" said Mrs. Murayama indignantly.

"The 200 block," she said, pointing out a window. "Next one over. Easy mistake. People do it all the time."

They got back into the car, pulled out of the lot, drove a short distance east along Lermontov Drive and saw that, indeed, right there, stood a second building looking exactly like its twin. A sign near the road listed a glass-and-mirror company, another specializing in granite countertops, an electrical contractor, a frozen-food wholesaler, and an upholsterer.

They were greeted by a woman who said everything twice, helpfully, not immediately as in an echo but after some minutes had passed. Perhaps to fill a lull or punctuate an exchange that had exhausted its fuel, she would repeat something: the best route home; the reason why her employer was not there (flu); the circumstances leading to this year's tax-return results, including the accountant's fee, which was higher than had been quoted.

"She can't afford to take time off, not at this time of year. Well, I suppose she could, but then she'd soon have no clients and I'd be out of a job."

The absent "she" referred to was the accountant. This woman, the accountant's office manager, who had met them as they trudged up the narrow stairway and commiserated with them over their mistake, had welcomed Mrs. Murayama and her son as though they were her dearest friends. It was a gift, he thought, the ability to create an instant rapport with people one hardly knew. It was a skill he lacked, despite having been an admired teacher. He recognized his deficiency and, without taking steps to remedy it, wished for it to be filled.

"We're all slaves to the machine," he said. The woman said nothing, looking as though she were waiting for him to elaborate. He felt his mother stir, restless and uncomfortable, beside him.

The women went into a meeting room on the other side of a glass wall. After the door was closed, he could still hear some of what they were saying. He sat on a moulded plastic chair in the outer room, where he flipped through the pages of a two-year-old copy of *Outdoor Life*. He would wait while his mother reviewed her taxes with the professionally amiable bookkeeper, and because Mrs. Murayama no longer felt confident driving on the highway he would drive her home.

He heard through the imperfect sound-barrier the woman ask about his sister's house, which had been damaged by fire five years earlier. She possessed, he imagined, similarly remembered details about her employer's clients' lives: significant milestones, the names of children and grandchildren. It was the sort of information that would create the sense of an established relationship without crossing the line drawn between friendliness and presumption.

Mr. Murayama filed his tax return himself every year. It was simple and convenient now that he subscribed to an online filing service. He entered the numbers where the form told him to and checked it carefully, part of him still wary of the new paperless modes of communication, before pressing the appropriate button. When he thought about the work he used to do, decades ago when he taught high-school English, he shook his head at how simplistic, almost trivial, so much of his life had become.

Nonetheless his brother-in-law considered Murayama a fool for doing his own taxes. "You wouldn't cut your own hair, would you? You wouldn't remove your own gall bladder."

The accountant's assistant had moved from introductory pleasantries—asking after Mrs. Murayama's health, recalling details about family members, sharing intel about the province's unusually hot weather—to the business at hand. Mr. Murayama knew this because the woman's posture had changed from fluidly relaxed, her right hand dancing gracefully the way an orchestra conductor might employ it, punctuating a phrase, eliciting a response, accentuating the message conveyed by a facial expression, to one that was defensively set. She was braced though not rigidly so: she had been tasked to deliver news that was out of the ordinary. This year an unforeseen wrinkle complicated his mother's taxation report. He could tell. Something was not right. His mother sat as she always did, in a consciously achieved posture, one that might be called regal without the comparison inflating to the hyperbolic. She sat as though her head were exerting a force pulling her spine upwards. As he watched the women, who sat side by side with their backs to him, Murayama was made to think of a student-teacher conference, the latter explaining to the former why she had done so poorly on a test or assignment. "Here," the instructor says, pointing, "and here. Do you see?" It was not good news. He saw this not in his mother, who continued to be unmoved, but in the way the accountant's assistant was speaking, her words at times clearly heard, at others indistinct. And he saw it in the way the woman moved, turning her torso mechanically on the pivot instead of merely turning her head. She was readying herself for the backlash should it come.

Mr. Murayama left the office without giving it much deliberation. At first, he considered driving away to see what his mother would do. How long before she noticed his absence? His better nature prevailed: no loving son leaves his aged mother stranded in a place of business, no matter how familiar to her the surroundings, without the means to get home. She had an old flip-style phone she rarely used. He doubted she had even put it in her purse that morning. It would be lunchtime in under an hour and though his mother hardly ate enough to sustain a bird, she insisted on maintaining regular meals. He recognized the same trait in himself, realizing that an unalterable system of habit was probably the reason why his mother was the age she was and why she enjoyed relatively good health.

He went quietly down the stairway and outside to the parking lot, leaving the car where it sat in a spot in full sun and no vehicle parked on either side. It would be an oven inside when it came time to drive home. He thought, *I should get one of those silvery reflective screens people put in their windshields to keep their cars cool.*

Then he thought, *I've been saying that for years. If I were going to get one, I would have done it by now. It was like, If you were really interested in getting married again, Hideki, you would have gone and done it, now wouldn't you? If you were going to buy a house instead of throwing your money away on rent all these* years.... *If you had been at your sister's instead of going away on that silly cruise....*

He began walking in the wrong direction and had gone a hundred metres before realizing his mistake. He turned, walked beside the curb (the street had no sidewalks) past the "200 Block" where he pictured his mother sitting stock still while patiently, maddeningly asking the accountant's assistant to repeat the salient details concerning her tax report. Or they were done, and his mother had the news firmly in her grasp and was processing it like an exceptionally slow metabolism. Or not. She could just now be standing up, looking around and not seeing her son. *Well,* he thought, never having entertained such a notion regarding his mother, *Cool your heels a while, okaasan. I shan't be long.*

When he reached the first building, the "100 Block," he opened the door expecting the large loud dog to be there again behind the glassed entrance of the first set of offices on the ground floor. The door displayed only the number 3. He couldn't see where the offices numbered 1 and 2 were situated, because the staircase was immediately to his left and no other doors were nearby. Though no lights had been turned on inside, he detected movement. Across what looked like a reception area with a round table and stylish, black, ergonomic chairs, something was going on in an inner office. Periodically every few seconds something flashed in the open doorway. It looked like a flap of fabric the colour of ash-dusted snow. His sightline wouldn't let him see definitively what it was.

When he tried the door handle it turned.

"Hello?" he said after taking a couple of steps into the room. As he progressed, his angle of sight into the inner office improved.

The man he had seen when he and his mother first arrived was seated in a desk chair that looked like the ones he had noted in the central room. Draped across his lap was the hound, whining softly to herself as though dreaming. A large pair of wireless padded earphones covered the animal's ears. The man wore an identical set. He leaned back in his chair, eyes closed. With one foot on the floor, he pushed gently to maintain the chair's rotational momentum.

Mr. Murayama expected the dog to sense his presence and to pounce defensively. *She must smell me*, he thought, *see me, surely, each time her head circles round close to the door.* The man didn't open his eyes. The animal seemed equally in bliss, listening to something that had to have been playing at the lowest possible volume. He wanted to continue watching, wanted to know what they were listening to. Why didn't the animal get dizzy and lose her lunch? To stay to receive answers to these and other questions, he felt, would be to put the man in an awkward, potentially embarrassing position, and so Mr. Murayama backed slowly away from the doorway, watching the dog in case she did detect him and spring to attack.

You lack an intrepid spirit, Hideki, he imagined his mother saying. *So do I. We are two of a kind, we play it safe. Your sister, on the other hand, is our opposite in that regard. She is a gambler, always looking for the quick pay-out, but never tending to the mundane matters that require our attention. Yearly chimney cleaning comes to mind. And that husband of hers—they might as well be twins, they're equally irresponsible. If only she had married someone like you, my son, a details person, the kind of man who gets his flue vacuumed religiously…*

MR. MURAYAMA was drinking a Mai Tai in the bar closest to his cabin when his sister texted to say that there had been a fire. He had been talking with an attractive older woman named Lily Gustafson. Lily's adult daughter, Greta, had gone to bed early with a migraine.

He missed much of what Lily was saying while he stared at his phone. His mother was spending Christmas with her daughter and son-in-law. No one had been hurt, but all his sister and brother-in-law's financial documents were destroyed. He excused himself to call his sister.

Lily was still sitting at the bar when he returned. He gave her a brief account of what he knew about the house fire. He told her there was nothing he could do short of spending a fortune flying home at once, which would be from Cozumel, their next port of call. He took a breath, let it out and relaxed his shoulders. His stomach remained knotted. It felt like guilt; he should have been there. He apologized for being so distracted and asked Lily to repeat what she'd been telling him about her daughter.

The Caribbean cruise was Lily's gift to Greta, who was recently single again. It turned out that Lily, an American, had a connection to Canada: her former son-in-law, Leif, an engineer, was born in Saskatoon. He lived and worked in Minnesota, where Lily was from. From what she gathered, Leif had been a bright but difficult child, not a reader, to his mother's chagrin, but a graceful, athletic boy who excelled at ice hockey. A scholarship in the sport took him south of the border to the University of Minnesota, where he set varsity scoring records that were still on the books. Leif's parents accepted grudgingly that, away from home and their aegis, the boy had blossomed, growing in confidence, developing an attractive personality, and discovering, contrary to what several of his teachers had said about him, that not only could he learn but he enjoyed doing so. He exchanged his student visa for a green card sponsored by his employer, an engineering firm that hired him before he graduated, and he began to make his life in America, his adopted country, one that he had come to love more than he did the country of his birth. Lily hoped that Mr. Murayama wasn't insulted to hear such a thing said.

"I can understand his choice," he replied.

Leif married Lily's daughter, Greta, a girl he had met and fallen in love with at university. They settled in Minneapolis, where Leif worked. His parents eventually stopped asking him when he and his bride planned to move back home. “This is our home,” he replied, barely holding his anger in check. Leif’s parents got used to travelling to Minneapolis-St. Paul every other year, usually for American Thanksgiving, always hopeful that Leif and Greta and their two daughters would be able to come to them to celebrate Christmas the next. It didn’t always work out.

“No,” Leif’s father would say by way of correcting the record, “it usually doesn’t work out.” Leif’s mother, a woman Lily liked and had come to think of as a friend, didn’t maintain a tally sheet of disappointments the way her husband did. She lived in the hope that this time, when Leif came to visit, whatever had kept him away the previous times would not be a factor, that he would have all the documentation he needed, with passport up to date and airline tickets purchased well in advance. Each period of anticipation allowed her to brighten and move with childlike ease, as though he were coming home for the first time after years away and had never let them down.

“I’ve been lucky,” Lily said. “Daughters stay close after they grow up. At least Greta has done and I’m grateful for it.”

AFTER THE PRESIDENTIAL ELECTION, Greta did not try to hide her grief at the result. She told Leif that she felt as though someone dear to her had died. “How could this have happened?” she asked, distraught, of everyone she encountered. On the Wednesday before Thanksgiving she took their daughters out of school and drove them to her parents’ house in St. Cloud. The plan was for Leif to come along the next day. He was finishing breakfast Thursday morning, preparing to wash up and get into the car, when Greta phoned. She told him she had decided to go away to Europe for the month of December with her best friend, a woman she had roomed with at college. The children, she assured him, would be fine. He could arrange after-school care or ask her parents to come back and stay with them. She needed this time away.

“Will you be back in time for Christmas?”

"Probably not," she admitted. His parents were expecting them for the holiday. It was expensive to have all four of them fly, but he had put the money aside. She told him it wasn't the cost or the anxiety-inducing airports. She loved his parents, loved visiting Canada.

"This is all on me," she said. "I need to jump off. You understand, don't you? Tell me you understand." He said nothing. "I'll be home in the new year, and everything will be back to normal, I promise. Let's talk about it when you get here, okay, Leif? Drive safe."

He wanted to talk about it now. Her phone went directly to message when he called back. When he did finally arrive, late on Monday, Greta wasn't there.

"She waited for you all weekend, Leif," said Lily. She offered to fix him a plate of turkey and vegetables. "Slice of pie? We've still got pumpkin. Or how about cherry?"

He told her he stopped to eat along the way. "When did she leave?"

"This morning. She caught the bus into the city and flew from there to JFK. That's where she was meeting Rachel. I imagine she's somewhere over the ocean by now. Or maybe they landed already, I should check. Sure you won't take a piece?"

In an email from London, Greta told him not to bother doing anything with her car. "Mom and Dad can use it, theirs is in terrible shape. I'll pick it up on the way back." Lily said that Leif must have wondered what the past years of marriage had meant to Greta, that she could have acted so impetuously. Lily knew what her daughter was capable of, but for Leif—and he told her this—her behaviour made him think of someone who had reverted from adulthood to adolescence, that period when flightiness and action taken contrary to one's best interest is understood and excused if not condoned. A good part of him was jealous that she should "jump off" in this way, without a care or a thought for others. Just watch what would happen if he pulled such a stunt, he confided in his mother-in-law just before he and his daughters drove home.

Leif chose not to call upon Greta's parents, instead hiring one of his neighbours, the daughter of people who lived two doors down from them, to babysit the children after school. It worked well, as far as Lily Gustafson knew. Nothing bad happened, not to the girls, although they did tell him one day that the babysitter invited two of her friends over and the trio spent the time gossiping and smoking cigarettes on the back deck. Leif asked his children whether they thought this was wrong. Did they feel that the girl had given them the level of care they deserved?

"We're not babies, Dad," they said.

"Then what didn't you like about what she did?"

"She ignored us."

Mr. Murayama asked Lily about the girls. Did they end up living with Greta or Leif?

"Funny you should ask that. Leif had them up till the divorce was made final, but he wasn't doing what you would call a stellar job. I'm not saying Greta is the world's best mother or nothing. The good Lord knows she has her shortcomings, changing her mind about something in the time it takes to go through a revolving door, and wanting to travel the globe instead of settling down. She spends as much time as she is able with her darling ones. As much as allows her to feel she's re-established the connection. The girls are with Gilbert and me right now. Gil's got our other daughter, Patsy, helping out while I take Greta all around paradise down hereabouts, making her feel human again, and so on. Divorce is a hard scrap in the ring, regardless of how common it's become. I'm thankful me and Gil are solid. Maybe even more in love than ever. And we are just plain crazy in love with those little girls. They were sure confused about their parents. I mean, they probably thought they were happy with their father. They said they were, in any case. What child really knows her own mind? The judge brought down his verdict. No do-over on that. Now that Leif is out of the picture, it's kind of a head scratcher that we had to go through the custody case at all. But here I am blabbing on about people you'll probably never meet. You said everybody at your sister's got out okay? That's a blessing."

"Wait, sorry," he began.

"You Canadians are always saying sorry! Hey, what's going on up there? Did you all do something bad or something?"

He didn't know how to respond and so he completed his question. "You said Leif is no longer in the picture. Did he move back to Canada?"

"He did go back there for a time, after he lost custody. Moved back in with his folks. I don't think it was a good decision. When he came back to Minneapolis, he was more depressed than ever. He kept coming to St. Cloud to talk to Greta. Her and the girls were living with us then. They would start crying whenever they would see him, said they wanted to move back to the city with him. We had a few tense scenes. Gil had to fetch his rifle this one time. You know, as a persuader that maybe Leif had overstayed his welcome. That young man was beside himself. I never seen anyone so lost. When he didn't come around demanding that everything change, those darlings had no complaints, none whatsoever."

"Where is he now? Did he stop coming?"

"I guess you might say that," she said, barking a bitter sounding laugh. "Where is he now? Depends on your belief system, I suppose. I know where his ashes are kept, if that's what you're asking."

"What happened to him?"

She told him. "Maybe you can wrap your mind around it. Me, I'm still turning it over. The sense of it eludes me to this day."

WHEN MR. MURAYAMA ARRIVED back at the parking lot of the 200 Block of Lermontov Industrial Park, he saw his mother standing in full sun outside the entrance to the building. His mother never took the sun. He waved to her as he ran to where he had parked the car. He rolled down the windows, turned the air-conditioning on full and drove up so that the passenger-side door could open as close to her as possible. He put it in Park, left it running and got out to help her into the car.

"I'm not going to ask where you were," she said. "You always have a plausible explanation."

"Have you been waiting long?"

"Long enough. I no longer expect the worst, though. It's one advantage of age and a fading memory. One sees all manner of disaster and knows that it is never as bad as one dreams it might be."

"Disaster?"

"I'm not remembering the quotation properly. It was something your father used to say. So much of what is quoted nowadays is apocryphal."

He reached across her to help buckle the seatbelt. "Were you pleased with the accountant's report, Mother?"

"That depends on what you mean by 'pleased.'"

He put the car into Drive, eased his foot off the brake, and brought the vehicle as smoothly as he could over a speed bump and back onto Lermontov Drive. He said, choosing his words carefully, "I meant, were there any unpleasant surprises?" He was braced for her to say something difficult or cryptic again. Instead, she shifted in her seat so that she was sitting as though he were her father and he had just admonished her about her posture. He glanced at her profile. She was smiling.

"I will be receiving a considerable refund."

"You are! Well," he began, not quite knowing how to continue. He was losing his ability to read her. *We are becoming opaque to each other,* he thought. *Perhaps it's for the best. It might simplify matters.*

"Yes," she continued, pleased with herself, "it appears I am able to claim the money I gave your sister and her hapless husband after the fire. You might recall that their insurance would not cover all the repairs. I'm not completely clear on the intricacies of the situation, but because I helped them with their mortgage and they insisted it be treated as a loan, I can write it off as a capital gains loss or some such thing. I will let you read the report when we get home, Hideki. You have a sharp eye for detail."

"Funny," he said, as they accelerated onto the 102, "I was sure it was going to be bad news."

"Were you, then?"

"I could see you through the glass. Something about the way you looked, your body language."

"Ah, you assumed the worst and decided to bolt. Thought I'd lost your inheritance, did you? You never did like unpleasantness."

"I'm glad I was wrong."

"Actually, Hideki, you weren't. Not completely so."

An image of the hound and her man, music lovers blissfully, languidly rotating in each other's company, filled his mind's eye. Headphones blocking all extraneous sound, the world forgotten, duty and difficulty forgotten in a bubble of suspended time. How he would love to be in their place right now.

She told him that his sister was suing her for an amount equal to the tax refund, many thousands of dollars. His sister and her perhaps-not-so-hapless husband were claiming that, given the purpose of the original loan, the refund should go to them. How her daughter's lawyer had found out about the tax windfall before Mrs. Murayama did was, the old woman supposed, one of life's mysteries.

"Then why are you smiling, Mother?"

"I can't say, precisely. Part of me says, Good for you, Daughter, you've got more spunk than I gave you credit for, and another says, Bring it on. That's what people say these days, isn't it? Bring it on? It's invigorating to feel this way."

ON ONE OF THE LAST DAYS of his Caribbean cruise, Mr. Murayama met Lily's daughter, Greta. They had arrived at the island of Martinique, from where he would fly home. Greta's migraine had finally passed and by chance she and Murayama were on the same shuttle boat from the ship to a pristine white-sand beach that was deserted except for them and a handful of other guests from the cruise liner. Lily had chosen to take a different excursion, a shopping trip into Fort-de-France.

Before returning to the ship, which looked like a dazzling city floating offshore, cruise staff members set up lounge chairs, food, and drink under a row of palms up off the beach. Shading his eyes with one hand, Murayama reached out with the other as if to touch the improbable vessel.

He asked Greta why she and Lily had opted for different activities that day.

"Oh, we just knew we had to," she said. "It's kind of a tingly sense we both have. Before we really start to annoy each other, we call a break. The weird thing is that we do it simultaneously. You know that feeling when you look at somebody and she's thinking the same thing and neither of you has to say anything?"

He said that he had not experienced such a tacit communication but imagined that it was wonderful to possess an ability like that.

"Lily told me about your husband. I'm very sorry for your loss."

She bristled, replying curtly, "What did she tell you?"

"That he shot himself."

"She shouldn't have done that." Greta stood and brushed sand off the backs of her legs. She wrapped a florally printed length of light cotton around her hips and strode purposefully towards the water. She had left her wide-brimmed straw hat beside the spot where she had been sitting. He brought it to her, and she put it on.

"I didn't mean to upset you."

"You didn't." They stood watching a billowing bank of grey and white cloud form in the middle distance between the ship and the horizon.

"I'm not looking for a relationship," she said.

"Fair enough." Something in her tone made him feel uneasy, as though she could hear his thoughts and was letting him know. The stronger swimmer, she had led him into dangerous waters.

She told him the deck and number of her cabin, adding that Lily was going to be out until late that evening, probably playing roulette or *vingt-et-un* in the casino. "She's pretty with-it," she added.

"Evidently," he said with a nervous laugh, wondering what his own mother would have thought or said about the situation. Including her in the comparison muddled the moment and made it feel the opposite of exciting.

"We're just two lonely people, okay? Nothing more."

When he touched her hand, she pulled away. "Not here."

That evening in her cabin she cried out, "Leif!" the instant before she climaxed.

Murayama felt himself beginning to come, but the sensation dwindled. Beneath him, Greta had her face turned to the side and she was biting the meat of her hand at the base of her thumb. Her moans could have been of pleasure or anguish. She seemed to want to climb a further peak. Her body and her head appeared to be at odds. He thought he heard her say, "Don't," but also, "Come on."

He began to move in sync again with Greta Gustafson, whom he would marry only to divorce three years later. He pushed against her as though she were an opponent. She responded, growing more fervent, more pliant. The mad joy was fleeting, he knew; too soon his head was going to burst like a milkweed pod and then it would be over.

He assumed that this would be the end of their brief encounter. He would fly home to Halifax. His mother would call him to help fix something in her house. At tax time he would drive her out to Lermontov Industrial Park in Sackville, wait while she conferred with her accountant, and drive her home again.

As he lay beside Greta, feeling the rise and fall of the ship at anchor, he thought, *Rest in peace, Leif, wherever you are. I wish I could have known you. I might better have understood why you did what you did.*

Who am I kidding? he thought. *I don't even understand me.*

Once in Jilani Park

His flight had been diverted from Houston because of a storm. She was on her way home from Atlanta to Vancouver after watching Elliot swim in the Special Olympics. Her partner, the team coach, would bring the boy home in another three days, after the closing ceremonies. No seats were available in the waiting area near her gate and so she found a chair several gates over. When she looked up, he was sitting across from her, looking at her as though they were newlyweds and she had just come back from freshening up in the washroom.

He looked prosperous, fifteen pounds heavier, his hair thinner, styled shorter and peppered with grey. He still had a smile straight out of a toothpaste advertisement. "You are looking well," he said, his smile having dimmed. *He's protecting himself*, she thought.

She returned the compliment and asked what had brought him here. He said he taught and practised orthodontics in Baltimore. She didn't tell him that she knew this already. He was on his way to Houston give expert testimony in a class-action lawsuit involving a product that had malfunctioned, a new type of implant.

"And you," he said. "What have you been doing with your life since the day you shattered my heart?"

THE SUMMER after she graduated high school and before starting her first year of university, Ambreen flew with her mother to Lahore to meet her fiancé. Her father had already been there for three weeks on business. As she knew from their Skype chats,

Sanjay, her intended, was lovely, both to talk to and look at. Their communication was stilted, however, given that they were never alone together and someone else was always speaking for or over them. In another life she might have gone on dates with the boy, who had two more years left to complete of his DClinDent in Prosthodontics at the University of Edinburgh. It was assumed that she would return to Halifax, take the first two years of her undergrad at Dalhousie, marry Sanjay, and finish her BSc wherever he set up a practice, which the families surmised would be either in the UK or America. Maybe Canada, who knows, they thought aloud like a cloud of conjecturing bees. It does become very cold there, does it not, Aswari?

That was the moment when she knew something was not right with her father. "Aswari!" they exclaimed, laughing. "Wake up!" He snapped out of it, took another sip of the Black Label his host had so proudly conjured from a locked mahogany cabinet, and caught stride again, regaling them with accounts of hundred-centimetre snowfalls and tossed mugs of tea freezing mid-air. Yes, he assured his audience, if the newlyweds did settle in Canada, the young man would require suitable protection from the elements. Ambreen leaned close to Sanjay to whisper reassurance: the snow was actually quite beautiful; he was going to love skiing; in the cold no one had to contend with mosquitoes.

But something was going on with her dad. Her mother saw it, too. Mr. and Mrs. Aswari should have been performing a well-rehearsed duet. They should have been finishing each other's sentences in the set-piece they'd mastered over the years, the soft-core Punch-and-Judy routine in which they pretended to be exasperated with each other but really were unified, a Gibraltar concerning this marvellous transaction involving their daughter. Papa Punch looked punch-drunk and Mama Judy looked like she wanted to brain him with the bowl of baba ghanouj she was holding for seated guests.

It wasn't until the fifth day, when Ambreen and Sanjay were walking through Jilani Park, an escort of sisters and aunts following at a distance close enough to say that nothing improper had transpired between the young couple but far enough away to allow them a modicum of privacy, that they had a chance to be themselves. He was nervous, and at first covered his discomfort with a running account of his accomplishments, academic and athletic, beginning in middle school. She didn't interrupt to remind him that he'd already told her these things online.

When he paused for breath, Ambreen said, "Did you leave any crumbs for your classmates? Your parents must have had to move into a larger house to accommodate all your cricket trophies!"

"I could tell you all about maxillofacial occlusion, but something tells me it would put you to sleep!"

"It wouldn't, I'm sure," she said, lightly touching her cheek. "Tell me about Edinburgh. Do you like it there?"

"It rains constantly and clothes never dry properly. I like my roommate. He's going for his DDS. We live in a desirable neighbourhood—Morningside—but how can I say this? Not everyone I encounter looks at me appreciatively."

"It's not forever," she said. He couldn't think of where to take the conversation from there.

Risking an intervention, she reached over to brush his forelock out of his eyes. "I love your hair. It's so thick. Also, you have beautiful teeth, not surprisingly," she teased.

Her intimate gesture had the effect, rather than driving him deeper into reticence, of reanimating him. "Oh," he exclaimed, "that reminds me of a funny story. Well, it starts off funny. It's about my last haircut."

"Hair is inherently funny, don't you think? I mean, it's relentless. Weeds are easier kept in line and are certainly better behaved." She couldn't think what about hair was particularly comic but wanted to encourage him.

"I thought I would get the stylist I'd had the last time I was in, but he'd since moved on to another salon," he began.

Two customers were in chairs ahead of him, an older man having his grey touched up and a younger fellow who did not look pleased with the situation. The stylist, a nervous, overweight youth, was trying to be pleasant, laughing to hide his anxiety. His customer was not laughing. Rather, he was scowling at his reflection in the mirror. Either that or he was scowling at Sanjay sitting behind him in the waiting area. Sanjay considered walking out. What kept him there, he had to wonder, especially after the junior stylist dropped his comb on the floor, and his boss, working on the dye job in the adjacent chair, intervened to complete the unhappy customer's haircut? Sanjay wanted to believe that he stayed because he didn't care how it turned out or that he had faith that somehow the stylist was going to give Sanjay a cut he wouldn't regret the instant he got home. What was it that ruled his behaviour most of the time if not the desire to be well thought of? He wanted to be the antithesis of the sourpuss who refused to crack a smile or say boo, and so when it was his turn to occupy the rookie barber's chair and be draped in the smock fastened tight at the neck, he listened attentively as the tyro chattered on about his two nieces, who, he said, were staying with him and his wife, and his dog, a Maltese poodle.

"You don't look old enough to have a wife," said Sanjay.

"Ha-ha! Thank you, sir, you are very kind to say so. I am told I look much the way I did when I was twelve!"

The dog was twelve years old, coincidentally, and recently widowed. The haircutter, whose name was Dodi, used the term without irony and bristled when Sanjay laughed and said, "Really?" Dodi recovered, becoming more relaxed as he told his story. Yes, he said, 'widowed' by the death of their younger dog, who was only eight. The dog had been having trouble walking. Their veterinarian recommended expensive knee-replacement surgery. Dodi and his wife got a second opinion, which led to the diagnosis of a brain tumour, and so they had to put the animal down. It was a humane decision, he told Sanjay, despite the dog's relative youth.

What made it difficult, he explained, was that this all happened during the first week of their nieces' arrival from Karachi. To say they were traumatized barely touched on how upset they were. Ten and thirteen and recently orphaned, they had not grown up with house pets. They adored Mitzi, the younger, afflicted dog, insisting she be carried everywhere they went. The older dog, Hector, seemed mystified at first by the girls' doting affection for his 'wife.' He trotted alongside the little girls, looking up constantly as if to ask, "Is everything all right up there?" and "When will you be able to walk again?" The expression on his face, as on Mitzi's, was one of perpetual concern. Even when their tongues lolled from their mouths, they looked worried. As Mitzi gazed down at her husband, it did seem that she was able to convey assurance. She was fine for the moment. He should not panic, as he was prone to, jumping up to place his forepaws forcefully against a human shin, running in circles, and barking loudly. He knew something was not right with Mitzi, something that couldn't be fixed with a mere joint replacement. He could tell from the way she smelled and by the filminess of her eyes.

Sanjay made encouraging sounds from the chair. Though he had never had a pet, he could imagine how difficult it must have been for Dodi. It made him think about a relative. He pointed out that as a society we don't hesitate to put an animal out of its misery, but a person suffering the early signs of an incurable disease, ALS for example, is refused their request for doctor-assisted suicide. This was what happened to his cousin, who was really his father's cousin by Sanjay's grandfather's second marriage.

"It's complicated," he said to Ambreen. "By the way, I like your father's associate. She seems very nice."

"His associate?" They were rounding the waterfall for the second time and Ambreen stopped beside a bench.

"Yes, we ran into each other in the lobby of the Pearl Continental, a few days before you and your mother arrived. They were waiting for an elevator. I was meeting friends for lunch at Bukhara, a superb restaurant, by the way. I will take you there. Anyway, I recognized your father from our chats and so I went over to introduce myself. We had only a few seconds because the elevator arrived quickly. They were headed up to the fourteenth floor to ink a deal. I believe that was the phrase he used."

"Really?" said Ambreen. "What did she look like?" She knew for certain that Mr. Gupta, her father's long-time secretary, had not accompanied him to Lahore. All his business associates were male.

"Can you picture Sunny Leone in Ray Bans and a leopard-print headscarf and turned out flawlessly in Givenchy? A beautiful woman, in other words. I hope I am at liberty to say that without making you angry. She was nowhere near as beautiful as you, of course!"

She didn't feel like helping him out. So this was her father's distraction.

"What happened to your cousin, the one who was ill?" She couldn't believe it. What was her mother going to do?

"He was quite old, almost sixty. He was so depressed about not getting the go-ahead, you know for assisted suicide, that he tried to kill himself all on his own."

"Tried?" She would have to keep an eye on her mother, stay by her side through this. She looked at Sanjay and thought, *I don't want to be married to you or anyone.*

"Yes. Failed miserably. Jumped from the second level of a shopping mall to the first, breaking both legs and shattering his pelvis. He will need a double hip replacement. That's what made me think of him, when I was telling you the story of the dog, Dodi's dog, the one they thought needed new knees except it was much more serious. I remember thinking, 'That's my cousin except my cousin has Lou Gehrig's Disease and no way out except a terrible, slow decline.'"

The man was laid up in a hospital bed, immobilized and still suffering the gradual loss of control over whatever parts he could still move, his arms, hands, head, and neck.

Eventually he would lose the ability to swallow and breathe.

"Now he wants to live. More than ever before."

"What about your nieces?" said Ambreen. She had to keep him talking.

"Not mine. Dodi's."

"Right. What happened to them after the dog died?"

"I asked him that very question. He said they were adjusting, but they weren't going to be around long enough to adjust to much. They were staying only a few weeks with Dodi and his wife before boarding a plane to Australia, to live with their grandmother."

"For good?" said Ambreen. *I'll go with them*, she thought.

"That depends on your definition of 'good.' They will probably live there permanently, if that's what you mean."

"When do we get to the funny part of this story, Sanjay?"

"I'm sorry," he said. "This is depressing you. Let us go back. Our honour guard I think is becoming restive."

"No, no, I didn't mean it that way. Please, go on. What happened to their parents?"

"It was a bus accident. The vehicle plunged into a river gorge."

Ambreen lowered her head and felt her throat constrict. Sanjay placed his hand on the nape of her neck.

After Dodi the haircutter told Sanjay about the bus crash, the salon's proprietor was suddenly and imposingly filling the space formerly occupied by his trainee. He had pushed Dodi aside, saying, "It is still too thick there," and in a flourish, a blur of scissor blades, he began thinning the hair around Sanjay's ears.

"How demoralizing," said Ambreen, somewhat recovered, "to have your boss not trust you enough to finish your own job."

"Demoralizing? Really? I don't think so. He was still learning."

"I know you wanted a good haircut. Did it have to be at the expense of that man's self-esteem?"

"I don't think he felt put down. I believe he relished the opportunity to be shown the correct technique."

"Ah, I see. So, if you saw me doing something wrong, say in our kitchen, you would push me aside and do it right?"

"No, of course not. Someone else, perhaps, a woman, someone more experienced in such matters. Not I."

"Not you," said Ambreen, shaking her head and narrowing her eyes.

Dodi the shunted stylist continued to stand nearby while he watched his boss finish cutting Sanjay's hair. It was an intense study, Sanjay could see in the mirror, and he told Ambreen this. "The expression on his face: he was making mental notes. Not taking it personally. Not going away in a snit or in tears, as one of my sisters might. There is training and there is humiliation. This was the former."

The salon owner removed more of Sanjay's hair in two minutes than his apprentice had cut in twenty. The man was working so quickly and deftly that Sanjay felt superfluous to the scene; he told Ambreen he could have been a corpse being prepared for viewing in an open casket. Meanwhile, Dodi watched his head the way someone cramming for final exams stares at an opened notebook.

Ambreen wondered about the poor, transient, parentless nieces. Were they still moping about Mitzi the dog who had been a warm, responsive, living thing to love and pamper? The plucky orphans. She imagined Dodi's wife had become so fond of them in so short a time that Dodi was worried she wasn't going to let them out of the house and onto that plane, the one that would take them to Perth. Sad, sweet, brave little girls.

What sort of women would they become, growing up Down Under? They would adopt an Aussie accent and the national slang, learn to be circumspect, perhaps, about what they did and said, so as to deflect attention away from themselves. This was after all the nation that detained undocumented arrivals in a concentration camp in Tasmania. They would probably marry boys to whom they were distantly related. They would bury their sadness and learn to love in a new way. They would stand in for their parents, in a way, earlier than most people expect to do.

Sanjay was saying something about prosthodontics. Smart

ceramics and the wonder of 3-D printing. She hadn't been paying attention. The escort brigade was closing in. Time to be shepherded home. She looked at him until he turned his head and their eyes met.

"You got a nice haircut, regardless," she said.

"Thank you," he said, as though responding to an accolade.

INSTEAD OF DRAGGING HIM through the pages of her life's album, she focussed on her father.

"Until the day he died he refused to apologize to my mother for having carried on that affair. Which, we discovered, had been going on for much longer than any of us knew, years in fact. He eventually gave the woman up. Unlike you I never met her, though I received regular intelligence from family and friends. My mother did her share of refusing, too, as in she refused to condemn him for his infidelity, refused to leave him when he asked her to, so that he could be with his princess. My God, it was martyrs all the way down!

"I was no help. As soon as I got back to Halifax, I thought about what I had committed to. I mean, think about it, Sanjay. I was supposed to wait dutifully for the next two years before rejoining you, me a clueless freshman and you this already accomplished physician becoming even more of a specialist, over on the other side of the ocean. It was like we were from different planets."

"We were betrothed," he said.

"I was seventeen. I thought my life was over."

"Yes, well…"

"You can't still possibly be angry," she said. "I know you've led a good life. Married, children, full professor at Johns Hopkins." When he expressed surprise that she knew this, she said, "You might want to review your privacy settings."

"I have not known a day of happiness since you broke our engagement," he said. He sounded like a hack from a bad melodrama. It reminded her of the moment, sitting with Sanjay in

Jilani Park, when she learned about her father's affair. It felt exactly like this, an immense, banal disappointment.

"Do you know for the longest time I was convinced that the families wanted me dead, that if you'd found me, you'd have killed me."

"That's absurd."

"Is it?"

"Of course! I'm amazed you would think such a thing."

"Do you remember that story you told me that day in Jilani Park, the one about your haircut and the widowed dog and the orphaned nieces? I've often wondered what became of those little girls. What sort of life did they have in Australia, and did they stay, and did they get another dog like their beloved Mitzi?"

Sanjay looked at her blankly. She saw that he had no idea what she was talking about and so she stood.

"I think that's me. They're calling my flight. It was so good to see you again, Sanjay. Don't get up," but it was too late. He was standing and moving towards her, awkwardly initiating an embrace. She let him encircle her with his arms but kept her hands up in front of her and her head tilted down, so that instead of a kiss on the cheek she felt his chin bang painfully into her forehead.

"Take care," she said, already turning away. Her flight didn't board for another forty minutes and so she kept walking, pulling her carry-on bag behind her, past her departure gate, past the security check area with its metal tables where passengers were putting their shoes and belts and watches back on, past the men's washroom and into the women's, where she went into a stall, closed and locked the door, sat on the toilet and waited. Her heart eventually stopped racing and her stomach settled, but the tears took a while to come. She was still a mess, sobbing in gasping, purgative, restorative moans when they announced that her flight home was now boarding.

Haida Gwaii

John might have thought of his final, incomplete pass as a sublime instant of frozen time. The moment contained infinite potential, as the small craft he was aboard achieved the zenith of its upward, tide-propelled motion and two pairs of hands grasped, simultaneously, the heavy block of dense, black, inert plastic, its chemical store similarly unrealized in its purpose. In that timeless frame, only possibility existed. The battery might, as the plan dictated, have been released successfully into the first man's grip, and thence upwards through the waiting chain of hands. Alternatively, John might not have felt confident in the moment, sensing that the hand-off could not have been made successfully, and so held on, subsiding with the wave to its nadir and from there prepared to try again. Neither happened, or such was the sense his brain made of the failed exchange. Except that in that infinitesimally short, infinitely unending tableau they made, neither man pushing, neither one pulling upon the object, nothing went wrong. If he could have said what it felt like, he might have likened the sensation to that of two magnets, their north poles approaching, touching, human exertion forcing them together while the repellant magnetism of each drove them apart. A religious person might call it the push and pull of opposing divine wills exerted upon a soul. Which would prevail? The eternal question. For John, neuroscientist, lapsed researcher into diseases of the mind, who would, until consciousness abandoned him, argue that the entity which was John Lauder Jones was the product of a similar biochemical reaction that explained why the heavy battery currently having such difficulty making its way to the top of that bleak outcrop could, once connected to a bulb, produce a strong beam of light and thereby save the lives of countless mariners plying the fjord-like waters of the Haida Gwaii, the potential of that static instant never changed. His final experience—this would have been comforting to his family, had there been a way to communicate it—was just that: John's hands, Oiler Kovalevsky's hands, holding not the weight of the object but whatever energy they in unison were producing to steal something from the continuum of heavenly nothingness. If someone had told him that God had plugged him into the battery, the battery into Kovalevsky, Kovalevsky into the other human chain-links leading up to the navigation light, and that beacon had inexplicably turned on to illuminate the heavy-lidded sky, the grey cottonwool draping the wet stunted fir and the slick black rocks, the metal sheen of the surging water, flecked white with castoff froth, John might well have said, "Of course He did! I felt it!"

FROM JOHN'S LETTERS HOME, his parents and siblings learned much about the *Thomas Darcy McGee*, the Canadian Coast Guard ship he had joined as a crew member that summer. The captain was a foul-mouthed crustacean named Dalton. His mates and crew respected him for his experience, though it was hard to say if any of them would have gone down with the vessel alongside him. In rough seas Captain Dalton slept in a tiny cabin attached to the bridge so that he could be alerted instantly to problems. Otherwise, he ordered, he was not to be disturbed. At first John found the old man's obscenities and blunt manner distasteful. After a few days he began to find Captain Dalton mildly entertaining, an irreverent crank who knew his stuff and wasn't above using his authority to play tricks on his officers and the chief engineer.

Of the three ship's officers, John liked the second mate, Roy Schurr, the best, a man without guile who reminded him of the old-time actor Gary Cooper. Schurr navigated the waters of the Haida Gwaii the way an experienced farmer ploughs the field he has cultivated since his youth: with unconscious skill, the sort of conservation even Nature herself might envy, that is, without a wasted effort or resource and with a knowledge of the topography, soil and drainage of the land so intimate it borders on the carnal.

The first mate, Chaim Meisner, was a serious young man who let John know early that he had his eyes set on a captaincy of his own. If Captain Dalton teased him more than he did anyone else on the bridge, the reason was that Meisner was already at the age of twenty-nine a better mariner, in a purely technical sense, than Dalton himself, a sailor with close to fifty years served on every kind of vessel imaginable. Dalton was too confident and too close to retirement to feel threatened by his first mate; he had experienced seas the young officer had only read about. As for his incessant needling, Dalton was by his own admission an incorrigible bastard who couldn't help himself. And so, knowing that Meisner would be still groggy climbing to the bridge for an 8 a.m. shift, Dalton once ordered the helmsman to hold the ship steady on a course crossing a line of fishing nets. The timing was masterful. John relieved the helmsman to begin his shift. Meisner, full mug of hot coffee in his hand, had a minute, maybe 90 seconds, to turn the ship hard away from the nets, stopping or reversing direction being out of the question on such short notice. He yelled at John, who had also just arrived and was paying more attention to the compass than to the thin line barely discernible in the bright morning sun reflected off the surface of the waters of the strait.

"Hard-a-port! Where have you got us headed? Who put us on this course?" he demanded, knowing as soon as he asked who it was who had sent them steaming at 12 knots directly into an 'incident.'

The captain returned to the wheelhouse to see what effect his prank had had on the mate, who didn't let the old man see that he was flustered. Meisner ordered John to take the ship, by way of a frantic series of wheel turns, through headings meant to circumvent the fishing boat and its nets. John concentrated on the officer's commands and the compass points only, having little time even to glimpse the object they were so intent on avoiding. Dalton chuckled to himself. Although he had failed to rattle his first officer, he had unintentionally succeeded in making John feel as though the mistake was his fault. Logic suggested that this could not be the case, of course, but exposure—Dalton's presence, the massive wooden wheel, the thick pane of glass separating him from the open air above the deck, the first mate's eyes falling accusingly upon him—undermined his confidence.

John tried to think of a time when, as now, he had nowhere to hide or flee. In school, standing before an audience, he had always been prepared, some would say overly so. He made sure he knew what was going to happen, what questions might be asked of him, what sentences or phrases were sure to elicit laughter or applause. In the lab he left nothing to chance. He read every report touching remotely on his research. He thought about, planned, and rehearsed in his head the method, the observations and measurements, the possible glitches along the way, so that when it came time to carry out a step in the study, he could predict the result. Now, feeling vulnerable and alive as never before, standing attentive and obedient at the wheel, he wondered what might have happened had he merely followed a hunch in his research, letting intuition rather than dogged preparedness and the expectation of predicted results lead him. For one thing, he would probably have dropped out of graduate school earlier. His mother would have intercepted him before that, taking him aside and reminding him how science, their version of science—cautious, measured, the opposite of adventurous—worked. How grant applications had to be worded to be successful. Go ahead, ride off in all directions, she would say. Just see where that lands you. Nowheresville.

Being one of four quartermasters on a coast-guard delivery vessel was not going to be his life's work, he knew that. He even wondered if he had the stamina and forbearance to last the summer. He had signed on as an ordinary seaman, but it became quickly evident that he lacked whatever instinct the other men had for remaining unscathed on deck. A full, swinging cargo net narrowly missed his head on its way into the hold. Ropes inevitably became tangled around his feet. He left decks and gangways dangerously soapy when he mopped them. The day he stepped into the bight of a heavy chain, moments before it and its anchor were due to be released to cascade over the side, chased by an immense navigation buoy, he was removed from deck work and reassigned to wheelhouse duty. As quartermaster he worked two four-hour shifts a day. It might be noon to four in the afternoon and again from midnight until four in the morning, steering while the ship sailed and acting as security while it stood in port.

Despite his own embarrassing deficiency as an able-bodied seaman, John realized that the other men in the crew had no idea what made them think and act the way they did. If he were to have asked them what governed the workings of their neurology, they would have looked at him as though he were insane. Nothing "governs" what I think, they would surely have replied. I think whatever I goddamn choose to think. They were oblivious to the chemical reactions underlying every signal, every impulse, from the clenching of a fist to the private curse meant for but rarely delivered to those in authority. They believed they were the masters of their fate when, really, they were like John responding to a series of commands from whoever happened to oversee the bridge that shift. Heredity, diet, childhood trauma, illness, chronic pain, positive stimulus, pollution, UV radiation, drug use, physical exercise, the conscious moderation of thought—these opened certain switches, closed others, caused certain hormones to be delivered while preventing others. Habit, learned response, automatic reaction whether it be beneficial to the doer or not, the deeply inscribed pathways of behaviour, none was easy to alter, though with enough time and the right corrective it could.

For a while he found the collective state of unconsciousness aboard ship refreshing. It was as though he had travelled to another world where the inhabitants, though adult, some middle-aged and older, were arrested in their personal and social development at the stage of early adolescence. When the ship was docked in port they trooped into Prince Rupert, where they drank until blind and had to be led or carried home. On deck, sober again, they tormented each other, especially those perceived to be weak, without mercy. A pair might bicker over an otherwise inconsequential slight: someone called someone else's truck less than manly; someone criticized another man's inability to loosen a lug nut; someone else refused to buy earplugs or move to another cabin rather than continue to lose sleep listening to his colleague's stentorian snores. John, being the one most easily identified as 'other,' learned to suffer silently those taunts related to his level of education, its having prepared him not to the least degree for a life at sea. It was the first time in his life he had ever been called stupid. The novelty was almost refreshing, until it wore off.

As the only quartermaster who was single, John spent part of every weekend confined to the ship while it was docked in port. It wasn't so bad, he wrote home. Sitting up all night, trying to stay awake, he cleaned the brass in the wheelhouse, rubbed lemon oil into the woodwork, washed the windows and vacuumed the carpet. Every hour he walked a prescribed circuit through the entire ship, turning a key in each station's time clock to show he'd been there. Back in the wheelhouse he was allowed to listen to the radio if it was played softly—he had to be able to detect intruders. He was not allowed to sit idly reading a book, but he could write. The difference, he decided, had to do with appearance: the authorities weren't concerned so much with his ability to hear or see someone trespassing on the ship as with his presenting an image of someone diligently engaged in a task. Reading was leisure; writing was work and hence the legitimate use of his time while in the employ of the Canadian Coast Guard.

He wrote what he was thinking and feeling, what the day had brought, his dreams, character sketches of crew members, the beginnings of stories he would never finish, all in a lab notebook he'd stashed in his duffel bag at the last minute. When he thought about what he used to record in similar pages, it struck him that record keeping was the part he enjoyed the least. It had to do with the pressure he felt to make his entries error-free, not simply the accuracy of his measurements and the rigour of his method but the handwriting itself. He had long given up trying to get his mother to let her team keep lab records on a tablet. No, she said, electronic devices were too prone to malfunction. Get it down on paper. The notebooks were hardbound and lightly ruled in graph-paper format, their paper acid-free. John would turn to his most recent entry and freeze, often shutting the book and walking away from it. The pages he had already filled seemed paltry. It had to do with the finite nature of the information they were communicating, and their so, so restrictive specificity. He would read over the notations, the symbols he knew even a PhD from another discipline would consider hieroglyphic, and all he would be able to think about them would be how inconsequential they seemed. Inert. Unattached to a larger narrative. And he, naively trusting that they would fit into the 'big picture' somehow, an immense and complex canvas even the brilliant Ursula Lauder Jones wasn't able to understand. This combination of drugs on these lab rats had this observable but not yet statistically reproducible effect on the mitochondria of the cells in that part of the animal's brain most likely affected by the disease.

"Sketch what you see under the microscope," Ursula insisted. "Don't take a photograph; draw the affected cells in the specimen. You think it's less accurate, and in one sense it is," she told them. "But we are hunting for something so elusive that we need to look that much harder and with greater concentration. A photo will show you everything indiscriminately; a careful drawing will include you, your questioning eye. I'm talking about perspective; I'm talking about what happens when someone with knowledge and training brings sceptical intuition to the search."

At first John, who did not possess natural artistic talent, resisted, but he worked at it and did improve. To a point. What stopped him was what he saw whenever he would review the previous day's notes: erasure, smudges, a line or a curve that he knew were not exactly what he had seen on the slide. He would be clenched, that was the only word for it, so knotted over an activity he could never master that he missed depicting the very thing, an essence, a bit of shading, perhaps, or a shape reminding him of something similar the way a jigsaw piece will suddenly announce its intended position as the puzzler holds it up to the light.

A ship's mate was always assigned to the vessel while it was docked. Unlike the quartermaster on duty, the mate didn't have to be present but on-call. He couldn't leave town or turn his phone off. The first and second mates usually came by early in the evening, once before returning to their beds at home, to check that the ship was secure. The second mate, Mr. Schurr, often brought something his wife had baked. They were married forty-six years, he would proudly announce, and it still felt the way it had when they were young, she eighteen and he nineteen, and first hitched. Not an emotionally demonstrative man—Schurr reacted the same way to a drunken seaman sprawled in the gangway net as he did to a buoy-chain improperly bolted to the deck—he could be betrayed by the slightest rash of colour rising from beneath his collar whenever he spoke about the love he had for his wife.

The third mate, Franklin Greatrex, did not show up at the ship the few times he and John were paired to serve weekend watch duty. Greatrex was about ten years older than the first mate and fifteen younger than the second. When Captain Dalton bellowed about something, everybody laughed because they knew it was for their entertainment. When the third mate yelled and cursed, they tensed up the way you might go cold when a drunk decides he doesn't like you and is still able to hurt you. Greatrex seemed permanently angry. He acted as though idiots populated the world and he was the only sane person left. John wondered if it had to do with Greatrex's being bottom man in a hierarchy of three. The man had experience, he had the training and ability, John's bunk mate told him one rare afternoon when they were both off-duty and away from port; but Greatrex put people on the defensive, people who had the authority to promote him, something they had failed to do. He had a particular hate on for Meisner, the first mate. The previous man in that position, a much-loved mariner who always made his captain look good, had retired. Greatrex assumed that he would be chosen for the post, vaulting over Mr. Shurr, who was closing in on retirement himself. In Greatrex's mind it made no sense to promote the older man only to have to fill the spot again in a short time. Who should parachute in, then, fresh from the Coast Guard academy in Sydney, Nova Scotia, but this hotshot, Meisner, who hadn't been alive the year the ship was built. Greatrex felt he'd been robbed of a promotion and all it entailed: better pay, more vacation time, and greater prestige, if such a word could be said to apply aboard a ship that was a glorified delivery vehicle, servicing the automated lighthouses and beacons from the northern tip of Vancouver Island to the Alaskan border.

John had never met anyone quite as disagreeable as the third mate. It made him realize what a protected bubble of civility, pretend or not, he'd grown up in. Alone with, and taking direction from, Greatrex, John was as likely to be called a cretin not intelligent enough to blink his eyes in unison as told to change his heading seventeen degrees to the west. Maybe the man mistook passivity for weakness. John still liked the job well enough to tolerate the third mate for four hours once or twice a week. Greatrex assumed that John had no recourse but to obey in relative silence and to submit to the bully's verbal abuse. Complaining to the captain was not an option. It was kindly Roy Schurr who communicated that bit of advice to him after overhearing one of Greatrex's tirades. Mr. Schurr made John think of a hunter explaining the significance of a wild animal's spoor or a farmer letting his neighbour the hobbyist know that ploughing his field with the contour of the land rather than against it will save him a whole lot of heartache come harvest time. Go crying to Dalton and you will reap the opposite of your intention, young man, Mr. Schurr warned.

Greatrex's favourite slight against him had to do with John's schooling. He could have sworn he hadn't told a soul that he possessed a graduate degree and was all-but-dissertation away from being able to call himself 'doctor'. Had he included his master's degree on his application? He must have. How was he to have known that this fact would be tilted against him to stomach-churning effect?

"Well, if it isn't Master Lauder Jones. Welcome to the wheelhouse, Master Lauder Jones. Well, well. This is going to be confusing, serving two masters. What a disappointment it must have been for you to arrive only to learn that this ship already had a captain. Bummer, dude! Relegated to lowly quartermaster. It's some kind of master, I suppose. It beats being called Masturbator, huh? Some kinda wonderful, eh, Master Lauder Jones? I'm going to call you Master JQ, you know, like GQ only uglier. Master JQ, the highly educated man, spending his summer up here in PR, BC, slumming his life away. What happened, you get caught shtupping one of your students, professor? I bet it was a pretty little sissy in tight pants just like you. You go for some of that, I just know you do, Master JQ. Tight little tush in lavender pants. Eyes front there, mister master. You have one job up here and that's to hold this pig on its intended course. I tell you the heading, you repeat it back to me, you turn that fucking wheel until the compass needle points to the number and you make damn sure it stays there. Think you can handle that, perfesser? Not too taxing for you? Should I lend you my calculator so you can figure it out?"

GREATREX WAS STEERING the workboat the day of the accident. Some aboard the *Darcy McGee* blamed him for it, calling him negligent for leading the job, the replacement of a navigation beacon's battery, in heavy seas. Others thought it was John's fault, saying the young scholar from Halifax should have stayed on that other coast, safely ensconced in his laboratory, where the chances of him hurting himself or others was slim. John, they said, lacked the head for deck work, which included, if necessary, the ability to scale a slick rock face in inclement weather and take his position in a human chain reaching to the top. Greatrex, to give him some credit, knew that the almost Dr. Lauder Jones probably could not have accomplished such a feat that day, and so told him to stand in the bow of the workboat, a 16-foot open inboard with a deep keel, and hand a 12-volt car battery to the first man in the chain. It would have been a tricky enough procedure in calm waters. That day the sea rose and fell a distance that seemed to John to be twice his height. Five deckhands and two oilers from the engine room climbed to spots on the rock face where they could stand, some just barely on narrow ledges, and pass the heavy battery to the person above him. Each manoeuvre was painstaking, from ascending and hanging tight to a stable foothold to reaching carefully, first below their feet to receive the battery and then up over their heads to the pair of boots above them, and potentially fatal, for the waters were cold enough that if a man fell in he had only a minute or two in which to be hauled into the boat before he lapsed into shock and drowned.

Greatrex had to hold the boat in position close to where the first man stood, which was just above the high-tide line. Though the sea that day was turbulent, making the boat rise and fall, pitch and roll, the tide was also ebbing in the inlet where they were working, so that as time passed, the highest the workboat rose each time it crested was a little lower than before. Greatrex had consulted the tide chart and visited the rock face first, alone, determining where each man in the chain might stand. It was a newly established beacon, and this was going to be its initial battery change. Farther south and on Vancouver Island, beacons ran off a combination of rechargeable battery and solar power. Up there where the sun shone even less often, solar wasn't a dependable option. Replacing the battery took a procedure that had more in common with a military operation than with the maintenance of civilian infrastructure. Position a squad as though they were stranded seals or puffins, in a line up the sheer, wet slope, and hope to whatever deity returns your calls that nobody slips and falls.

What did fall overboard, twice, was the battery John was trying to hand off to the nearest man. Greatrex swore loud enough to be heard, above the roar of the wind and the surf, by everyone there. He cursed John's name, calling him incompetent, uncoordinated, weak, fearful and every other deficiency he could think of, as he revved the motor angrily to keep the boat in place close enough to the rock without colliding with it. Standing upright in the bow, John couldn't maintain his balance well enough to complete the pass, and so he took to kneeling on the triangular surface formed near the apex of the bow. It was the only way he could control his part of the exchange, after dropping the battery, a first time and then again. All the way back to the ship to retrieve another battery—they had a supply of ten for the eight beacons being serviced over the course of the week—the mate upbraided him. He repeated the tirade on the return trip. Did John know, did he have the slightest notion, what this was costing the Canadian taxpayer, in materiel, man-hours and Greatrex's health? Did he have any idea just how incredibly inconvenient this was?

"Each of those seven men clinging to that wall is thinking about how he is going to kill you, Dr. Frankenstein, just so you know. I can't be held accountable for what they do to you. Another twenty minutes in this rain and they'll be shivering so hard they won't be able to hang on. You will have seven possible and preventable deaths on your hands. How about that as an outcome, Master JQ? John Q Rotten. Useless egghead. Knob-wart. You ever had to deal with that kind of thing when you were jacking off into your Bunsen burner? I didn't think so. Write this one up in your lab report. Experiment resulted in me killing seven innocent men because I dropped the g.d. battery! Not once but twice! And these are no ordinary batteries, by the way. Each one costs half a grand. That's right. We should deduct the loss from your pay. Two fielder errors resulting in seven dead teammates. What if every time a player flubbed the ball one of his buddies had to die? Unthinkable, right?"

It continued, the litany of reproach rising and falling like the swell itself, at times lost in a howl of wind, at others clear, lacerating, as though the man were pouring his vituperation directly into John's ear. Aside from its hateful purpose, the mate's stamina was impressive. That he could sustain such an attack and never repeat himself deserved recognition.

Except for one unavoidable swell while they were sailing back to Rupert from Port Hardy, John wrote that he didn't get queasy aboard the ship. It was a different feeling being a passenger in the bow of the work boat. Being so close to the water and experiencing each rise and fall as though they were a fishing buoy bobbing on the surface, he quickly would have understood what it was to be green with sea sickness. Probably the only reason why he didn't void the contents of his stomach while serving as point man in the delivery of the battery to the brigade of crew members waiting, shivering, cursing those responsible for their present state of tenuousness on the rock face leading to the beacon at the top, was that he had not been given time to eat his lunch before being seconded by the third mate.

The ship had dropped anchor out in the strait, still visible and out of the lane, where it wouldn't impede traffic, of which there was blessed little, a few small fishing boats, the occasional seaplane landing or taking off, the rare yacht up from the Lower Mainland or farther south. Greatrex told John that the captain was doubtlessly watching them, and so it behooved the newcomer not to do anything that would afford the old genital crust a reason to crow. It seems that one of two possible states of mind take hold of people as they approach retirement in their career: either they double their efforts to achieve a level of professionalism that will remain, being most recent, memorable and emblematic in the minds of any who might think about their soon-to-be-absent comrade; or they decide no longer to give a flying fig about the job and whatever legacy might attach itself to the outgoing, as in, leaving, employee. Captain Dalton occupied the second of these. He would be remembered, but not for his seamanship.

John was thinking that the three-strike rule must be in effect as they approached the hand-off point, a third battery in the bottom of the boat. Greatrex had run out of insults and was wrapped in silent bitter rumination on the general state of his luckless existence. As for John, two-time butterfingers, author of the growing discomfort suffered by his superior and the seven crew members clinging to the outcrop, the novelty of being deemed a failure had him thinking more like a curious spectator than a penitent last-chancer praying to make up for his mistakes. It wasn't that he didn't care what they thought of him; he wasn't hewn of insensitive material. What allowed him to hold his head up, to put off feeling defeated by the situation, was his history. Nothing else could account for it. All his life, except for losing Danica, John had been sheltered from humiliation, and once the suffocating cloud of lost love had cleared, he was able to convince himself that her leaving had little to do with anything he had done or failed to do. It had been a biochemical change in her. In response to him, the way he stimulated her senses, the pheromones he sent into her nasal passages, whatever neural response we prefer to call love simply shut down, refused to comply, and failed to recognize signals. He would have had as much control over it as over the weather. Residual longing remained, naturally. He could still be ambushed by what can only be called a ghostly visitation upon him by her essence, triggered no doubt by an aroma, a visual image, a snatch of melody, none of which he was conscious of as an original pathway back to her, but was, in retrospect, obviously so. It frustrated him when his attempts at putting these sudden and overwhelming sensations away from him didn't work, when in fact he was letting himself engage in capitulation, the wilful sinking into his feelings, wallowing there, despite all he understood about what was going on in his frontal lobe.

Greatrex interrupts, shattering the shelter of John's thoughts. "Last chance, Master Fuckwit. After this we got no more to spare."

It is close to a relief to hear him say it, say anything, finally, after the choppy transit from the ship to the barren crag atop which the light stands. The sky has dropped in the interim as though its seemingly permanent bank of cloud has grown too heavy to be held up. Any lower and they'd be working in thick fog. One of the men in the chain shouts something indistinct as he waves. John returns the greeting, a truncated, self-conscious gesture he hopes will be taken for an apology. He tries to identify what went wrong with the first two attempts. What did he do or fail to do to send the battery to the seabed? He wishes that this time the third mate could somehow steady him from behind so that when John leans forward with the load in his hands he might feel less weak in his abdominal muscles, which have never been particularly strong. Such bolstering is impossible, he knows, given that Greatrex must keep hold of the rudder wheel while throttling in reverse to maintain the boat's position. To that, John adds the sensation, imagined and potentially nauseating, of Greatrex's hands placed on his body, wrapped around his waist, perhaps, or gripping the back of his belt. He thinks he could stand it if it afforded him the stability to stay upright and in position kneeling on the bow's platform while he reaches forward at the perfectly timed intersection with Kovalevsky, the oiler perched closest to the water.

He needs a strategy, and he needs to communicate it to Kovalevsky. As Greatrex brings the boat into position and begins the process of revving the engine periodically, turning the screw in reverse to counteract the force of the swell pushing them towards the rock, John yells to Kovalevsky, "Can you hear me?" The oiler gives the thumbs-up sign and nods yes. "Five up-an-downs!" John yells.

"What?"

He isn't sure if Kovalevsky didn't hear or doesn't understand what John is proposing. He tries again, holding his hand up with five fingers splayed.

"Five times up and down," he calls, motioning a rise and fall with the same hand now held flat and parallel to the surface of the water. "On six I hand off to you. Got it?"

"Roger that!" Kovalevsky calls back, nodding in the affirmative.

"On my count, then."

"Say what?"

"ON MY COUNT!"

"Roger Roger!"

John expects to hear the mate's hectoring voice behind him, saying something like, "For the love of fuck, Doctor Doolittle, get the lead out. Let's do this. It's not astrophysics," but in place of that is the sound of the motor groaning every four or five seconds, the water smashing into the rock, exploding, sliding down, and the wind, deafening, incessant in his ears.

KOVALEVSKY WAS THE MOST EXPERIENCED seaman on board, John divined through overheard conversations and the few encounters he had with the man. One of these happened during a weekend duty when the ship was docked in Prince Rupert. As the tide rose and fell, the gangway, looking like a metal ladder with railings, a pair of small wheels at dock-end, and rather than rungs a flat, roughened rubberized surface, had to be adjusted to allow pedestrian access. This entailed untying the lines securing the walkway to the ship and refastening them to make for a shallower or steeper angle. Sometimes the gangway pointed up from the dock to the ship's deck and sometimes down. Access might, at low tide, be to the boat deck, where the wheelhouse was situated. At high tide, the gangway angled slightly upwards to the main deck. Below the gangway was always strung a precautionary net meant to catch anyone or anything that might slip over the side while coming aboard or disembarking. When John was first shown how to adjust the gangway and test the safety net, he wondered how anyone could possibly end up caught like prey in such a ropy hammock. There wasn't much more width to the netting than to the gangway itself, only perhaps a foot on either side.

"I guess stuff gets dropped over the side," John offered. "Boxes, luggage, phones."

"Not that often," said the man training him. "It's not there to snag things so much as people. You'll see. Friday, Saturday nights in port, that there net saves lives."

The night John discovered Kovalevsky lying in the gangway net, the oiler was not to be roused. John didn't have the strength or leverage to lift the man out onto the deck, and so he found a blanket, covered him with it, made sure he was still breathing, and let him sleep it off there. A wispy rain fell, the permanent meteorological state in Rupert. In three entire months of summer, John wrote, he had felt the sun on his face twice. The gangway formed an overhang that kept Kovalevsky relatively dry, not that it would have mattered to him in his present state of inebriation whether he was soaked or bone dry. More often than he would have ventured out of the wheelhouse otherwise, John checked to see how the man was faring. It amazed him that someone could sleep so soundly while lying in such an uncomfortable position. He wondered how much liquor the man had consumed and how often this happened. John had read about benders, usually in novels, in which entire days, whole weeks of time were lost to extreme intoxication, with levels of alcohol poisoning that should had led to toxic shock, organ failure and possible death.

Sometime between 3 a.m. and dawn, when John startled awake while seated at the wheelhouse map-table and went outside to check on him, Kovalevsky had gotten out of the net. Who knows where he went. He could have wandered back into town, found his way to wherever he lived off-ship, or made his way into his bunk on board. John wasn't about to go looking. A quick perusal of the water under the gangway suggested that the man hadn't fallen in. If he had and drowned, wouldn't he be floating? John was too tired to be overly bothered by not knowing the answer to this. He knew he should be more concerned about his colleague's well-being. Had ship work made him hard or was this merely his fatigued brain bypassing its sympathetic functions? It didn't matter and wouldn't until he'd been able to sleep ten hours or longer. The vague thought that in this state of exhaustion he might be capable of unfeeling violence came to him before wafting away. Being so tired was the same as suffering a psychosis, he knew that much. Kovalevsky was all right; logic dictated it. If the oiler had had the wherewithal to land in the cargo net rather than the water, he was more than capable of extricating himself from the thing when he woke. If he was an alcoholic, he was possibly more able to make important decisions and manoeuvre his body safely around obstacles than was John at this moment, this end-of-shift, waking dream. Still, still, he thought as he lay on his bed without having gotten undressed, I should determine his whereabouts. This final word echoed before John dropped into a dead sleep.

"ONE!"

The way Kovalevsky was perched, he was turned so that his left shoulder and side hugged the rock face. His feet, right in front of left, pointed parallel to the wall. His head was turned to face John and the rising, falling bow of the work boat. He held his hands out as though ready to receive a lateral pass of the ball in a game of rugby.

"Two!"

Back-splash from the surge of water coming off the rock had soaked through John's clothes and slickened the surface upon which he knelt. He was going to have to get off his knees into a crouch and eventually stand upright if he was to bring the battery high enough for the hand-off. How to do that while holding on to the blasted thing, which was growing heavier with every second, and maintain his balance at the same time seemed near impossible. Something was destined to go over the side.

This time, John vowed, it was not going to be another battery.

A Shock of White

Donnalee Vance was taking twice as long as she needed to shop for food. She liked it in the new grocery store, its bright lighting, wide aisles, soothing music, and occasional announcement over the public-address system. Even the wait in line at the checkout register was pleasant, with magazines to peruse and sometimes someone she knew to talk with. She wasn't interested in learning how to use the self-checkout machines. She liked one cashier in particular, a woman who never lost her patience if an item wasn't marked with a price code and who always had something nice to say, about the weather or what Donnalee was wearing or the latest exploits and general development of Donnalee and Dick's two sons. Donnalee didn't get her this time but a woman who was equally efficient though distant and taciturn. It made Donnalee uneasy, with little to do aside from unloading her cart and flipping through a copy of *Shape* or *Us*.

The boy who transferred her bags to the trunk of her car was Mark Hallam, a classmate of Gord's. They used to play on the same city-league hockey team. Gord didn't play last year. He quit all extracurricular activity to concentrate on his schoolwork. He had set his sights on a scholarship to Acadia, her and Dick's alma mater, and should have gotten it, as far as she was concerned. His marks were higher than he'd ever achieved: mid-80s, very respectable but not good enough for entrance money. He'd done well in English, his highest mark, Mr. Murayama's class. Mr. Murayama—Dick knew him better than Donnalee did, Dick having taught at the same school—was not one to win any popularity contests. He was tough, you could even say inspiring, making his students work for it. Nothing wrong with that. Gord did get a little money from the province. It covered the cost of some of his textbooks, but he'd been crestfallen not to have gotten the full entrance-scholarship that his friend Les had to Mount Allison. Dalhousie was out of the question: too close to home for Gord's liking, too hard to get into, too expensive. It wasn't the end of the world, she told her boy. She'd been putting money aside for years, secretly, fifty or a hundred siphoned off Dick's paycheque every month. It had been more when Dick was teaching. His present boss, Lionel Mountcastle, was a cheapskate and a tightwad, as far as she was concerned. She could understand Dick's reasons for retiring early. Teaching was a young person's game. You needed energy. You needed to understand the kids, what they were saying and their interests. What she could not wrap her mind around was him spending his days cooped up in that tiny shop with that weirdo, Irma Zlotsky. Donnalee suspected that Irma had a thing for Dick going back to when they taught together. They left teaching within a few years of each other. Then they ended up working part-time in the same framing store, first Irma, who told Dick about it. Donnalee tried hard not to be jealous.

And Gord, her Gordie, her serious little man so worried about his future. Don't sweat it, she reassured him, wanting to add, whatever you do, don't end up like your father. Gord tried so hard to please, offering to stay home and go to the community college to save money. She wouldn't hear of it. "You are accepted at Acadia, young man, and that is where you are going to be educated."

The bag boy, Mark Hallam, wore his hair longer than was fashionable. It was black except for a streak of white running through it and hanging down over one eye. Someone told her that a shock could do that early in life, even in the womb. He tossed his head to move the bang aside. She remembered watching him play defence. He wasn't the best player on the team, and skating backwards was difficult for him, but he made up for it with an aggressive style of play that landed him in the penalty box more often than anyone else. Some of the other parents expressed dismay, even disgust at his bruising bodychecks. Secretly Donnalee felt a thrill whenever she saw him send an opponent crashing into the boards. Mark Hallam also had the team's hardest slapshot. Part of her felt shame that she should spend more time watching this boy—the team's enforcer, as Gord referred to him—than she did watching her own son, who played left wing, usually on the same shift as Mark. She left that scrutiny to Dick, who couldn't sit still in the stands while Gord's games were in progress. Instead, he stood down beside the arena's boards, where he called out encouragement to the players. Gord was a strong skater, technically better than Hallam, though he lacked the taller, heavier boy's drive to dig the puck out of the corners and fight for possession close to the net. Dick kept his language in check as much as he was able, though once or twice a period he could be counted on to let loose a creative stream of invective. It was often directed at Gord, who would have missed an opportunity to score or stop an opponent when he should. His teammates teased him by calling him "Come On Gord For Christ Sake Gord Get In There And Fight Gord!"

As far as she could tell, none of Mark Hallam's family came to see him play. That year Dick and Donnalee sat through an entire losing season in cold rinks all over the place, in Bedford, Dartmouth, Cole Harbour, Lower Sackville. It was Gord's swan song as far as hockey was concerned. Hallam had his driver's license and his own car. All that winter, Fridays before school, Gord rode with him to hockey practice. He had to get up at 4:30, wash, eat, dress and be ready when Hallam arrived to pick him up at 5. Donnalee was usually awake then, too. As soon as she sensed that Gord was up, she would lie in bed listening to him move around downstairs. She worried about him driving out to East Hants so early in the morning with Mark Hallam, who, as much as he was nice to look at and exciting to watch play hockey, scared her. He was too rough, off the ice as well as on. He didn't seem finished. A certain refinement was lacking in that young man, as Mr. Murayama might have expressed it. Maybe he frightened her because he was finished, set at age seventeen for life, and she was worried that Gord might stop developing and end there, at Mark Hallam, more man than boy, hardened, independent, smirking, sinister with his vampiric shock of hair that looked like a lightning bolt. Mark reminded her of Dick in his younger days, before he put on weight and lost definition. Stopped being passionate about things. Except, of course, during Gord's hockey games. Now those too were past. How was a mother supposed to prevent this from happening to her baby boy, the hardening followed by the growing soft? Gord, she was thankful, still let himself be exuberant, silly, boyish, and unconsciously sweet when unaware he was being observed.

One Friday she slipped out of bed and went to the window after hearing Mark Hallam's car, a restored Plymouth GTX with its distinctive purr, pull into the driveway. She parted the curtains to peek out, hoping to catch a glimpse of the boy. Dick woke and asked what she was looking at. Startled, as if icy fingers had raked the back of her neck, she recovered enough to reply that she was just watching to see that Gord got away safely.

"Safely? It's not here you should be worried about him, it's out there on the 102."

"They don't use the highway. They take the secondary roads."

"Is that what he told you?"

"Yes, it is. Are you saying he's lying? Why would Gord lie about something like that?"

"He knows you don't like him driving on the highway."

"I don't…when he's at the wheel."

"Oh, so it's okay when his friend is driving. You trust him more than you trust your own son."

"Mark's been driving longer, Dick. Gord just got his license."

"I don't see why you don't let him take your car to hockey practice. There's nobody out on the road this time of day."

"Well," she said, "because Mark is already driving out there every week. It wouldn't make sense to run two cars when they didn't have to. You said yourself the price of gas is going to bankrupt us."

"So, if Mark weren't already available with his car...?"

"Of course. Gord would have to take mine. Or would you let him drive yours?"

"I'm only saying he's safer going with Hallam."

"No doubt you're right, Dick."

"Then why do you need to keep looking out the window?"

"I don't. As usual, you've made me acutely aware of my error in that regard."

MARK HALLAM grabbed multiple bag-handles in each hand, confident in the plastic's ability to hold up under the weight of its burden. Donalee thought, *you break anything in there, mister, and I'm sending you back inside for replacements.* As soon as she had formed the thought, she knew she would demand no such thing. *I really should get a bunch of those cloth bags*, she thought, as she stood beside the open trunk while he loaded it with her grocery purchases. She admired the effortless way he transferred the bags from the roller bin to the car and the surprising gentleness with which he placed and arranged them. She thanked him, smiling, waiting to see if he recognized her. He glanced at her through his bangs, head down, as he stepped up onto the concrete walkway under the store's overhang.

She thought, *He probably thinks I want to give him a tip*. Unlike Dick, she wasn't in the habit of tipping bag boys, delivery people and the like. How much was customary? She opened her purse, rummaging there until she had snagged two dollar-coins. He was already moving the next set of red plastic bins into position along the roller track. His back was turned. The car behind her in line wanted to advance. Calling his name would cause further delay.

He didn't seem to feel the late-August chill rising off the harbour, wearing as he was only a thin short-sleeved shirt and tie as part of the store's dress code.

She walked back up to the driver's-side door of her car, a sensible little Kia the colour of linen.

"Say hi to Gord when you see him," she heard Mark say.

For an instant she hung awkwardly between being seated and upright, her right leg inside the car, her left one still on the pavement. She leveraged up and out, hauling on the roof of the car and the opened door. "I will," she said. "Thanks for asking, Mark. Nice to…"

"Same here. Tell him I'll give him a call sometime. When he's home. When is that? Soon I hope."

"Yes," she said. "I'm not sure, exactly. Whenever the job finishes up there. He's not the most conscientious letter writer."

She felt her smile was broader than she expected it would be, out of proportion to her desire, which had been merely to say hello, or not to say anything while committing the subtle act of admiration from afar. He was handsome. The hardness she remembered and expected to see wasn't there in him now. He seemed almost bashful with her. Was he embarrassed to be seen doing such menial work? Gord had said that Mark was dating a girl who was a year younger than he. Rebecca Sleight. Donalee wondered if they were still together.

She started the car and pulled it ahead, turning into the main thoroughfare leading out of the parking lot. Becky Sleight, if she remembered correctly, was one of those sweet, pixie-like girls too perfect for the corruption of the modern world. You wanted to protect a girl like her from grime and violence and exploitation. It was incomprehensible that Mark Hallam should attract someone as apparently innocent as Rebecca. Who am I to judge? she thought. She was as inexperienced as Becky and about the same age when she met Dick. Now look at me, mother of two strapping boys, one headed off to university. Were Mark and Rebecca still going out? She could ask her son Jamie, but he would wonder about her motive. What was her motive, anyway, and what did she intend to do if she learned that they were no longer together? Call him up? Invite him over to the house when Dick and Jamie were away?

"I must be losing my mind," she said as she drove. At a stoplight she lit a cigarette using the plug-in lighter beside the radio and took a deep drag, her first in weeks. The light turned green. Donalee hesitated, unsure whether she should drive with the cigarette in her hand or butt it out. Dick didn't approve of her smoking. He was going to be able to tell. The car behind her tooted its horn twice, not aggressively but to say, hey, snap out of it.

As she began to move her foot off the brake, a car careened through the intersection and across her path. It seemed to be accelerating and skidding sideways at the same time. Afterwards, when she tried to remember the details, the policewoman patiently posing questions and pausing to get Donalee a space blanket because she was shivering so much, she was certain the driver had not applied his brakes before hitting the light standard. It was a man, she learned on the scene. Who it was she wouldn't find out until a few days later, after the next of kin had been notified. He had been drinking for days, apparently, inconsolable after the drowning death of his son. It was in the newspaper. He was a writer of some kind. Donalee had never heard of him. But then Dick told her that the man's daughter had been working for the summer at the frame shop, and Donalee thought, *how awful, first her brother and then her father.* It was the sort of grief you might never recover from. And then for no reason she thought about Mark Hallam again, and her own father, whom she'd adored. And then her husband, who grew, obscuring everything else. A desperate urge, close to panic, took hold of her, and nothing else mattered. She didn't want to think about anything until she was home, safely enclosed in Dick's embrace.

The Sumerian

A gang of them played touch football and road hockey on Atworth Lane, the cul-de-sac where Mate Speedwell lived. He owned the two hockey nets they used for goals; their battered aluminum frames strung with netting that had many times been repaired with whatever twine was at hand. Speedwell made you feel important. It was game-off without you, the party paralyzed until you arrived. Your ability to lope with deceptive speed down the middle of Atworth Lane to the spot where his expertly thrown spiral pass dropped softly into the basket of your two hands was, in his parlance, frightful.

"How did you do that, Gord? I wasn't even looking. They were all over me. All I could do was close my eyes and let fly. How did you get there so fast? You are one horrendous talent, Vance."

He was, until they switched teams. As an opponent, Maitland Speedwell, named for his mother's family, the investment mogul Maitlands, was a demon. "All over you" was a common phrase where Mate was concerned, as was "You got Mated," gentler on the ear than its cruder translation. Mate's fingers raked your ribs, his elbows rudely explored the unprotected area around your kidneys, his heels applied dissuasion to your instep. The same boy who minutes before had been a welcome pair of shoulders for Mate's celebratory arm could become, without so much as an acknowledging wink, a punching bag, terminus for the toe of his boot. Such a switch from ally to foe always left Gord dazed, and so, years later, when Mate asked him to be his navigator, Gord was conditioned to be wary.

He did say yes, as much to mitigate his doubt as to give him confidence in his supposed ability to keep one eye trained on the odometer, another on the map and instructions lying in his lap, and a mystical third on landmarks he had never paid much attention to before and which would soon be whipping past the window too quickly to identify. He knew what car rallies were, their goal and the means of attaining it, but had never been in one. He didn't have his license yet, though he was taking the drivers' education course on Wednesday evenings at his school. Mate had had his license for a month but wasn't supposed to drive after dark at all or in the day without an adult sitting in the passenger seat beside him.

The distance between them had begun to widen even before they reached high school. By then Atworth Lane, suiting its design, had grown quiet. Homework, afterschool jobs, girlfriends and organized sports kept them away from street play, much to the relief of the Speedwells' neighbours. Gord kept to himself unless invited out. Studious, he liked getting high marks despite not being particularly passionate about what he was learning. Mate joined a loud, obnoxious group of *agents provocateurs* who congregated before and after school, and between classes, in the foyer, hanging off each other, sharing girlfriends, singing outrageous lyrics, loudly announcing their loves, hatreds and indifferences. Their boisterous knot appeared to be a static entity, be they stoned in someone's basement rec room on a Saturday night or sitting in obligatory assembly midmorning in the school auditorium—Mate and his mates were often on stage promoting school spirit with equal parts ennui and verve—or stumbling home from Argyle Street early on a Sunday morning.

Because he was quick but relatively short, Mate played guard on the basketball team. If he'd asked Gord to watch, Gord might have done so, though not with the same enthusiasm or loyalty as before. Mate didn't call him to come over to his house anymore, and whenever he did acknowledge Gord at school it was with a mocking tone.

To say that he felt left out is to overstate the importance, sway, and ability to disturb of the Reprobates, as they called themselves, a group that included the Hyman brothers, Sacha and Gad, sons of the doctor who performed one of the first successful penile reattachments. The boys acted as if this accomplishment were the one bit of news in the universe meant to stunt their social development. The only remedy for such embarrassing notoriety, they decided, was to organize an event that required the racing of automobiles, scores of them, faster and farther than what passed for safe recreation.

The rules of the rally were that each car in the competition could contain two people only and that no one except for the route's designers knew where they were supposed to be going. Everyone paired quickly, settling predictably into boyfriend-girlfriend cars with male drivers and female pilots, perhaps not the combination most likely to lead to successful completion, given that the girls generally ignored maps and tended to navigate by way of familiar landmarks and past association, whereas the boys drove while focused dangerously on the odometer and on those instructions they could remember or, more often, on their usually erroneous conception of what the ideal route should be. Mate, who wanted intensely to win, thought that his navigator should be the smartest person he knew, regardless of that chosen brainiac's lack of experience or their now strained friendship. Gord was duly flattered.

THE DAY OF THE CAR RALLY, Speedwell insisted they call him the Sumerian. Maybe he thought it made him sound mysterious and accomplished, a man of a lost civilization. The name suggests mild threat, although not high danger. What you'd risk crossing the Sumerian, with his strange symbols and his suggestion of greater dynasties to come, might be your reputation or your credit rating. Still, for so ancient a name, it did connote currency and sophistication, in the way a professional wrestler might achieve wider recognition by starring in a romantic comedy about childbirth or a self-mocking TV commercial for an anti-itch cream.

That year he and Gord were taking the same advanced-technology course designed to prepare them for engineering at university. The teacher was Ms. Olenska, new to the school that September, in her late twenties or early thirties, someone who looked like she curated art exhibits, attended gala fundraisers and marathon raves with equal aplomb, and knew what kind of wine to drink and which golf club to use. She was overqualified to be teaching high school, possessing two graduate degrees, one in physics and the other in art education. One of the first things she told them about herself was that she made all her own clothes, which looked like what you see on the fashion channel, only more practical and designed for real women you see out in the world.

The class quickly divided into two groups, those who were in love with her and those who refused to believe she knew anything about machines. Predictably the scoffers gave her a difficult time for a few weeks, sitting at the back of the room and coughing snide remarks whenever she spoke. Finally, sick of the subterfuge and its effects, she singled out the ringleader, none other than Mate Speedwell, and challenged him to a duel. The two of them would bring their cars in to the auto shop, she said, and race to see who could change the spark plugs and motor oil and lubricate all the necessary moving parts the fastest. At the word 'lubricate' Mate smirked suggestively and gathered appreciative laughter from around him.

She beat him by ten minutes and forty-three seconds.

Order descended upon the class.

Seemingly incongruent for a first lecture in a class about technology, Ms. Olenska talked about the Sumerians. They had the oldest-known written language, she told them, adding that we still don't know everything about the relationship between cuneiform and successive scripts. Their mathematical system was based on the number sixty rather than ten. They were probably the first to live in autonomous city-states. We are still writing stories, painting pictures and thinking about religion the way the Sumerians were before their demise four thousand years ago. Her point in beginning with ancient history rather than math or problem solving or team building was to remind her students that what we create can last a long time, not necessarily in a physical state but through its influence.

When Speedwell announced that his classmates were to call him "The Sumerian," he was braced for laughter. Anything said in a tone of proclamation was automatically greeted by derisive cackles. But it was a fitting moniker, one possessing an elusive cachet. They now knew a few things about the Sumerians from Ms. Olenska. The most titillating was that this ancient civilization grudgingly accepted the tradition of *jus primae noctis*, the king's right to be the first to sleep with a bride on her wedding night. Gord didn't know what a Sumerian looked like, but figured that Mate, with his slightly hooked nose and easily tanned skin, passed for one as well as anybody did. Who among them was better suited to be a man of a lost civilization?

And so, the Sumerian gives Gord the nod to ride shotgun, he decorates both sides of his dad's car with cuneiform symbols done in multi-coloured water-soluble paint, and don't think it stops there. He gets his mother to sew tunics out of bed sheets and Gord feels like he's wearing nothing at all, a mini-dress ending mid-thigh. Sandals—who knows where he got those, a costume-rental place, probably—with straps that crisscross around the calf almost to the knee. Identical wraparound sunglasses that make them look like aliens from a bad sci-fi movie.

In a way it didn't matter if they got back in the car and tried to complete the course. In those fifteen minutes before the rally began with a loud report from a starter's pistol, they were memorable, captured by the yearbook photographer, laughed at, fussed over, the recipients of catcalls and lewd advances meant to uncover what lay beneath their brief smocks. For Mate, this attention was air and sustenance.

As quickly as it came, attention in the parking lot shifted away from Mate and Gord and toward Ms. Olenska and Ms. Phelps, a PE teacher, who arrived in Ms. Olenska's vintage MGB, its top rolled back. They were made up to look like Amelia Earhart in leather helmets, goggles, fleece-trimmed leather bomber jackets, white scarves, jodhpurs, riding boots. They sat up on the backs of their seats and blew kisses to the assembled. As soon as Mate saw them, he bristled, still angry about having been shown up in the oil-and-lube competition after class. She made a flourish of leaping out of her cool little roadster and coming over to wish the boys luck.

They reached the head of the queue after sitting uncommunicatively, inching ahead, staring at the back of the car ahead of them. Mate's tension wafted off him. Gord wished he would at least ask him if he knew what he was doing or in what direction they should be heading. The instructions assumed his ability to read the odometer, in this case an auxiliary trip meter that could be reset, and to read a compass mounted between them on the dashboard.

They received their send-off; their departure time noted. They turned right at the Willow Tree onto Bell Road and drove until they reached Sackville Street, the nearest intersection that matched the first change of direction indicated on the instruction sheet. Gord told Mate to turn left and proceed along Brunswick. By the time they reached the intersection where Gord thought they should be, he knew he'd made his first navigational error. The number showing on the trip meter was the same as the distance from the school parking lot to the first checkpoint, where they needed to get their rally card stamped, but there was no checkpoint in sight. Brunswick was leading them onto the Macdonald Bridge and across the harbour towards Dartmouth. If he was reading the instructions properly, after the first checkpoint they were supposed to travel a considerable distance in the other direction.

There was nowhere to turn around so that they might retrace their path and discover where he had made his mistake and so they drove all the way across the span. "Don't worry," he said, "I'll subtract the extra mileage in my head." He was certain they had missed the first checkpoint. Mate knew it, too.

"How do you even get yourself dressed in the morning, Vance? How is it you're able to find your way to school?"

He added that he knew exactly where they should have turned. After that, the boys didn't speak at all while Mate drove. Once across the bridge Gord suggested they turn into the parking lot of the Dartmouth ferry terminal, where he could review the instructions and try to figure out where he'd gone wrong.

Gad Hyman's girlfriend Tanya was sitting reading a book at a wooden utility table at the edge of the lot, near the sidewalk. Gord got out of the car, said hello, and asked her what number checkpoint this was. "Four," she said. "You're the first ones here." She stamped their card, saying nothing about the fact that it was otherwise unmarked, and Gord scrambled back into his seat. Before he'd closed the car door, Mate revved the engine, angrily threw the stick into gear, and spun the wheels to leave rubber on the pavement. He muttered something Gord couldn't make out, reset the trip meter, and looked at him sceptically.

"Where to now, genius?"

"Back across," Gord told him, to find the first three checkpoints.

They drove west then south, through and out the other side of the Rotary. Gord had no idea where the next checkpoint might be. They passed scrubby brush, desperate-looking apartment blocks, saltbox houses and rusty trailers. It all looked like the sorrow of a fading dream.

"All we have to do is make it to the final checkpoint and not be last," said Mate.

"What about the stamps?" Gord asked. So far their card had only the one.

"We don't need no stinking stamps," Mate replied in a lame imitation of Cheech and Chong. He had a theory. Knowing the Hyman brothers, the route organizers, he thought that the final checkpoint would have to be at the highest point in the city, because Sacha and Gad were, one, always talking about getting high, and two, wanting to be pilots, first in the air force and later with a major airline. The airport, he surmised. But Stanfield International was in the opposite direction, at least a twenty-minute drive away.

"The Redoubt, then," he said, referring to York Redoubt, the fortification built in the late 1700s. "That's the highest point. It has to be there."

They wound along Purcell's Cove Road heading southwest. Mate made the car accelerate, and as he hunched forward at the wheel, his face clouded by whatever inner storm had him in its grip, he continued to speak in a relaxed, almost nonchalant way. Who cared if they finished the race or not, he said. At least they weren't sitting bored in a classroom. Maybe he'd try his hand at professional car racing, as if all he had to do was show up in a muscle car and drive like this, fishtailing around tight turns, the righthand tires of the car wandering onto the gravel shoulder and back. The contrast between his placid demeanour and the speed of the hurtling car was disconcerting, as if Gord had awakened to a situation that seemed real but could also have been the product of hallucination.

They were close enough to the centerline of the narrow road that an approaching car had to veer onto the gravel shoulder to avoid collision. A moment later they heard a siren growing louder behind them. Gord turned in his seat to see the same car they had just encountered gaining on them, a removable cherry light now flashing on the roof. Mate's reaction was to speed up, until he saw that he couldn't outrun the unmarked car, which, when the boys finally did slow, pull over onto the gravel shoulder, and stop, contained an off-duty constable who had been driving home from playing in a charity hockey game. He made a point, after looking askance at their costumes, of marching them back to his car so that they might look through the rear window to see his equipment bag taking up most of the back seat. The handles of two goalie sticks formed an acute angle opening toward the opposite window. He was astounded, astounded, he repeated, at the abject stupidity of boys their age. He said he would rather get into position without a stitch of padding and face the hardest slap shot than share the road with idiotic killers like Gord and Mate. Did they have the faintest idea how much trouble they were in?

They weren't in trouble, only Mate was. The policeman said that when he finally caught up with them his speedometer had reached 160 km/hr. The speed limit was eighty. He confiscated Mate's license and keys, told him to lock the doors of the car, and ordered the boys to get into his car. Mate begged him to let him drive his father's car home. The man only shook his head and said, "You don't get it, do you?"

GORD SAW HIM, years later, in a restaurant in Toronto. It was summertime. Gord and his two daughters had driven together from Halifax to see family. They had met his sister-in-law for lunch. As they finished their meal, Gord stole glances at Speedwell, sure that he had seen and recognized Gord and was actively refusing to acknowledge his existence. Fair enough, he thought. Mate had every right to relegate him to his memory's waste receptacle. Gord hadn't emptied his yet, his sin, that of navigational incompetence, continuing to rattle inside, but the container was tightly lidded. As a result of his speeding infraction, Mate was penalized the maximum number of points, lost driving privileges at home for the better part of a year and had to take the driving test again when his license came up for renewal. Gord phoned him to apologize, the day after it happened, expecting Mate to tell him not to worry about it or that it wasn't Gord's fault. He hoped he would make a joke about it and say something like, 'Hell of a ride, huh, Gord?' They could turn their shared experience of failure into something exclusive, a bold story, an adventure others might envy them hearing about.

The only thing Gord remembered Mate saying was, "I guess I asked the wrong person to be my navigator."

Gord's party left the restaurant before Mate and his companion did. It was a small enough space that they had to pass close to Mate's table on the way out. Gord's daughters were in good spirits after having eaten and were excited about the coming shopping spree with their aunt.

Gord had a flash, before Mate looked up, of seeing the four of them from Mate's perspective: *Gordie Vance has done okay for himself; I underestimated him; clearly he's not the screw-up I assumed he was.* Pure conjecture, of course. When Gord thinks about that moment now and applies time's corrective, Mate Speedwell resolutely refuses to look up, and they exit without Gord and Mate saying boo to each other. Given the choice, between his having seen Gord and been reminded of that painful time in their youth or his not having recognized Gord Vance, his erstwhile navigator having come to mean no more to him than did the harried waitress who served him an overpriced burger, Gord takes the former every time.

Aubrey

Aubrey was the one who told Cary about John. They met by chance on Spring Garden while negotiating the temporary walkway that wound through the road construction. All he said was that Cary should call Merin, who had heard about the accident from the RCMP.

Cary liked Aubrey, liked him and Merin together. Aubrey might have been the most unpretentious person Cary had ever met. Aubrey hadn't had the easiest go of it. He could be walking along, listening to Yo La Tengo, Sons of Anarchy, or The National, his favourite groups back then, and he would start to drip sweat and fight for breath, his heart beating faster than it would if he were running. He was no runner, didn't have the build for it. Overweight, he knew he had to do something about it.

Nothing helped until Aubrey could reach home or the Barrington, whichever was closer. Merin kept the name after she bought the theatre from Aubrey's mother. At that time, Aubrey's father lived with his new wife somewhere in rural Manitoba, where he was from. Aubrey's mother lived in a condo near the Public Gardens. It suited her. She lived on an inheritance from Aubrey's maternal grandmother and volunteered at the QE Hospital. Aubrey and Merin would go over to have Sunday supper with her once or twice a month. She didn't press her son to do this or that, but Merin detected disapproval: about his choice of girlfriend, lack of ambition, and his continued involvement in the running of the movie house, the place where he had grown up and where he'd always felt safe. This all emerged for Merin gradually and indirectly. His mother would call him, when she knew he was busy in one of the two projection booths, to ask for help: changing a light bulb in the kitchen; opening a jar; carrying a heavy patio chair inside from the balcony and down to her storage space in preparation for winter.

"Go. Just go," Merin would say. "It's fine. I can keep an eye on things here."

The movies they showed were no longer reel-to-reel on celluloid film, and so unless a glitch in the software governing the digital projector caused a stoppage, which had yet to happen, they could start a flick and fall asleep in the booth until it was almost over. Aubrey missed the old-style projectors, the lightly clacking sound they made, the whirr, the heat of the projection room caused by powerful bulbs.

He could watch the same movie twice a day for a week and not tire of it. Sameness and regularity gave him comfort. It took him longer than it should have to get used to Merin's new haircut, for example. One day she came home sporting a much shorter style. The bangs were gone, replaced by a style in which the sides of her head had been shaved, and what remained on top cascaded in a slant across her right eye. "He almost left me over that cut!" She was only half joking.

Merin met Aubrey the summer before she bought his family's theatre. Home for a visit, she'd brought with her a box of manuscripts, poetry book submissions, and after two days of reading, feeling as though the container were refilling mysteriously each time she looked away, she decided to take in a show, something light playing at the little independent place downtown, a 90s rom-com. It was what she needed to help clear her mind of so much earnest overreaching for meaning, the obscure imagery, unfortunate expressions that meant significantly other than what the poet had intended, and personal revelation better left in a therapist's office. It was a weekday evening, the earlier of two scheduled showtimes.

Aubrey was selling tickets, his mother, standing beside him, running the refreshment counter. His father must have been in one or the other of the projection booths. Merin didn't recall meeting the man that evening.

Their debit machine wasn't working and Merin didn't have enough cash in her purse for a ticket. She asked if she could watch the movie and promise to come back to pay afterwards. She didn't think she had enough time to find a cash machine before the show started.

"It's just downstairs," Aubrey said, "near the entrance. Look for the lottery-ticket kiosk. The bank machine is right there."

"Yes, but I hate having to walk in after the lights have been turned off. I have terrible night vision. I'm as good as blind in the dark."

"Don't worry," he said, "I have a torch. I can lead you to your seat."

She thought, *torch rather than flashlight*. Bluenose accent but British influence, one or both parents. She loved these flecks of the realm that clung to Canadian English, as much as she knew she was supposed to blue pencil them into oblivion.

"That's nice of you to offer. I wouldn't want to put you out."

"Oh, no problem at all," he said, smiling. It was a lopsided grin. One of his eyes was almost closed. The other looked at her without guile. It was like looking into a baby's eyes.

She said, "That's not the only thing. I really don't like coming in once the movie has started. That sounds like something ripped off from Woody Allen or *Seinfeld*, I know. And I know what you're going to say, that there are ten or twenty minutes of ads and previews and that I could probably go down the street, order a cup of coffee, drink it and be back before the feature presentation had even started, but it's hard to explain to someone, anyone who doesn't share this quirk. I suffer from an intense aversion to missing out on things. You know? What I paid money to see?"

"FOMO."

"Technically not a fear," she said.

"Technically you haven't paid anything yet."

If anyone else had said that to her, she might have bitten his head off. What was it about him? He was devoid of subterfuge.

"You make a good point," she said, aware that she was holding up the line and that the time remaining before the film was due to begin was quickly running out. "That's fine. Sorry, really, to be such a bother. I'll come back another time."

"Next screening is at 9:45."

"Yeah, a little late for me."

"This is its last day."

"That's okay, I wasn't dying to see it. I was only—listen, don't worry about it. Really." She turned to leave.

"You were only what?" he called after her, past the person next in line at the ticket counter, a man betraying his displeasure at being ignored and talked over.

Merin stopped, turned around in the foyer between the two screening rooms. "Why do you want to know?"

Aubrey's mother appeared at his side. "You'll have to excuse my son," she said. "He does like to engage. Please go ahead in," and she handed Merin a ticket, the kind that came in long strips all in a roll and you used them instead of cash to pay for beer at outdoor events. "Pay when you can. Enjoy the show."

Merin thanked her, feeling awkward to have been singled out, but intrigued by what had transpired. She said it felt as though she had been chosen. Tag teamed. It would have been just as easy to let her leave. How could they be sure she would return to pay? Wouldn't others demand the same treatment? She wasn't even dying to see *You've Got Mail,* a movie she'd somehow missed all these years. If she had taken the time to answer Aubrey's question, completing her broken utterance, she would have said that she was looking for diversion, an entertainment that didn't demand anything of her except passive consumption of predictable fare. Nothing provocative, nothing to shake her belief system, her grooved ways of perceiving. A formula, delivered in a bright, familiar pattern but which felt nevertheless like a surprise, a shiny new trick.

For all that, once she was seated, she couldn't concentrate on the movie. She kept looking around, expecting Aubrey to be standing in the aisle looking at her or leading a customer to a seat, his 'torch' trained on the floor to minimize bother to the audience. She thought about movie dates she'd been on, few of them enjoyable or even satisfying, for this very reason of hyper self-consciousness: she could never not be thinking about the person sitting beside her. What was he thinking? Did he consider it a good scene or one superfluous to the action? Why was he touching the back of her neck in that particular manner? Conversely, why wasn't he trying to touch her? He's breathing loudly: is he aroused, or does he have a cold? If she were sitting alone in the dark, she knew, she would fall effortlessly into the story, as though she had left this world and entered that other one, gigantic, vivid, magnetically attractive. It could happen while she was reading, also, engrossed in a book to which she couldn't wait to return. The critic in her would grow mute. She would stop questioning except for, What will happen next?

After she used her surprise inheritance to buy the Barrington, Merin was asked the same question many times: Isn't this a rather expensive way to enjoy what everybody can watch for far less money? "I mean, Mer," said someone she had considered a close, sympathetic friend, "like, come on. I have been known to watch the same movie lots and lots of times—*The Princess Bride* springs immediately to mind—preferably with months in between. Ideally years. But every single day? How are you not going to die of boredom?"

She would smile, crinkling her eyes thoughtfully as though the question had not occurred to her until that moment, or it had, and she was delighted to be answering it. "I don't think so. I'll be very busy with everything else to be done."

She didn't reveal that she had only the vaguest idea what went into running a successful movie theatre. She knew she had to sign on with a distributor and order titles well in advance of showing them, but how long in advance? How did she go about finding out what was coming? From the distributor, she surmised, or trade publications. That shouldn't be so difficult to arrange. Does one do business with a single provider or many? Can I bring titles in all on my own? Gradually, with Aubrey's help and his mother's, Merin's questions found answers.

After acquiring the business she had almost no money left, and so she embarked on what proved to be the frustrating excursion of returning to the bank, asking for another loan, one to tide her through the first months of operation, wondering why the financial institution had not recommended she take out a line of credit for just such a necessity, being naively shocked when she was turned down, and, finally, on the banker's advice, attending a weekend seminar where she picked up the basics: what a business plan should look like (why, she wondered in amazement, had they let her buy the Barrington without one in the first place?); the rudiments of balance-sheet bookkeeping; tax planning for small businesses; advertising and promotion. The brilliant idea (to her) that she hire an accountant, that is, as soon as she could afford one. The unknowns of ticket pricing, liability insurance, pertinent city by-laws, and the launching of special events. She knew she wasn't going to be afforded much time to sit quietly in the dark, revelling in the erotic catalysis of Campion or the stylized mayhem of Tarantino.

What her crazy undertaking had going for it, and what she had going for her, was a point of focus, something heretofore missing from her life. Until becoming the proprietor of the Barrington, she was someone who lived in reaction to what was tossed at her from the wings. Reacted admirably, as her father would have said, but nevertheless was forever having to roll with whatever new set of circumstances was carrying her along: school, friends, boys, jobs, cities those jobs took her to. She sometimes wondered, *Was I too accommodating? Should I not have stopped at some point and identified my priorities, as my mother was always suggesting I do?*

Being a reader, she gravitated towards literary employment. Being the daughter of Douglas Lauder Jones certainly didn't hurt her chances when she reached important junctures. Grad school. Editorial work. She became what each new situation required of her, comporting herself in such a manner that no one mistook her for a rival though all considered her smart, industrious, and pleasant to be around if somewhat eccentric, her fashion sense a singular example of her quirky originality. She didn't become paralyzed thinking about herself, successfully avoiding such soul-searching quagmires as, *Where am I headed in life?* and *What do I want to have achieved by such-and-such a date?*

She let some people come close, huddling confidentially over coffee or cocktails, telling her delicate details about themselves perhaps better told to a priest or a therapist. She knew instinctively the appropriate depth to which she should accompany these souls laid bare to her. And so she would commiserate, holding advice to within unimpeachable limits, so that none could come back to her, six months later, broken across the ribs of some romantic wreck, and accuse her of sending them off in the direction of disaster. Safety first, her *logos. But*, she wondered, *have I been too safe?*

She preferred the camaraderie of mixed-gender groups, fluid congregations within which pairing-off was tolerated if it didn't disrupt the integrity of the whole. She liked the cohesiveness and plasticity of her gang, a mix of people she'd been at school with, work colleagues, those she'd met at poetry readings and book launches, the occasional online hookup, and the rare blind-date setup who turned out to be genuine. He was usually someone more interested in conversation and friendship than in sex, and ever so much a welcome relief from the usual sort of guy who asked her out.

Sometimes she would stand back and look at them and try to imagine having gone to high school with them. They certainly resembled those boys from her adolescence and yet, strangely, it was as if they had undergone a metamorphosis in the intervening decade. It felt as though, upon graduating, these boys had been handed a playbook, one unknown to people like her. In it, she imagined, were set down certain inalienable truths about romance, except that the word 'romance' appeared nowhere in this Lad's bible. 'Engaging with the target,' 'Seduction,' certainly. 'Scoring' as both verb and gerund. 'What a woman wants, what she responds to, what she expects you to do to win her, what she might not know yet about her desires,' etc. As if she were a trophy, big game, or a jackpot to be scooped up on the roll of the dice. It often seemed that the boy / man / prospective lover was looking not at but through her to a teleprompter set up just behind her chair, seen just over one shoulder. He might appear confidant, charming, relaxed, all that, and there were moments when she felt herself relaxing, too, laughing at his story, looking into his eyes, and wondering what it would be like to see them upon waking in the morning. Really, she would remind herself, everything she knew about the male of the species came from having a father and brothers, hardly informative sources in this regard. John was an enigma. The brother she had grown up admiring, being jealous of, and thinking unbearably annoying, at different times and in varying measure, had given her relatively little to go on (though he would have pointed out the inadvertent pun in the word 'relatively'). He had plied the same choppy seas she had but had suffered comparatively little emotional injury, staying high and dry until the day he ran aground on a reef named Danica. Secretly Merin wished someone would fall hopelessly for her the way John had for Dani. There had been one boy, Sid—what was his last name? They'd met working summer jobs in Ottawa. Whatever happened to Sid? He talked about journalism as a career. They'd clicked, they had chemistry. He made her laugh…

So, somebody like Sid—Beausejour, that was it! Someone without guile, unacquainted with the Playbook, sensitive, funny without being silly, someone to coax into the light, a co-pilot, someone she could count on through the years. At which point she would laugh at herself and say, "Merin Lauder Jones, you haven't the foggiest notion what it is you want. You are so messed up, it would take a junk mover an entire week to sort through all the detritus in your psychic attic."

Then she met Aubrey and bought a movie house. After that, everything started to make sense.

Until it didn't.

Newlywed

Zachary and his wife were taking in the Jack Bush retrospective at the AGNS when he spotted the woman he used to live with. She had her back to him and was looking intently down at a display case where the artist's sketchbooks were laid out.

They were there as guests of Zach's mother, Joyce, a devoted patron of the gallery, it being the focus of her week, usually. Joyce had painted as a young woman before getting married. Art, the visual search for beauty and meaning, was still the way she stayed in touch with the divine. Not that she would have put it quite that way. Those were Zach's words.

The woman Zach was watching, Anya Lauder Jones, moved slowly from piece to piece. Joyce couldn't see the young woman's face, but from the look on her son's she knew who it had to be. Joyce had liked Anya and had become friends with her in a way that didn't exclude Zachary but could easily have existed without him. Joyce wasn't sure yet whether she and Annette, Zach's wife of eighteen months, would ever become friends in the same way. She hoped it would happen. She just wasn't sure yet that it would.

Zachary and Anya. How happy they had been together. They were still teenagers when they fell in love. Joyce felt that her own youth had been bound up and reflected in that pure, simple love between her only son and a girl Joyce felt nothing but warmth for, none of the jealousy mothers assumedly feel for the girls who steal their sons' hearts. Circumstance contributed much to the strong bond between Joyce and Anya. It had been an unusual relationship from the outset. Anya's father and eldest brother died the summer she met Zach. A year later, Anya's mother was diagnosed with lymphoma. Had the disease been triggered by a grief the widow couldn't quell? Joyce subscribed to that theory, unsubstantiated by anything other than intuition.

By then, Anya Lauder Jones had already become like a third daughter in the Ferryman household, she was over at Zach's house so often. Anya's mother responded well to treatment, her cancer lapsing into remission for five years. Although Joyce never became friendly with the woman the way she did with Anya, she admired Dr. Lauder Jones. Joyce always referred to her formally in that way though the woman had a fine first name, Ursula, which suited her. Ursula Lauder Jones was reserved and elegant, patrician. Some might have thought her high-strung, though in Joyce's estimation the tension perceived by some in Ursula Lauder Jones was merely proof of the woman's preoccupation with her research. Hardly the perfect hostess—she left the work of entertaining to her husband Douglas—she nevertheless welcomed all who crossed her threshold with the sort of inscrutable smile a portraitist would want to depict. Though it played no favourites, all who had that smile directed their way felt singled out and recipient of an intimate embrace.

Anya would often say that she could not have survived the years of her mother's illness without the support of the Ferryman family. One of them would get Ursula to her medical appointment whenever Anya couldn't. Anya had one remaining brother, Cary, and a sister, Merin. Cary was away at school in the States. Merin ran a movie theatre downtown, the Barrington, and, according to Anya, "wanted to be more available than she was able." Anya didn't elaborate. The Ferrymans made sure Anya and her mother had food in the refrigerator and pantry, hearty meals prepared, frozen and ready to heat, the lawn cut when it became unruly, the driveway cleared of snow after a blizzard. She could not have survived without them, could not have completed her degree at NSCAD. When she thought Anya was working too hard, Joyce would tell her to take a break, and if Anya refused, Joyce would say, "Zachary, do something. Take the girl to a movie. She's going to develop a hump always hunched over her books that way. Go for a walk. Go for a drive and make out. I need to set the table for dinner, so please, move all this! And while you're at it, dear, check in at home. Your mother will forget who you are."

Anya said that Ursula preferred to convalesce alone, which Joyce found hard to believe. No one chooses to be on their own if they're ill. Anya was avoiding having to see her mother so weak. It was a natural response. Given the choice between a house dimmed and muted by cancer and one filled with chatter and light, which would you take? Still, to bury oneself in schoolwork, spending so relatively little time with one's own kin—what was Anya running to, Joyce wondered, it being evident what she was running from?

Zachary accepted Anya's presence in the Ferryman household without question or analysis. She was his girlfriend, after all. He was happy to be in her company, sharing her with his family, occasionally (not often enough for his satisfaction) spiriting her away to explore the marvellous ways their bodies corresponded. He didn't question her ability to move from the languorous aftermath of sex so quickly to the esoteric intricacy of art theory, as though she had thoughtlessly stepped through to another plane of existence. With Anya it was both simpler and more complicated than an act of avoidance. If she were spending so much time with the Ferrymans merely to avoid having to be with her dying mother, would she have been able to concentrate so well on her studies? Neither Zach nor Joyce thought so; Anya was being driven to succeed academically and artistically by a force neither of them recognized.

Joyce suspected that her husband Wilfred understood Anya's compulsion to excel. It took a mind that could block everything else out, the kind of exclusionary focus that risked alienating those who loved you. The driven ones like Wilfred, a mathematician, tended to be blind and deaf to cues, apparently obtuse beyond belief at times that called for sympathetic perceptiveness. They missed their children's musical recitals, championship sports-contests, convocation, and award ceremonies. Sometimes they were away, travelling for business, but just as often they were gripped by a problem they almost didn't want to solve, so greatly did they enjoy grappling with the puzzle. It could be the only time they were truly happy, truly themselves, unbeholden to anyone, unencumbered by obligation. Wilfred understood Anya; they were two of a kind, and maybe that was another reason why Joyce grew so fond of the pretty waif with her moppet's head of dark curls, large, violet-coloured eyes, slightly asymmetrical oval face, and an unwavering approach to whatever or whomever she faced.

Joyce thought that perhaps there were only two kinds of people: actors and spectators. The difference boiled down to one's field of vision. Do you take a spectator's panoramic view, all the better not to miss anything, or, like an actor, zero in on the matter closest at hand, one's lines, this present scene, such that everything outside one tightly defined circle can be eliminated? Zachary was a spectator, hyper-conscious of everything around him; Anya had been an unconscious actor, in a way, unaware of being watched and so intent on the moment that she could miss great swaths of significance.

Joyce wondered what her son was feeling at this moment in the Art Gallery of Nova Scotia, seeing Anya again? He was married to Annette, with whom he was still suspended in newlywed bliss a year and a half later. Joyce didn't know her daughter-in-law all that well. It was perhaps too early for unguarded intimacy. If she never became as close to Annette as she had to Anya, what of it? Joyce was all that much older now. History, it was said, never repeated itself. Circumstances did recur, events reminiscent of past experiences, what had been suffered, relished, or merely endured. It was that no one could be that age again and no one who is that age now can fully comprehend what you, with all your living, memories sharpened and memories lost, are trying to tell them. The present air is different, the light, the seasons. Language has mutated, mores evolved into alien codes, and—Joyce had not thought this possible—history itself abandoned, unremembered except by those studying it as a discipline. For Joyce to reproduce what she had loved with Anya Lauder Jones, they would each have to climb into a time machine and travel backwards, and still it would not have been the same. Annette, she noticed, was not one to reveal intimate details about herself. Joyce used to be the same. The young woman would open up in time. After all, one married, spent decades coming to understand this stranger in your bed, studying him at times the way Jane Goodall studied her beloved primates. Joyce felt she knew Wilfred now as well as she knew herself. She had not given much thought to his family, however. "I didn't marry them, I married you," she once said, referring to Wilfred's brothers and parents. "I don't see why I should tie myself into knots trying to think of ways to please them."

"You do not have to please them," he said. "You don't even have to please me. Just be yourself, Joyce. They're not cannibals, they aren't sharpening their knives. In fact, they're hardly giving you a second thought. I can tell you without a word of embellishment that the members of my family are some of the most self-involved people you will ever meet. You are significant to them only in so far as you now hold a place in their egocentric universe. I call it the Ferryman Egoverse."

"But you're not like that," she said. "Were you adopted?" She didn't want to admit, despite his assurances, that Wilfred was worrying her. This was going to be her first extended period spent with his family since meeting them at her and Wilfred's wedding. There hadn't been enough time then to see the real people hidden behind tuxedoes, frocks, flowers, and best behaviour.

They were indeed not cannibals, Wilfred's charming two brothers and their parents. The Ferrymans were warm, witty, aware of their surroundings, publicly self-deprecating, and kind to Joyce, treating her with nervous cordiality as though she were a war refugee or a weary traveller whose plane had been diverted to land near their humble little town. She lost count how many times one of them told her she was "doing fine," before the ceremony and afterwards at the reception. "Joyce," they exclaimed, "you're a natural!"

She liked Wilfred's older brother, Cedric, a bit less than she liked Jonathan, the younger, probably because Cedric made a stinging weapon of his vulnerability and undressed wounds. Effete, moody, solitary and not happy about it, Cedric latched on to Joyce immediately, making it clear to her from the outset that he understood she was a victim of some unnamed abuse, just as he was. Jonathan, a financier, countered Cedric's self-pity by insisting on taking nothing seriously, mocking what people were saying and what they were wearing, smiling like a mad hyena, and obstructing the caterer and her staff so often that a formal complaint was lodged with Joyce's mother. Who, according to murky tradition, was supposed to be the one in charge of the wedding in all its urgent detail but who early on found it all too much to handle and so retreated to dim corners, undiscoverable, whenever she could. This left the brunt of the logistics falling to Joyce. It was her wedding day; she was meant to float about in giddy relief, thanking guests for attending, for their gifts, for just being so generously alive, offering them daintily wrapped morsels of her cake, all the while trying to think of the perfectly personal, intimate *bon mot* that the second cousin once removed would remember fondly long after the rest of the day had been forgotten. Instead, Joyce became adept at speaking out of the side of her mouth to strangers in starched white uniforms, never letting her smile drop, and thinking that the least someone could do for her was to refill her punch glass and bring her a ventriloquist's dummy to hold.

Nobody was eaten that day. Wilfred's characterization of his brothers and mother and father didn't reveal itself to be true until months later, when his parents' health—his father's mental state and his mother's spine—began a rapid decline. Regrettable things were said. Joyce put it down to the pain they were suffering. Wilfred's dad, last of a breed of stalwart travelling salesmen, retired though hardly long enough to have been said to be fully enjoying it, began to suspect that his son Wilfred and daughter-in-law Joyce had married for one reason only, which was to steal Mr. Ferryman's savings and use it to finance a political revolution. Mrs. Ferryman dealt with her chronic back pain by consuming enough alcohol to mute most sensory information, including her husband's paranoid rants. When Wilfred's father zeroed in on Joyce, calling her a fascist, of all things, Wilfred didn't step in to defend his wife soon enough for her liking. His justification was that the old man was losing his grip on reality. She shouldn't take it personally; Wilf, Sr. was only picking on her because she was the least-known entity; last in, first clobbered. She didn't laugh. Jonathan and Cedric didn't help matters, referring to Joyce as Eva Braun loud enough for her to hear, teasing that she was a bottle blond and was going to dye all her husband's white shirts brown. Wilfred, as the middle child, played conciliator and peacemaker, continuing in that guise almost unconsciously, and convinced his brethren to lay off. It wasn't funny, he insisted, threatening never to speak with them again, at which they laughed. Wilfred was known to age through multiple seasons of life without communicating with his brothers. Whom was he supposed to be kidding?

Mrs. Ferryman's decline came quicker than her delusional husband's, hers accelerated by her discovery of prescription opioids. Vicodin plus booze, an unholy duo. The official statement from the family (absent their father's input, which would have mentioned something vague but ominous about the Deep State) was that the dear woman died of natural causes, 'natural' being something of a family motto. "Why, you're a natural!" "Natch." "Fuck ecology; oil and gas are as natural as you can get."

A meager funeral: Mrs. Ferryman had had few friends. Those who numbered themselves among her close acquaintances and confidants gradually receded when they heard about her condition, and some when they became unlucky enough to be smacked by what had become an uncharacteristically scathing tongue. Funerals and weddings, thought Joyce; how they are more alike than not: a bunch of loosely connected people who hardly know each other gather to witness a ceremony of passage, one into a light-filled but far from certain union, the other into probable darkness.

Mr. Ferryman lingered in the wasting prison of dementia for the next twelve years, most of them spent in an institution designed for people suffering with Alzheimer's. It wasn't a question of whether you were going to get it, Joyce thought after her only visit to the place where Wilfred's father resided, but when. It made her shudder to think that this hell of confusion was what awaited them all. Not I, she vowed. I'll jump off a skyscraper first. I'll O.D. on pills. This was still the most theoretical conjecture, Joyce being then barely out of her twenties and the mother of three. The children's newness and vitality drowned out all signals suggesting that death was even a possibility. Death took the elderly and those who hadn't taken care of themselves. Joyce adhered to a shade of Ayn Randian libertarianism that surprised even her at times, whenever she expressed an opinion supported by its stark tenets. Why, for example, should she have to pay, via taxation, for the health care of people who had abused their bodies? Why should she help cover the cost of chemotherapy for a lifelong smoker? "Well," Wilfred would say, a man no one could accuse of espousing socially progressive beliefs, "that cigarette smoker paid a hell of a lot of tax every time he bought a pack. I don't condone his habit, but I defend his freedom to make the choice."

"How is addiction a choice?" she countered.

"You're right. But he did choose once, or a handful of times, at first. After that, the drug decided for him. But here's the thing. Does that mean the rest of us abandon that person to a fate nobody would choose? I'm talking about premature and often horrible death there, Joyce. Are you saying that we collectively have no obligation to care for that poor bastard?"

Joyce was foremost a rational person. She knew when an argument made sense and when it didn't. This is to say she knew her husband was right and that she should concede, but damned if he didn't have that ghost of a smirk invading each side of his mouth—she called it his twitchy face. He couldn't help it. He looked too pleased with himself, smug, and that would not do, no, not at all. And so, she dug in, heard herself say the most untenable things, extreme statements which, if she had heard someone else say them, she would have condemned instantly. But when you are horn-locked with a man whose face is all triumphant, making you feel as though he were mocking you for being alive or for having your own ideas—well, screw that. He was going down.

"I DON'T THINK your mother likes me very much," said Annette.

Zachary looked at her cautiously. They had come home from the gallery after dropping Joyce at home and he wasn't sure what to expect. Annette knew all about Anya Lauder Jones, Zach's first everything: first girlfriend, first adopted sister, first close friend, first person ever stolen from him by his mother, first lost love. Zach had been forthcoming about Anya before he and Annette became serious about each other. No secrets, they agreed solemnly. She knew about their year together in Timmins when Anya and Zach did so much for those suffering economic hardship and so increasingly little for each other. In turn, Annette told him about her obsessive fan-love for Michael Jackson, which had lasted well past the time anyone in her right mind could have found the pop star attractive. She revealed that she had had a two-year relationship with a man who was convicted of tax fraud. She admitted to her inability to become sexually aroused in the bathroom or near running water.

Zach had watched Annette watching the reunion of his mother and Anya. Annette seemed horrified at first that the women should be so demonstrative and loud, to the point of hyperventilation, joyful shrieks, and copious happy tears in the middle of an art-gallery showroom. Alarm changed to tentative pleasure on Annette's face. Introductions ensued. A docent intervened to ask them to be quiet. The four of them moved out into the public concourse. Zach hung back a bit, standing beside Annette while his mother and Anya fawned over each other. He kept waiting to feel Annette's realization, thinking it would radiate like a heat source, fearing it would include anger. Instead, she was placid, curious in the patient way an excluded person waits until it is time to be let into a conversation. It made him wonder if the person he'd married was capable of strong emotion. She was watching the two women gush over each other, basking in the sun of their mutual affection, as though they were part of the gallery's larger collection.

It wasn't until she and Zachary were alone that she let him know that she was upset. "I'll get over it," she kept saying. "It was a surprise to meet her that way. You know, through the prism of your mother's regard for her. I always thought I would meet her, your first love, under more controlled circumstances. A dinner date, perhaps. A foursome, she and whoever, you and I, in a quiet restaurant with soft, low lighting. Adult. Where I could watch you being gracious and nostalgic, but at the same time letting me know there's no longer anything there, that you feel nothing but kindliness towards her, and otherwise emotionally detached."

"That's exactly the way I do feel," he said.

"Really? You didn't utter a peep, Zach. You stood back like a shy little boy and let your mother make a fool of herself with that girl."

"She's hardly a girl anymore. And you're not being fair. Anya and I stopped being a couple long before my mother…"

"Yes?"

"They never stopped being close, that's all I'm saying. It was harder for my mother to say goodbye to her than it was for me."

"But you lived together in Halifax. Before moving to Ontario, you said. You got an apartment together."

"That was my mother's idea. I was content to live at home."

"Now that sounds like revisionist history, Zach. Don't make things up just to spare my feelings. I'm not jealous, really I'm not. I do think you're not completely over her. Someone who, I believe, you resent in a way. Or maybe it's your mother you resent, having to share Anya with her, even as a memory."

"Now who's being over-imaginative?" he said testily.

"Someday you'll tell me everything about Anya Lauder Jones. You'll trust me enough to do it without attached filters and without embellishment. Because I have a right to that much, don't you think? Being your life partner and all."

They were still so blindly in love that making up after an argument felt as heady as the fight itself, even more so. It bothered him, though, that she should scold him for being untruthful about Anya. He wasn't built that way. He wasn't complicated enough to devise ways to withhold the truth from those he loved. His mother could have told Annette that about him. It was only that Anya had never felt like a real person to him, even while they were a couple. She had seemed more like a character out of a storybook, one about a plucky orphan who overcomes adversity to thrive and make life better for others. He wanted to say, "Talk to my sisters. They know more about Anya Lauder Jones than I ever did. Talk to my mother, who doesn't hate you, by the way. That's just Joyce. Give her time. Before long you'll be bosom buddies, best friends forever."

Mountcastle

Harbourview United

Tiger, Tiger
Taking flight
In thy Cadillac at night
What immortal hand or thigh
Could make thee drive it so awry?

The markets were in a freefall. The announcer on the radio invested the news, no longer new having led for a week now, with what to Lester Mountcastle sounded like glee. It couldn't be, he knew, but lately there had been little else, every headline establishing a new low. The dollar hadn't been this devalued since he was fourteen and trying to convince his brother Evan, younger by two years, to take over his afterschool paper route. Nowadays, newspapers, so few dailies left, were delivered by adults in cars. You no longer paid some neighbour kid who stood nervous or gloomy in your doorway while you hunted for coins. Now it was a deduction from your bank account or a deceptively cumulative charge on your credit card statement. Come to think of it, who subscribed to print news delivery anymore? He'd switched to the electronic version years ago. What if this were the crux of the current disaster? Value no longer resided in something you could hold in your hand.

He was driving home after a meeting with his investment counselor, although they had not attended the meeting in their accustomed roles as broker and client. Lester was the head of the board of deacons at his church, and Dorothy Gale, the young woman who kept her keen eye on his portfolio, chaired the committee overseeing the sale of the church building. Lester, who had grown up attending Harbourview United, could not remember a time when he and his family did not go there for Sunday morning services. Although not the church of its denomination closest to the house where they lived, the only residence Dr. Mountcastle had ever known, it was where his Uncle Forrest had been the minister and so Harbourview became their church without question or discussion. It had been a happy time, those years of rising early so that he and his brothers, Evan and Lionel, would have time to eat breakfast, bathe, and dress before first service of the morning, at 8:00 o'clock. They would stay for the second service, at 10:30, the children passing that hour in the Sunday school classroom. They had their books and weren't by nature rambunctious boys.

From the outset, Forrest de Quincy Mountcastle, D.D., had been out of favour with his church's board of deacons. He was seen to hold and promote from the pulpit certain progressive views concerning the role of women in society and the acceptance of same-sex love in the world and in the church community. He introduced modern popular music to the service, with guitar playing and a singalong feeling to the rendition of hymns, something that did not sit easily with the older members of the congregation. When the Reverend Mountcastle sat on the altar steps with the children at the front of the sanctuary before they trooped off to Sunday school, he told them stories that often left them wide eyed with fright or laughing uproariously, neither response deemed appropriate to the time and place. His hair having gone grey and then pure white before he was forty, he kept his leonine mane long and brushed straight back from his forehead. Often, before the children had stood to follow their teachers through the door that led upstairs to the classrooms, one or another or the whole gaggle of kids would have messed his Santa-white hair so that it fell all in disarray into his eyes. Lester would try to sit closest to his uncle to be the first to commit the act of dishevelment before dashing away from the big man's demonstration of mock outrage. His thick head of hair raked back into place with strong fingers, he would regain his solemnity, the general hilarity surrounding him subsiding, only to have the hush punctured by a shriek or a giggle—it really was too hard to maintain one's composure under the circumstances—while a picket fence of eyebrows, in the first few rows of pews, in the choir lofts behind him and to the left and right of the altar, would elevate in unison, righteous concern abounding. Not until Lester was old enough to stay to hear the sermon, and then for only a few months before his uncle moved to another church far away, did he see how quickly his beloved uncle could alter his bearing, turning once again into the stern but loving spiritual leader he was. After the great man left and was replaced by a series of interim preachers, going to church became an event Lester and his brothers endured but rarely enjoyed.

DOROTHY GALE had thought about changing her name or going by her middle name, Selma, but nothing else felt natural or right, and fewer people these days recognized hers as the full name of the heroine in *The Wizard of Oz*. She didn't look at all like Judy Garland, being tall and square-shouldered, with narrow hips, a short torso in a bit of a stoop from sitting hunched over her computer. No one would call her pretty, though they would say she had a pleasing face. She wore clothes that accentuated her strengths, and she kept her straight brown hair cut short enough to lend it shape and body.

She would have given anything to be able to sing. She sat where her family had always done, in the third-row pew to the left of the altar and closest to the wall, somewhat hidden from view by a large pillar. She loved watching the choir, and imagined herself in their midst, holding her music folder at the correct angle in front of her so that she joined a collective effect that was painterly and architectural, the carmine-red leather folders moving in unison with the breath, pages turned as one as if smoothing the sections of a divine suit of armour. Their robes were white. The purity of it, she thought was angelic, Arctic, expansive. *Look to Heaven,* it said to her, *and be reminded you are alive,* dazzled by God's grandeur. *Rejoice,* the contrast in colours said to her, though they could also be blood spilled on a winter battlefield.

Before his ouster and long before Dorothy Gale began attending church services at Harbourview United, the Reverend Mountcastle spent a small fortune, all that was contained in his discretionary fund and some that was not, outfitting the choir with these new robes and music folders. Her mother still referred to him as 'that hippie preacher' and 'that bohemian with his funny ideas,' that is, a suspect and possibly improper man. Dorothy pictured someone who looked like Dr. Mountcastle, only older, but it wasn't a convincing portrait. She could not bring herself to believe that Lester Mountcastle, director of the board of deacons, could be the least bit rebellious. Lester Mountcastle the freethinker? Lester Mountcastle rolling around on the sanctuary floor in a state of ungoverned mirth? No, sorry, does not compute, as her father used to say in his *Lost in Space* robot voice. She loved her old dad, who was almost the same age as Dr. Mountcastle. In her estimation they were equally worth studying, equally a lost cause, equally endearing.

When she told him how much money the church had left after the new roof and how much was still required to fix the leaking foundation, the corroded wiring and decrepit plumbing, he looked like he was going to cry. He held off. Men like her father and Lester Mountcastle didn't release their emotions in that way. Not in front of people like her. She knew the strength of his connection to the building. He would never confide in her his bewilderment at the state of the church's affairs, its uncertain future. He didn't have to; she could see it troubling his eyes, feel his uneasiness charging the air between them. It made her worried about him, although not in the way she might be worried about her father in a similar situation.

The real estate company hired to sell the building erected a large sign the size of a small billboard beside the church. Everyone knew the asking price, an obscenely large amount to many in the congregation who could remember buying their first house for less than ten thousand dollars. The price was not displayed on the sign, which was visible from the busy city street that ran up from the waterfront.

When Lester was a boy, his father told him in confidence that one night, when Mr. Mountcastle was a university student and boisterously drunk in a gang of his residence mates, they went bowling at Benson Lanes (the building long since demolished) and, afterwards, smuggled three ten-pin bowling balls out in their backpacks. They went to the top of this same street, Morris, that ran beside the church. It was early in the morning, the traffic almost nil, a car every ten minutes or so, usually a taxi. At the bottom of the hill was Lower Water Street and beyond it the harbour, but before that stood a gas station, long gone, displaying a large balloon in the shape of a bowling pin. It was tethered in place as a marketing attraction: with every tank of gasoline, customers got a free game at the bowling alley.

"I'm telling you this, Lester, not because I'm proud of what we did, but to let you know, son, that in a few short years you will be the same age I was, and you are going to feel the urge to do some pretty strange things."

"Like rolling a bowling ball down Morris Street?"

"Yes. Resist the temptation. You have no idea what sort of havoc you are capable of wreaking on your surroundings. A boy is an ungovernable beast. Remember that. I'm of the firm opinion that young men in any group larger than three constitute a dangerous mob, despite what your Uncle Forrest might say. Mark my words and act accordingly."

Lester wasn't told the details of the damage done to the gas station by his father and his father's university friends. He could well imagine the impact made by a heavy ball accelerating down a slope deemed too steep to be the venue of the annual Boys and Girls Club Soap Box Derby. He liked to think about his strait-laced father acting delinquently. He thought, not without a twinge of regret, that in his fifty-five years he had never done anything as impetuous, silly, or destructively fun as that, not even as a boy. Too late now. The world was in a bad state and was too serious and fragile a place for such boyishness. Perhaps he had taken too much to heart his father's warning. Fun: a limited concept. Lester preferred contentment, the enjoyment of living that comes of a sense of honour and gratitude at being alive and in following God's path. He could be just as easily not alive or never having been at all, he reasoned. The chance of his never having been born overwhelmed him when he thought about it too much. The exhilaration that often brought him to the verge of panic was—had to be—just as powerful as any childish acting out of hormonal madness. Being alive—it was more than enough.

Dorothy Gale had said that the sale of the church building would eliminate Harbourview's debt and leave them with a handsome cushion to bring to the merger with Chalmers United, a suburban church in the west end. The question remained: once the congregations became one, who would oversee the use of that sum? Would they, the Harbourview emigrants, now homeless, a lost tribe, remain separate for the purpose of administering that nest egg, or would they hand it over, dissolving the last vestige of their former existence, and let whatever church governance, newly formed, take over? Trust each other, and trust in the guiding hand of God? Believe, console, and forgive the sins of distrust and jealousy, at the very least. It was a very large sum of money, to one who had never enjoyed an overabundance of it. The debt, accumulated over decades and at an interest rate far below the usual, given that the lender was their national association of churches, had long ago ceased to register in Lester's mind as anything terribly troubling. He found it not difficult but unusual, perhaps, to conceive of amounts that large, and because the note was held by a populous benevolent body, he did not suffer the worry a personal debt of that relative magnitude might have caused him. But to lose the old stone, erected a century and a half before he was born, and to have been the one to sign that beloved structure away after it had existed for so many generations, the steady, faithful tide in and out of families like the Mountcastles, the gentle but inexorable flood of the devoted and the hopeless in equal measure through those thick wooden doors—would his name forever be linked to the sale and to the failure it represented and would that memory be infamous? Or would he be quickly forgotten, and the transaction lost to history?

If he had been more courageous and Dorothy older and more experienced, they might have hammered out the kind of deal other congregations in bigger cities had made, in which multimillion dollar sales of church land allowed their antique structures to be connected to apartments and retail shopping concourses, leaving the place of worship intact while rental revenue from commercial and residential tenants secured the church's survival. Not quite the revenge of the moneychangers chased from the temple, but close. Success in this regard took *sang froid*, luck and timing. It also took an ideal location. Was theirs such an address, well enough suited for that sort of shotgun wedding? He wasn't sure. But Dorothy would know. He had never pretended to have a head for such matters. All he could think about was the loss of the sanctuary. It had been his childhood citadel, God's fortress, the place of ultimate safety.

AFTER HIS LAST PATIENT of the day, a walk-in complaining of pain in his first, upper right premolar, Lester called Dorothy at the bank where she worked. There had to be a way to save the church. All he got was the central voicemail. Because he didn't know the number of her extension, he hung up. She wouldn't be at work the next day, a Saturday. He tried finding her home-phone number. There were seven Gales listed with the first name indicated by the letter D, and he wasn't about to start dialling them. He knew he could find her in the printed directory of church members he had at home. Normally he would have waited. He was, after all, a man who made his livelihood remaining calm and exuding confidence while invading people's mouths to intercede on behalf of their teeth.

He had resisted a recent offer to join a large dental clinic opening close to home, preferring to work out of a small office downtown with a single hygienist. Dental care—not anything to rush or compromise. Those storefront, strip-mall practitioners didn't take enough time with a patient, their every procedure itemized so that all a dentist had to do was touch a screen to tally the bill. Dr. Mountcastle had heard all about it from Norris, who had come to work for him as a dental hygienist after a brief internship at one of those corporate-run dental mills.

"I tried, I truly did, but I couldn't work fast enough, according to their protocol," Norris said.

"Their what?"

"That's the word. Protocol. Your basic de-scaling, flossing, and polishing should take X number of minutes, no longer, regardless of the patient. It didn't matter who could be sitting in the chair, a child with a tiny mouth or a lifetime smoker or red-wine drinker. And I wasn't supposed to converse, aside from basic instructions. Can you picture me mute, Dr. Mountcastle, I mean not chatting with my patients? Asking them about their weekend, how their kid's hockey game turned out, you know, putting them at ease? I even got—listen to this—I even got chewed out for explaining to this little girl what I was doing with scaler. I was like, 'Don't you worry about a thing, sweetie, this isn't going to poke holes in your pearly whites. Holes are what we're trying to prevent.' Slap a price on that? Well, I'll tell you, she got relaxed, calm, not exactly happy but, like, suddenly she was five years older. So, who's going to be a repeat customer? Who is not going to have to be dragged back in here for her six-month follow up? The firm didn't care about shit like that, excuse my potty mouth. So, I have to say, I thank my lucky stars I saw your ad when I did, Doctor, or I'd still be doing things I don't believe in. Or, worse, down on the street doing something I swore I'd never do for money, enough said about that."

Norris wasn't the best dental assistant Doctor Mountcastle had ever employed, but the young man was a pleasant, competent presence in the office, filling in for Mrs. Hurdcraft, the receptionist, when she was late, which was most Monday mornings, answering the phone, dealing with bills and insurance claims as easily as he accomplished his own work. What Norris did on his own time was his business. All that mattered was that the patient got the best possible care.

Harbourview United had never been as open to the LGBTQ+ community as, say, the Unitarians or Cooke Street Anglican, but neither had they ever turned someone away because of sexual orientation. After Lester's Uncle Forrest left ('was hounded out' was the phrase his mother used), the new minister set a far less progressive tone, and for some years garnered a reputation for being less welcoming to those who espoused 'alternative lifestyles.' It wasn't something Lester thought about much while he was growing up. He couldn't say he had a strong opinion about homosexuality, one way or the other. What Pierre Trudeau had said, that the state had no business in the bedrooms of the nation, resonated in him when, still a boy, he had first heard it. He remembered thinking that the state, in the form of his parents, had no right snooping in the bedroom of Lester Mountcastle. Though he had wanted to post just such a declaration on his door, he was astute enough even then to know that it would only arouse suspicion. The intimate truths he was discovering about himself were too personal and potentially too embarrassing to risk disclosing. He was lucky that his parents had been as hands-off about his privacy as he had been furtively 'hands-on' about his body. He still believed that what other people did alone or together was entirely up to them.

After closing the office for the day, Lester drove out to Dorothy Gale's bank. Except for the automatic-teller machines, one just inside the entrance, the other outside and around the corner, the building was closed. Dorothy told him that they were going to remove the outside machine because it was too vulnerable to being tampered with and because a woman had been robbed while she was using it.

"In broad daylight! Four in the afternoon, with people waltzing past, nobody batting an eye. I tell you, Dr. Mountcastle, what next?"

He enjoyed the folksy way she spoke, as if she had just halted the harvester she had been driving and had a notion to chew the fat a while, swap stories, it needn't be anything earth shattering. That was the way she was when she was explaining the progress of his investment portfolio. Speaking plainly, she took the time to explain the meaning of terms, acronyms, and the like. "And such like"—she often ended her lists that way. "There's way more to it, Dr. Mountcastle, but I won't bore you with it. Suffice to say you're holding your own." *Well, yes,* he thought, chuckling to himself, *we have an entire, head-above-water, shared existence, don't we, Ms. Gale, unsaid, inexpressible. Loneliness makes me think these things, do forgive me.* Most days, if he wasn't looking at himself in the mirror, he still felt eighteen.

He hung around the entrance until a teller opened the glass door leading into the bank proper. He said he was an acquaintance of Ms. Gale and wondered if he might have a word with her.

"I'm sorry, sir," said the woman, someone he recognized, though not as one of his patients, "she's already left for the day. Would you like me to leave a note on her desk?"

"No, that's all right," he said. "I'll try to reach her another time. Or another way. I was in the vicinity." He thanked her, thinking, *That wasn't too strange! Now she's going to think I'm a stalker or an ageing suitor who's lost control of his faculties!*

The weekend loomed, dark, voluminous, a flapping tent billowing before him. He had thought about working on weekends, but that would mean hiring another assistant. Lester didn't want to do that. Norris was working just enough each week to qualify for benefits, and it was against Dr. Mountcastle's principles to take that away from him by splitting the week between Norris and someone new, even if the result was more money for the practice.

What can I say, Mr. Scrooge? I've no head for business. Makes me more of a Fezziwig, don't it? Thank goodness for people like Dorothy. The economy was making him anxious, certainly, and he was worried about his investments and savings, the relative security of his eventual retirement. The best way to counteract panic, he had learned, was to leave his statements unopened for a few weeks before looking at them. On Dorothy's advice he left his money where it lay, in a conservative, diversified portfolio, knowing that to take it out or move it around would most likely deplete it. She had taken his 'temperature,' as she liked to call it, his (relative) acceptance of the amount of risk he was willing to live with over the long run, that period being another ten years, 'if all went according to plan,' another of the clear-eyed Ms. Gale's favourite phrases. Undoubtedly the all-too-recent market collapse had decimated the Lester Mountcastle Exit Plan. It surprised him, though, that he wasn't more upset about the loss. He was healthy for someone in his mid-fifties, and he liked his work, even if some of his patients feared his dental instruments almost as much as they feared death. Even so, if he had a self-image, it was that of the Happy Dentist. Was that an accurate assessment of his general state of mind? If it weren't for the impending demise of his church, it might be right. He knew in his heart that he could lose all his money and keep going. There was no small assurance in that.

I'm still here, he thought. Still filling cavities, still shovelling the walk, watering the garden, collecting the Offering on Sunday and chairing deacons' meetings. He was eating better now that he had joined a supper club of singles his age and older, many of them from the church, with a few new faces. More women than men, a three-to-one ratio, meeting every Wednesday. They were down to seven members of Diners' Destiny, as someone had christened them, someone from outside the group. Seven now that Jack Harmony and Indira Salwaz had bowed out after getting married. Lester didn't miss Indira's cooking all that much, anyway. It never tasted like the Indian food he was used to at the

Bengal Gardens restaurant. And Jack Harmony, the sanctimonious prat—Lester caught himself, took a deep breath. Well, he thought, I'm not going to miss him. Indira was welcome to the man, to him and his fortune.

The club was down to two men, Lester Mountcastle and Gordon Grainger, a former patient who had found a new dentist and had made a point of letting Lester know the reason why. Grainger had let an ache in an old filling become so bad that the tooth had to be reamed out in a root canal. His insurance had lapsed because of an irregularity in his health plan—reduced coverage after retirement—and as a result he couldn't pay Lester for all the work right away. Lester let him pay in installments, which he did for three months before defaulting. A letter came accusing Lester of unprofessional treatment, though not in specific terms. In it, Grainger threatened to bring legal action for pain and suffering if Doctor Mountcastle did not immediately release his records to the new dentist and—the nerve of the man!—forgive the balance owing. Lester was relieved to be rid of him. The outstanding $600, though not an amount he could afford to waive every day, had in this case been worth the termination of their professional relationship.

It was difficult not to take the affair personally. Lester took pride and the utmost care in his work. It troubled him that he had sent Grainger away without arranging to protect the root canal job with a crown: Grainger had waved it off, refusing to pay extra for it despite Lester's warning about possible cracking and infection. Too late now. Let the new dentist handle it. He wondered who it could be, knowing most of the practitioners in the field, especially those who had clinics downtown. The suburban operations were another matter, largely unknown to him despite Norris's reportage. Lester knew he had to let it go; he had done his best. The unsettling thing was that here was Grainger, back in Lester's social sphere, all chummy as the only other male in the supper club, with so far nothing said or hinted at concerning the past difficulty between them. It was as if they'd not met until the day Grainger turned up at an Anne Cherney's with a Chopstick Tuna casserole he insisted he had made himself. When Grainger smiled, Lester saw the gleaming porcelain of a new upper plate of dentures. They could not have been cheap.

SID BEAUSEJOUR liked Dr. Mountcastle, but he swore, if his dental hygienist started pressing his groin into Sid's shoulder, as he usually did once Sid was lying back settled in the chair, he was going to look for another dentist. Sid was the only one in the waiting room. The old bird behind the glass, the receptionist, looked to be asleep. None of the magazines on the table beside him interested him. In the sports section of the newspaper, he read that the Blue Jays were leaving their star hitter in the starting lineup despite the outfielder's dismal, 0 for 23, showing at bat. On the back page of that section, he read that the food critic who had helped raise the standard in British restaurants was dead at the age of ninety-four. *I have become a reader of obituaries*, he groaned inwardly. Maybe he was feeling more than usually mortal. Professional sports would carry on. The Jays' star would not remain mired forever in a slump. Eventually he would recover his mojo. Or not. He might never get another base hit let alone homer. Nobody could say. He might well hang up his spikes before taking the field in the upcoming doubleheader against the Reds, bequeath his mitt to the bat girl, return to Santo Domingo and accept that job offer to be a spokesman and ambassador for a bank, attracting clients with his fame, giving them a taste of the country's storied culture and long history, and posing with them for photos in front of the Catedral del Santa Maria la Menor.

After reading about the life of an heiress to a fortune amassed by her father, a manufacturer of bathroom fixtures, Sid scanned the local announcements for names he might know. Most of the deceased had lived longer than he ever expected to last. One of them was his age, forty-nine. He was surprised, although, surprisingly, not frightened. It was natural, he rationalized, to think that he could have been that formerly alive, now fondly remembered, person. There but for the grace of God, chance, or fate, went Sid Beausejour. It wasn't a particularly morbid feeling. It was mostly the sense of having discovered a new game: Life and Its Various Unpredictable Termini. It made professional sports, even the embarrassing soap opera surrounding Tiger Woods and his beached libido, seem inconsequential, not only small and silly but counterproductive, possibly even dangerous to the common good. What did it do to the collective psyche that young men barely out of adolescence playing a game that involved striking a ball with a piece of wood should command so much attention and money? All those passive hours spent watching sports on TV. To think that he used to care passionately that a certain team be victorious, not because it represented his city, not that its fortunes and his were linked, but because it was 'his team,' almost equivalent to 'his family.' It made just as much sense to say that Sid had chosen them because their mascot was adorable or that he could see himself dating one of the cheerleaders, particularly the blonde Pixie who doubled as the morning weather girl. It was beyond ridiculous. 'Sport,' as the British called it—not something he missed. Better to honour the recent dead than to lose his life to the marrow-sucking sink of inane fandom.

He was about to put the newspaper down when he recognized a name, the mother of a woman he used to know. The deceased, a neuroscientist, had had a distinguished research career. The obituary indicated that one of her daughters, Merin, was married to someone unknown to Sid.

Merin Lauder Jones. It wasn't the first time he'd thought about her. Sid liked to know where people were now, what they were doing with their lives, those he'd once been friends with. He wasn't usually interested in resurrecting the acquaintance; he thought of it as the antithesis of networking. The honoured friendship was now sealed, its one-time intimacy private, accessible only as a memory.

They had met many years before, in Ottawa. He had been eating a sandwich in Major's Hill Park, beside a gracefully organic sculpture composed of varnished wood slats. The installation looked like the inside of a giant shell. Merin had a summer job leading tour groups around Parliament Hill and the nearby attractions. Sid was between the second and third year of his undergrad and working for a backbencher, his local MP, a family friend. He was practically volunteering to get the work experience. Though Sid threw himself assiduously into the job, his boss didn't have enough for him to do. When he wasn't being lent out to other parliamentary offices—to stuff envelopes, sift through clipping files in the library, answer phones and occupy reception desks for absentee secretaries—he wandered the Byward Market and along Elgin and Sparks Streets, trying to catch a glimpse of his future.

Merin and her group shuffled close enough to the bench where he was sitting that he could hear her voice. Her audience, somberly rapt, nodded and turned their heads in the directions she indicated, respectfully keeping the lenses of their cameras capped until she had finished telling them the significance of whatever they were looking at. He was fascinated by her voice, the intonation of which made him think of someone older and from a previous generation. She reminded him of Katherine Hepburn: upright, angularly poised, bright, purposeful.

She raised a small yellow pennant attached to a pole above her head and moved quickly along the path in the direction of the river and the statue of Samuel de Champlain. There, he surmised she would tell them about the intrepid explorer and his astrolabe, the sophisticated piece of navigational equipment Champlain had lost somewhere west of where they stood now, a hundred kilometers up the Ottawa River. Sid imagined her telling her group this fact and hearing their reaction. How careless of the Frenchman. There was no excuse. Did he not know how important the astrolabe was? He should have been guarding such a valuable instrument with his life.

Abatement and Delay

> That we would do
> We should do when we would, for this 'would' changes
> —*Hamlet*, Act IV Scene vii

That summer, as soon as the school year was over, Evan Mountcastle set himself a goal to return to his neglected education and read those texts he had read either not well or not at all when he was a student. He thought he would begin with Shakespeare, the Riverside edition, bought second-hand from his roommate, a nervous but amiable fellow who told Evan to pay what he thought was fair, which, it turned out, had been the negligent sum of nothing at all. Evan took the dusty, scuffed, spine-split volume from the spot where it sat on the bottom shelf of a small, cherrywood bookcase in his study. His mother had built the case during a short-lived spurt of self-improvement after the death of her father. Someone had told her that the best way to overcome grief was to produce something substantial, an object she had never made before, and so in the evenings twice a week she went to her children's school, where she learned the rudiments of woodworking. The result was a solid, attractive bookcase with a satiny finish. One could not say, however, that she rid herself of her sorrow in so definitive a way or with such a pleasing effect as she had when she created the handsome piece of furniture. All Evan could remember of that time was his mother's intense focus on the craft of carpentry, her workbench beside the furnace in the basement, where she spent every free moment practising what she had learned in class, and her distant, distracted air when she came back upstairs.

The pages of the Shakespeare seemed hardly touched, though the cover looked as if the book had served as a prop under something heavy or as someone's sled. One of the first things he would do in his new job, he decided, was to find someone who could repair the book's binding, the school's art teacher, perhaps. Recovering the book was the right thing to do, he felt, regardless of the way it had come into his possession.

This packing away of the books in his study was the last job left to do before the movers came. Everything else in the house was either wrapped for the move or placed securely in cardboard cartons. He had been putting off this task until the last minute, an act of procrastination that could be interpreted, he supposed, any number of ways. One was that, of all the places where he, Steph and the kids had lived, this house was the most comfortable and this little room, not much bigger than a landing on the way up the stairs to the attic, had been the first home office Evan had had all to himself. Before that he'd had to make do with the dining-room table, where he would open his laptop, mark papers, and write letters and reports, the first drafts of which he did archaically by hand. And so, although the new house had an even bigger room he could appropriate as his study, he was reluctant to leave this one—and it didn't even have a door he could close. He preferred the ever-open entrance. The children were more likely to come talk to him in the evenings if they could see him sitting in profile at his desk as they passed by on their way to and from each other's rooms. Maybe he was thinking of this house is the last one where they all had been together without the inevitability of the future and, as it barged its way into their lives, the disillusionment it would bring.

Brynne wanted to stay in the city to finish her senior year of high school. To say that she was upset with her father for moving them at this point in her life was to understate the case. It wasn't that she couldn't have stayed, boarding with one of her girlfriends' families or either of her uncles, Lester or Lionel. She was mature for her age, the most responsible seventeen-year-old in her circle of friends. With her parents, sister and brother moving less than an hour away, what was the big deal? All her father could come up with when she asked was that soon enough she would move away for good. Why accelerate the process?

The books fit easily into their boxes. He knew to use the smaller of the cartons to limit the weight of each. Oversized books lay on top. He could hear Stephanie talking on her phone downstairs in the kitchen. The movers were supposed to be here by now, and so she was checking on their ETA. It was the sort of thing he had to do all day in his work; he hated having to do it at home. She, on the other hand, didn't mind doing it. On the phone she was fearless. He was the opposite. Dealing with a delinquent student, getting the story straight, one-on-one, face-to-face, he worked with the icy-smooth competence of a labour-relations arbiter. Talking with parents on the telephone, on the other hand, he dreaded: it was inevitably fraught with hidden traps. For some reason, as soon as he was unable to see a face and read an expression, he lost confidence in what he was saying. He worried that this move to a new school and position, from vice-principal to principal, was going to expose him for a fraud. Finally, the nightmare runs, he will have risen to the ceiling of his ability. A school principal had to speak to a deep cross-section of the community. The face-reading talent that had made him a successful classroom teacher and a respected, effective disciplinarian, he worried was going to abandon him or be of little consequence in his new role.

The Riverside Shakespeare in all its heft was the only book not packed and he had run out of small cartons. Like Evan after him, the book's original owner had given the Bard no more than a cursory scan. Who could read so many plays in such a relatively short time? It had been impossible. At age twenty, he remembered, he hadn't been able to sit for longer than half an hour before falling asleep with the book in his hands or standing up and changing into his running togs. The young aren't built for sedentary pursuits. Still, one of his daughters might appreciate having the Shakespeare. He was thinking it would be Angela, dreamy in a prolonged fantasy lately, the result of having travelled to New York with her school's orchestra to see *The Ring of the Nibelung*. She'd even told them that she wanted her name pronounced with a hard letter-G in the German style. It had effectively eliminated her diminutive. No longer was she sweet Angie, at least until the next intense obsession took hold of her.

Evan thought about the one who had lent him the book, never to be compensated for it or to get it back. Galen Pritchard. They had mutual friends in their residence hall their first year of university and were cordial acquaintances more than they were friends, seeing in each other qualities they recognized in or desired for themselves, and it was in the light of that familiar reflection that they agreed to join four others in a student house off campus the following September. Galen Pritchard: the name written in ink and crossed out with heavy double strokes on the inside of the cover. Evan had known almost nothing about him except that he had grown up in Saint John, was the first in his family to go to university, was doubtless overwhelmed when he arrived at Dalhousie University, and appeared to get along cautiously well with everyone he met.

Evan noticed immediately that the boy's spoken English sometimes contained glaring grammatical errors. He confused 'I' and 'me' in the objective case when the object was plural: for Betsy and I. He must have come from people who considered it impolite to say, 'me'. And the past participle of 'to lie' threw the boy for a loop, the act of prostrating himself, not the act of committing an untruth. Evan did not correct him, thinking that do so would have branded him a prig and a bore, the absolute last labels he wished pasted to his forehead. *When was the last time you got worried about what anyone thought of you, Vice-Principal Mountcastle,*

Lord High Executioner? Brynne's voice in his head. Decades, he was sure. Still, it was going to be a blessing, perhaps even a life extender, not to have to mete out another punishment upon a student. He believed it changed one's DNA to do so, day after day, basing his theory on nothing but intuition.

He still would rather overlook philistinism in a peer than attract criticism by correcting the flaw. Did that brand him a coward? It must, in a certain regard, as he policed his school from behind the fortifications of his office. Those he sent home with suspensions from school sometimes told him what they thought of him for doing so and often in harsh, hurt-filled, unflattering terms. What would the world be like if we told each other exactly what we thought of them? It would not be pretty, that was for certain. But what a relief in the aftermath. Might the original feelings change in the crucible of such truth telling?

He wondered if Pritchard had changed as much or as little as Evan had in the ensuing decades. He'd always assumed that the boy had returned to New Brunswick, but nothing said that that had to have been the case, especially since points west held more opportunities. Or he might have stayed in the Maritimes.

Newly minted a teacher at twenty-three and anxious about unencouraging job prospects, Evan applied to a school in an outpost of Newfoundland and Labrador, almost accepting the offer of employment when it came. The hidebound words of his bigoted father put an end to that idea. He said, "Evan, if you move to that godforsaken place you will never land a decent job anywhere else and I will cut you off at the knees," by which the man in his hackneyed eloquence meant that the trust fund Evan and brothers were supposed to have access to when the youngest of them, Lionel, three years Evan's junior and five years younger than Lester, turned forty, would be closed to him. Lionel's fortieth came and went, their father the old insurance hustler took his final, smoky breath two years later, and what do you know: the money was never there in the first place, as in, it was all a fiction perpetrated to make sure they followed paths sanctioned by their father. Lester was never a problem in that regard: DDS, church deacon, pillar of the community. Lionel—well: shopkeeper. What kind of life was that? One with no safety nets. The strange thing was that the old liar made more of a fuss over Evan's choice of profession, school teaching, than about Lionel's. "Lionel is different," he would say. "Lionel is special, he possesses a unique talent. It would go against God to squelch such a gift." Lester knew what he wanted from the beginning and always found a way to make it happen. The money for his education and for setting up his dental practice was found, borrowed, eventually repaid. Brilliant Lester, scholarship winner, wunderkind with laser focus, the man without a burdensome social life to distract him from his studies and his goals. He was the only one of them, their mother included, who still went to church. They, the congregation, were losing that ugly old cave, freezing in winter, stifling in summer. Their numbers were dwindling; those who remained, many of them, were frail ghosts hanging on; an ambulance would stop beside the back door about once a month now. They had to sell out and join another church. Evan loved his big brother, but really, was it all worth the heartache? He knew how much the loss of the sanctuary hurt Lester.

It was a devastating failure for a man who was not used to failure.

Their father didn't worry about his youngest or his eldest son. In Evan's case, he hoped the boy would labour at something meaningful and salaried for the remainder of the sputtering, fearful, oblivious final days of the twentieth century, and when Evan had matured properly, he would emerge, after a fashion, like a debutante, and if he wanted to continue to teach high school, well, that would be his prerogative. The 'trust fund' would allow him the choice not to do so if he didn't want to. Evan could apply himself to philanthropy or hedonism, it didn't matter, just so long as he pursued his goals with panache and brought no disrepute to the family name.

Family name! Their father talked as if theirs had the distinction of a Dupont or Molson. And what about Lionel, whose existence was the most precarious of all? Why had the old con artist not put pressure on him to follow a more financially secure path? It didn't make sense.

It never had.

By the time reality had obscured—no, shattered—Evan's hopeful window on the future, he had been teaching longer than his best-before date, in a semi-rural school outside of Bedford, and he was tired, jaded, homing in on depressed, and wise to the many ways a man of his vintage could be disappointed in life. Now that their father's treasure-filled chest was seen never to have existed, all that stood between Evan and collapse, he believed, were Steph and the girls. There was no storied legacy. The vault stood empty, echoing, mocking. He was pathetic, as sorry for himself as a spoiled baby, and he was not proud of the prolonged pet he enacted, the ranting, the phone calls to his mother and brothers, the indignant face he showed to the lawyer who executed their father's will. Evan pulled all the shopworn clichés of his disappointment and anger out of his raided pockets and shook them in the face of whomever was within range. He drank. He swore off drink, apologizing to embarrassing effect. On Lester's advice he moved his modest investments into the most cautiously blue-chip savings certificates possible. He scrutinized himself ruthlessly, considered his career options without once feeling grateful that he had a career, a job that paid well enough for him and his family to live comfortably, and decided to hightail it out of the classroom. Forgetting or ignoring how much he loved to teach, he set his sights on administration. He would fashion himself into someone hardnosed, a well-paid, highly respected, even somewhat feared, principal educator.

Evan had colleagues who were in worse shape than he was. Their children were many of them horrid, though rarely without reason to be so. These darling prodigies would crack up in scandalous, predictable ways, crying, "Wake up, Mom and Dad, look around, put down that paper you're grading, put down the drink, the pill bottle, take off the blinders, because I'm acting out here, as the saying goes. Hello-o, I'm like puking after meals, I'm sucking down lemon gin before I reach the eighth grade, I'm a fellating genius, I'm stealing twenties from your purse," and so on. Relative to such nonsense as that, Evan was a lucky man, a thankful husband and father. He acknowledged it every day. Why, then, was he feeling the way the futon couch in his study looked: slumped, unable to hold its shape?

He remembered the day Brynne came to him, clutching the Riverside Shakespeare, and asked him to read her a story from it. She couldn't have been older than four at the time. The book was half her height and about the same width. She'd thought that here was goodly bedtime fare, more than enough to delay the Sandman a long while. She tottered under the weight of the book, her hair wet from the bath, nightie obscuring her bare feet. They couldn't convince her to wear slippers on the cold plank floors of the old farmhouse, this same structure, the one she insisted she could remember from when she was an infant lying in her crib, the house she said she would always miss the most, love most. Her feet were always hot. They would find her sprawled sideways in bed, the covers having slid to the floor, her bare feet cooling in the night air.

Onto her father's drowsy lap she plunked the printed brick, a two-fold slap to his negligent conscience because it reminded him that he was supposed to be a teacher of literature and yet much of this work of genius remained unknown to him. It also told him that he had not been paying strict enough attention to his child, not that he was able to address her immediate need. What had he said? 'Oh, hon, that's not for kids. Let's go see what the Berenstain Bears are up to.' Or, 'When you're a little bigger I'll read you some of these old stories.'

Sure, when you're like me: middle-aged, disinherited, disappointed, discouraged. That's when these tales will begin to mean something to you.

Nature Boy

They couldn't call it true Second Summer, this balm of honeyed sunshine and short-sleeve temperatures. There had to have been a frost first, she said.

"I can't believe we haven't had one," said Lionel. "It's been so cold lately."

"It hasn't," said Laurel. "You've been too sedentary, is all."

He reminded her that he used to be able to run for an hour or more without stopping.

"That was thirty years ago," she said. "You were nineteen and you couldn't sit still longer than ten minutes at a time. Such energy."

"You and your silly numbers," he said.

Halfway up the ramp he began to breathe with distress. She suggested he stop and wait until she had gone inside and returned with a wheelchair. One was usually folded just inside the entrance.

"No," he said, "this is ridiculous. It's twenty steps away."

"Lean against the railing here. It'll take me all of a minute, tops. Why are you being so stubborn?"

"I—a week ago I walked all the way out to..."

"Let me do this for you, Lionel!"

"You can't keep ditching your life to come hold my hand."

"It's only the second time. Stop being such a pain."

He brought his elbow up so that his arm rested on the black iron railing. He watched her stride confidently, purposefully up the concrete ramp to the clinic entrance. Where would he be without her, his annoying Laurel, the Missus Doctor Gaudry?

Now that she had disappeared, panic took hold. What if she didn't come back? What if she had never been his best friend these past thirty years, ever since that morning when he'd stumbled groggily into the shared washroom on their residence floor to hear her sobbing in a stall. He knew the quality of those gasps. They were angry, self-pitying, desperate, and despondent in equal measure. He brushed his teeth, waiting for the intervals between sobs to lengthen and the crying to subside, before trying to coax her out. She would tell him later that something in the way he spoke, as if he were building gradually to the most hilarious punchline, made her feel safe and curious, like a child being lured by a fun clown onto the merry-go-round.

When had that been? "After Halloween," she'd said, "and I couldn't believe we'd never met until that moment."

"Our rooms were at opposite ends of the hall," he reminded her. "Besides, I was so nervous I hardly said a word to anyone. I got up in the morning, ate breakfast in my room, caught the bus to class, and was sure everybody knew I was an impostor."

"I find that hard to believe," she said. "I thought you were so together, Lionel, the way you patted me back into shape without making me feel burdensome. You talked me up and out of the darkest well of lovesickness. It felt like grief, only more pathetic. I think you even helped me with my face. Yes, you did. What if somebody had walked in on us?"

"That depended. If it had been the girl in the room beside yours, I probably would've expired on the spot. On the other hand, who cared? There you were, someone in need of help. You don't think twice in that situation, do you. In a way, you saved me as much as I you."

"Can I confess something?" she said. "I had no small crush on you, Lionel Mountcastle, even suspecting early on that you were never going to be my P.C."

"Personal computer?" he said, mockingly aghast. "Progressive Conservative? Prehensile cattail?"

"Stop!" she cried, the back of her hand pressed against her mouth, as if trying to keep frothy draft-beer from spurting out her nose. "You know what it stands for. Did you never play Princess in the Tower?"

"And you, my damsel, for whom were you in distress, dragons notwithstanding? What's his name, I'll slay him for you! And why are we drinking this swill?" He'd looked around the grubby tavern at their dorm mates. "Don't you agree there's something more than a wee bit Night of the Living Dead about the term 'pub crawl'? You and I, my dear, should be sipping a Pink Lady or a sere gin Martini. You were never made for beer, and neither was I."

Laurel pushed the button that opened the doors and wheeled the empty chair onto the ramp. Two small, patient-transfer buses that hadn't been there when she'd entered the building idled in the paved lot bounded by three hospital buildings. Lionel stood where she had left him.

He was draped over the railing, arms crossed, the metal tucked into his pits, hands in a tight grip the way one might against the force of a strong wind.

She pushed the wheelchair past him, turned around and came back up the ramp. He sat, tried to lift his feet onto the rests. She made sure the brakes were engaged before coming around in front of him, squatting, and placing his feet one at a time on the grooved metal rests.

"Sorry it took so long," she said. "I had to go all the way to the top floor to find this one. Are you secure? Away we go, then."

"Away we disappear."

"I said I was sorry, Lionel."

"No," he said. "I meant me. Away I go, into the ether, one atom at a time."

"Please let's not. If you're looking for pity, you've got the wrong girl."

"You've always been the right girl for me."

"Get the button, will you?"

With the back of his left hand, he tried pushing on the large metal disk with the handicap symbol on it. "Look at me, all the power of a newborn." He tried again, with both hands this time, and got the doors to swing open slowly.

As they waited inside the clinic lobby for the elevator, he said, "Here's one I've never been able to figure out. If as we age it's not the recent but the distant past we remember, our youth increasingly more than our years of maturity, and if youth, its health-crammed vitality aside, is generally accepted to be a time to get through, to survive and transcend while we learn without appearing to do so about how to be an adult, then what mean-spirited practical joke is this we're stuck in? I mean, come on already! We know zip. We think, erroneously, that we have it all figured out. We're self-conscious to the point of asphyxiation. We're sheathed in skin eruptions that could trigger a pandemic. Our days and nights are photo negatives of those lived by the rest of humanity. And when we finally make it to that time of wisdom and enlightenment, our so-called golden years, it's *this* we're destined to remember best? Sharply, in precise detail, things, events, humiliations we have thankfully forgotten about most of our lives? Until this moment of our decrepitude, when it all comes flooding back?"

"Oh stop. You're talking as if you're a hundred and all you can remember is your adolescence."

"I feel it," he said. "Look at me. I can't walk ten paces. I'm that old geezer I would have condemned to an ice floe. No really."

"You've got the virus," she said. "You've been vaccinated. You're not going to die."

Laurel pushed the chair into the elevator and got Lionel turned so that he was facing the door. For the first time she felt as if she were more than emotional support. He needed a haircut, the back of his neck woolly and, where the hair was thinner it was stringy. Time for an Ascot, she thought, like those worn by old wags still in possession of their vanity. Lionel's shoulders sagged forward; his back rounded. A memory of her father as an old man, or, rather, a middle-aged man made too soon old, swept over her. The elevator had been timed to allow the slow of limb to board and leave safely without anxiety. And it seemed to her that the compartment's ascension had been similarly retarded. If they didn't reach their floor soon, she was going to suffer her own panic attack. She gripped the wheelchair handles tightly, riding out the light-headedness that broke in a wave over her.

Lionel perked up in the waiting room, sensing that she needed to see him once again funny and attentive to the world beyond his affliction. He rose from his chair to walk closer to a corner where games and books made a play space, and watched a little girl stuff a floppy, long-legged, cloth frog into available holes. When she looked up at him looming over her, she ran to where her mother was sitting.

"Can't blame her," he said, seated again beside Laurel.

"I can," she said in a whisper. "Little wuss."

They didn't have to wait long before Lionel's name was called. Lionel insisted Laurel come into the examination room with him. The nurse weighed him, recorded his height, and wrapped a blood pressure cuff around his upper arm. "It's always through the roof on first reading," he said. "Classic white-coat syndrome." The nurse brought them down the hall to another room where she hooked it Lionel up to a monitor that took his blood pressure automatically every few minutes. She closed the door behind her after saying that the doctor would be with them soon.

Laurel stood reading a poster that gave tips to new mothers about breastfeeding. The baby reacts to the mother's stress level. It reads body language better than it does verbal language, the newborn does. That makes sense, she decided. Like a dog. We enter the world with abilities more canine than human.

Lionel had gone to a zone far away. He sat as the nurse, the old doll, a veteran, had instructed him, with his back straight, his arm resting easily on the surface of the desk beside him, and his feet flat on the floor. He breathed deeply and evenly through the nose. How could a man who only a few minutes ago had been so panicky and helpless that he couldn't make it up a gentle slope now be this warrior of relaxation, the Zen master he was imitating? He'd always been determined, not in the way some men are determined, with muscles tensed and a flinty look of resolve on their faces, but more fluidly. Lionel could be a river, flowing where he had to and doing it magnificently, not because it was expected of him but because the balance of the earth warranted it. *Oh, Lionel,* she thought, *mud child, Golem built by squirrels, nature boy, don't fall apart on me yet. I couldn't bear it.*

Prospectors

While they waited to see his doctor, Lionel told Laurel a story from his youth. One Friday night in August, not long after Lionel's fourteenth birthday, his father showed up at the cottage with a boy from Lionel's hockey team. Billy Fischer was a grade ahead of Lionel in school and not somebody he spent any time with off the ice. It wasn't that they weren't friendly with each other; it was just an odd assumption for Mr. Mountcastle to have made, that Lionel and the Fischer boy were chums.

They put up a small tent beside the cottage, since there wasn't room for everyone—Mr. and Mrs. Mountcastle, Lionel, his brother Evan, and now Billy—inside the tiny three-room structure, and the teammates slept out there. Billy was newly enamoured of the song, "Johnny B. Goode" by Chuck Berry. God only knew why. By then, 1950s rock-and-roll was considered dated and embarrassing. The boy must have been nervous. That was Lionel's explanation of Billy's odd behaviour. Why else would he keep Lionel awake much of their first night together, singing songs, telling risqué jokes, and filling the tent with flatulence?

Billy was taller than Lionel and he swam competitively. His training showed in the long sleek curve of his spine, the way his shoulders lifted so easily and completely out of the water when he did the butterfly stroke, and in the loose suppleness of his thighs. It didn't take long, half an hour at most, before news of the new boy's presence on the beach spread to all the cottages where there were girls old enough to be interested in a good-looking boy who made a show of swimming like a dolphin. He was everything Lionel wasn't—clownlike, happy-go-lucky, flirty—and Lionel quickly despised him for it, having been complacent in his belief that those girls, three sisters of the family from whom the Mountcastles rented their cottage, friends of the sisters, in two cottages at the far end of the beach, and another girl who was sometimes part of the group, sometimes not, all wanted to be with Lionel despite his reticence.

At breakfast the next morning, Mr. Mountcastle announced that Lionel and Billy were accompanying him on a road trip to look for silver deposits on the shore of a lake two hours north of them. For Lionel it was going to be a relief to leave the beach behind for a while. The girls wouldn't be fawning over Billy Fischer, for one thing. But it also meant that Lionel and his guest would have no one aside from Mr. Mountcastle, the expedition's mastermind, to distract and entertain them.

When Lionel's father was a young husband in his early twenties, he worked for a mining exploration company in northern New Brunswick. He was convinced that a forgotten silver mine lay near Bathurst. Not far from there was Petit Rocher, where he brought his wife and baby to live soon after Lester was born. Lionel's mother told stories of being there through the winter, not knowing a soul or a word of French, and listening to radio broadcasts of the local hockey-league games her husband played in. She would sit in the kitchen of the house they were renting, trying to stay warm beside the oil stove, and listen for his name. He was something of a star, a tall, black-haired, rangy centerman who hung around the middle of the ice surface waiting for the pass that would send him on a breakaway. He wasn't much of a defensive player, Lionel's old man. You wouldn't find him digging the puck out of the corners, especially not in his team's own end.

What, really, was this trip and Billy's presence all about? Lionel wondered what was going on in his father's mind. It didn't occur to him then that his mother had probably asked her husband to take Lionel away for a few days, but now, looking back four decades, he was certain that this was the case. They weren't bad boys, Lionel and his brothers. The opposite was true. Having three teenaged boys to mind, or two or one alone—it would not have made much difference to their mother, since the Mountcastle boys were helpful around the house, obedient, usually pleasant and self-sufficient. There had to be another reason why he was being singled out and removed from the beach. He knew his father well enough to know that his old man's idea of a good time had almost nothing to do with his youngest son, who was perceptive enough to see his father for the man he was, someone more at ease with his drinking buddies than with his family, a man who wanted to recapture the halcyon days of youth at the expense of his responsibilities as one charged with the care and nurturing of children. Sons. In his father's mind, sons were challengers. It was not a good idea to get too comfortable with them.

If Billy Fischer had not been in the car, Mr. Mountcastle might have confronted Lionel about the strange behaviour Mrs. Mountcastle had witnessed. By present standards, it wasn't all that strange. Lionel happened to be a typical adolescent male who had yet to see real live female nakedness, having had no sisters and a crippling shyness that kept him well removed from girls his age, even as thoughts about sex consumed him constantly and obsessively. He had looked at photographs in skin magazines, lurid images that fuelled his imagination and helped relieve momentary tension, but a substantial part of his psyche demanded the real.

Lionel had thought he was undetected spying on his mother while she changed her clothes. The old cottage they rented had a knothole in the wall near the floor and beside the front door, and if he stood outside near the bottom of the stairs leading down to the beach, he was almost at eye-level with this peep hole, an angled aperture that let him see directly into the front part of the bedroom—if you could call such a spartan, doorless enclosure a bedroom—used by his parents. It was the space where his mother slept and which she shared with her husband those Friday and Saturday nights of the few summer weekends he made it up to the lake. When Mr. Mountcastle was there, he was usually restless, pressing his sons into canoe trips across the lake. Or, apparently, to long-lost silver mines hours distant by car.

"In my defence, may I say that she was not completely innocent in this."

"What do you mean, Lionel?"

"I mean, she knew I was watching her."

THE COTTAGE the Mountcastle family rented—a three-room shack, to be accurate, solidly constructed though it was—had been built in such a way that the two dividing walls within the structure ended to form a short corridor running across the front, parallel to the beach. The rooms at either end, the kitchen and the parents' bedroom, fronted on the exterior wall, while the middle room, where Lionel and his brothers bunked, was enclosed by a wall that had an opening for a door onto the corridor, but no physical door one could close, only a curtain, and two glassless interior windows flanking the room's entrance. Thick curtains hung across these openings, also, to offer a modicum of privacy. No such curtain hung in the room where Mrs. Mountcastle slept and changed into and out of her bathing suit. None was deemed necessary. It was understood that the boys should avoid that end of the cottage and that when they left their room, they either turned left into the kitchen or went straight out the front door.

For Lionel's mother to have been seen changing into her pink striped bikini—she was proud of the fact that she could wear a garment that many of the other mothers on the beach could not—seen, that is, by her youngest son as he stood almost under the building, its four corners seated level on raised concrete-blocks, with the slope of the beach rising under it, she had to be standing close to the front of her bedroom, close to the white-sand beach, the sound of the waves continuous and beckoning, so that the voyeur's sightline could take in that brief section of the room that was exposed and not hidden behind the interior wall shared by the boys' room.

"I suppose what I'm trying to say is that, yes, I was a horny kid obsessed with female nudity, indiscriminately, but that for me to have seen my mother under those circumstances, she had to have been aware of my eye framed in that convenient knothole. Otherwise..."

"Otherwise?"

"Yes?" he said.

"I would have had you horse-whipped," said Laurel, "either way."

"We never spoke of it."

"What would you want to hear her say, Lionel, if she were alive today? That she knew you were watching her, and she chose to do nothing about it? Would that have changed anything?"

"I think it would."

"In what way?"

"I wouldn't still feel so goddamn guilty about it."

EVERY OLD PROSPECTOR worth his rock hammer knows of a lost mine somewhere, an Eldorado of untold riches, and if he can pull together the right people, the necessary financial backing and the time to pore over geological-survey maps, pinpoint the most probable spot, gather samples, have them assayed, if he can bring about these few crucial steps in the process, then, well, watch the hell out is all he has to say on the matter. That, in essence, was Lionel's father.

It was cool enough in the evenings for Lionel to wear his father's old hockey jacket. It was made of black wool felt with yellow cotton trim and it had the name of the town on it as well as the sponsor of the team, the Irving Oil company. Lionel was proud to wear it. It had his father's jersey number patched on one arm near the shoulder, the number 4, Jean Béliveau's, and, on the other, the years 1962-63, which corresponded with Lester's first year of life. Lionel expected people to stop him in the street and comment. It was such a distinctive jacket, surely someone would recognize it.

He couldn't say what depressed him most about the town, the drab, sagging storefronts with their chipped, peeling paint and rusting signs or that he made no discernible impact while wearing his father's team jacket. Billy tagged along good-naturedly, making wry comments about the quaintness of the main street, the single-nozzle gas pump anchored to the sidewalk in front of what appeared to have been a general store, but which now looked abandoned or still in operation without identification. The locals would have known what the store was. Why bother with a costly sign when everybody knows what and where your business happens to be?

Lionel looked around and thought that summer in a place like this would have to be the deadliest, dullest time a person could pass anywhere on the planet. He wanted to be back at the lake with its sparkly sand, lying on his narrow cot in the rustic, leaky-roofed cottage, listening at night to the ceaseless lapping of the water at the fringe of the beach, the sky brimming with such celestial light as was impossible to see in the city. In this decrepit little town his father believed his future lay, and Lionel's, his brothers' and even that of some of the residents.

"They were welcome to it," said Lionel. "Fathers mean well, but rarely do they get it right. I'm speaking of their attempts at assistance in the social growth of their offspring. We want what's best for our sons and daughters. We think we know, by dint of our experience, especially our mistakes, what is best for them. Invariably we get it wrong. My father decided he was going to deal with his son's voyeuristic tendencies by hauling him away from the nexus of his libidinous spying for a few days, the better to address and recalibrate the mechanism that had tripped over into perversion.

"I can just hear him," said Lionel. "He says, in response to my mother, 'First we get the little bugger away from his knothole. Remove the temptation.'

"'Then what?' my mother asks.

"'Well, for one thing, stop getting changed in front of open doors and windows.'

"'So, this is my fault now.'

"'No, of course not. How could any of this be your fault, Monique?'

"'I don't appreciate your tone.'

"'He's a healthy teenager. He's discovering his…'

"'You can't even say the word. No wonder he sneaks around.'

"'Do you want me to be more direct with him?'

"'Yes,' she says. 'Talk to him. Let him know it is not all right for him to be doing this.'

"'Oh, you don't have to worry. He is going to come away from this experience knowing exactly what is what.'"

"And did you?" asked Laurel.

AFTER EXPLORING what little there was to see in Petit Rocher and finding no one who knew Mr. Mountcastle or recognized the garment his son was sporting, they drove to Baie de Bouctouche. The boys watched him chip away at rocks at one end of the flint-strewn beach. Billy appeared to be fascinated. They were the same, Lionel thought, Billy and Lionel's father. They had the same sultry features and dark hair women loved, and they shared that easy way of inviting, attracting, and holding their attention. He would have given anything to be that confident.

His father showed them some samples. He pointed to silvery striations in the newly broken chunks of rock. "Galena," he said. It was proof that what he sought was nearby. Billy looked impressed. No doubt, thought Lionel, the boy was wondering how he might be included in this lucrative undertaking. Billy was full of questions for Lionel's father. Do you just start digging, and if so, where?

How will you know there's enough silver for a whole mine? Do you have to buy the land before you're allowed to dig? What if somebody wants to come along and steal your silver? How do you protect against that?

Mr. Mountcastle was pleased to answer the boy's eager questions, as if he were his own child or a student in a class he was teaching. Lionel had not shown the least interest in geology, much to his father's disappointment. It was one more thing they did not share. Galena, he thought. Isn't that a place, and isn't it associated with lead rather than silver? Why did he bring this annoying boy along? Why did he invite him? We're not even friends. Billy's a lazy player. He has that one move he's perfected, the one where he draws the goalie way right as if he's going to switch the puck to his backhand and try to tuck it between his pads, except that what he does is he holds on, fades a second or two longer than expected, holding on to the puck, his body moving right, and at the last possible moment, just as the goalie is about to take a swipe at the puck with his big cumbersome stick, Fischer lifts it deftly over the goalie's right shoulder and into the top corner of the net. It was a neat trick, Lionel had to admit, and, until a goaltender learned to anticipate it, it almost always worked.

Mr. Mountcastle surprised them—surprised his son; Lionel couldn't speak for his teammate—by announcing that they would check into a motel for the night instead of driving back to the cottage. The sun stood high above them still. Lionel knew it would be dark before they could make it back to the lake. Nonetheless, he'd had it all worked out in his mind, how they would drive retracing the route, and how he would be magnanimous in anticipation of their return, sitting quietly or talking generously with Billy or listening to one of his father's long, familiar stories about life as a young prospector. On the access road that ran behind the cottages strung along the beach lining their bay, the headlights of the car would pick out each mailbox, each named neighbour. They had summered there most of his childhood and he had the order memorized. He thought about the different families sitting quietly, contentedly in the simple comfort of each cottage. Sun, wind, dry sand, tall pines—the residue of each was concentrated like a perfume at day's end. He had had it in his mind to re-enter that realm before the sun set. Someone would build a bonfire. In warmer clothes than he would have worn in the day, he would sit on the sand, burying his bare feet close to the fire's warmth, and watch winking yellow spots of light, similar bonfires, appear like the beads of a necklace all around the lake. Someone would have a guitar, they would sing songs and tell ghost stories, the best parts of the day would be prolonged and preserved before the arrival of sleep, the great extinguisher. Even to miss one such evening of the too-short, precious summer was unthinkable.

The motel room contained two double beds, a television, a low, two-drawer piece of furniture that you couldn't call a dresser between the beds at their heads, and a wooden kitchen chair. The room smelled like stale unwashed hockey equipment and cigarette smoke too old to be attractive to even the most desperate nicotine addict.

"You boys make yourself comfortable. Play a game of cards or something," said Lionel's father. He tossed an old deck of playing cards on the bed the boys were meant to share. Lionel looked disbelievingly at his father. Somehow, after realizing that they would not be driving back to the cottage that same day, he had pictured each of them in his own motel room or he and his father in one and Billy in another. This, the three of them jammed into a single, foul-smelling, threadbare, unclean motel room in a strange town where nobody knew them, had never occurred to him. *Am I really that clueless?* he wondered.

"I'll be back in an hour or so," Mr. Mountcastle said. "Be good, you two. Don't do anything I wouldn't do."

After Lionel's father had left, Billy said, "I like your old man. He's a cool guy. Do you think he really knows where there's a lost silver mine or is he making the whole thing up for our benefit?

That would be okay if he was. I don't mind. Because I know what he's doing, what this is all about."

"You do? Really," said Lionel. "That's good. That makes one of us."

"He's doing it as a favour to my dad. I guess they're like drinking buddies or something. Mine calls yours, says, 'Hey, Lionel's father, this is Billy's father, got a favour to ask. My boy is, shall we say, *developing* in a somewhat speedier fashion than maybe his mother and I are prepared for. Specifically, I am talking about the boy's dick, his trousers, and the fact that the first has a problem staying within the confines of the second, if you catch my drift, Mr. Lionel's father.'"

"You have a girlfriend?"

"Deed I do. We are being forcibly separated, against our wishes, might I add. The official line is that it's for our own good. We're supposed to cool it before—how did her mother put it? Before something regrettable happens."

"Are you, like, you and her…?"

"You better believe it, Pontiac."

"What's it like?"

"You mean you've never done it?"

Lionel shook his head, his face flushed.

"My God, Lionel, it is the abso-fucking-lutely best feeling in the entire universe. No drug could possibly match it."

"I guess you miss her a lot."

"Do I ever. It sucks being kept apart like this. Big time. It feels like I'm gonna explode sometimes. I mean, if a half good-looking girl walked through that door I would jump her bones, no hesitation. I wouldn't even ask you to leave, I'd be that into it. You could stay and watch, it wouldn't bother me in the least. You could even have a go after I was finished. If you were into it, that is. Assuming."

"Oh, yeah," said Lionel, "definitely I would be. Thanks."

Billy lay back on the other bed, the one Lionel's father would be sleeping in, and threw his arms back over his head in a gesture of abandonment. "I can't believe you've never had sex. This we must remedy. It's crazy. Like, what are you, too shy or something? Talking to girls, I mean, at first, before you get good at it, that can be stressful. They really pay attention, really really close, and they remember everything, every detail, even after you forget what you said. It can be pretty freaky. But after that first time, and after you get the hang of it? I'm telling you, it's fantastic the way she'll start to relax and come around and warm up to you. She'll start paying more attention to your face, especially your mouth. And touching her hair, playing with it, wetting her lips with her tongue. Oh, man, the anticipation! It's almost as good as finally getting there."

Lionel looked around the room. The creaking, saggy beds, the grimy walls, and the smell, like old cheese—it all seemed to be mocking him the way Billy was on the verge of mocking him for his naivete. Smugness in the tension at the edges of the mouth, the darting, mirthful glances in Lionel's direction. The probing, unsettling questions: exactly how far *had* he gone with a girl? He didn't want to play with himself for the rest of his life, did he? Did he mean to tell Billy that he had never seen a real live naked girl?

"I've seen one," said Lionel.

"Good for you. Who?"

"A woman."

"You have to be more specific," said Billy.

Before he caught himself, before the implications of what he was about to reveal sunk in, Lionel told Billy about the knothole and watching his mother change into her swimsuit.

Lionel felt uneasy: his father had said that he would not be too late, only an hour. Lionel didn't want Billy to know that he was worried. He wished his dad would walk through the door now, if only to dispel the awkwardness that had filled the little room. They should get to sleep, his father had said, and not wait up for him. Tomorrow was going to be a full, busy day. He was going to find somebody in town who knew something about the old silver operation and see if he might get his hands on a geological survey map.

The boys sat side by side on their bed watching *Rambo* dubbed in French. Billy made a gag out of providing a running translation, non sequiturs which made Lionel laugh. "Take me to the disco or I decapitate your chickens one at a time with my giant spoon. That is a darling pair of pyjamas you are wearing, Mr. Evil Man. Be prepared to be castrated. Oh, please, Mighty Rambolicious, spare my life. I am unworthy to bear your children or lick your gleaming pectorals. My, what a bulging package you carry. Do I employ the correct word?"

The movie ended. It was still light outside after nine o'clock. When Billy suggested they get outside to explore the town, Lionel didn't care what he meant by it. It was going to be a relief to get out of the stifling room. He was finding it hard to breathe. Billy had said nothing about Lionel's revelation, his perverse confession. Instead, he had talked further about his own experience. What the older boy had talked about so suggestively, what he had described in details that made Lionel nervous and excited, Lionel hungered for more. That phrase, 'when you're inside,' displaced everything else Lionel could think about. He wanted to tell Billy that he too had intense sex-thoughts, that images of naked women preoccupied him to the point of turning him into a sleepless, dysfunctional, blunted, stupid wraith. He spied on his mother when she changed her clothes. How sick was that, how unworthy. How impatient he was to return to that knothole. Being here in this village in the Miramichi felt like an exile from which he might never come back.

Billy locked the door with the key from the outside. *I should be the one to do that*, Lionel thought.

"What did you do?" asked Laurel.

"Nothing. We walked the length of the main drag and back. Nothing was open. We came back to the motel, got undressed, got into bed, making sure we were lying as far away from each other as we could be, and fell asleep. I didn't even hear my father come back in."

"You know what I'm going to tell you, don't you, Lionel?"

"What's that, Laurel?"

"That you have to forgive yourself and that it wasn't a waste of time. Not by a long shot."

"We never found the silver mine," he said.

"That's not what I'm talking about and you know it."

He knew. The doctor arrived, finally, to examine Lionel. When Laurel stood to leave, Lionel asked her to stay. She smiled, seemed genuinely pleased, and he thought, *I love you, my dear, dear friend.*

The Capuchins

Merin Lauder Jones was a partner in Capuchin C.C., Inc., a corporate-communications firm consisting, Sid discovered, of Merin and her husband, Vincent. Sid learned this when he met her for a drink in a bar he liked on the waterfront. Always arrive armed with information, his guiding rule. He didn't want to be ambushed. Then it occurred to him that he didn't have to act as if he were on assignment. After all, he wasn't interviewing her for a story. She was an old girlfriend, one he remembered fondly though she had been the one to call a halt to the romance. He'd thought they'd been as close to bliss as a couple could possibly get.

She recognized him first, before he had time to stake out a spot from where he could watch the door and choose his moment. She was already there, sitting at a table with another woman, who was as expensively attired as Merin. The friend stood and got out of the booth, ostensibly to let Sid slide across the padded bench. But before he could do that, Merin stood and embraced him, holding him at arm's length to try to assess the years in his face. Releasing him, she introduced her companion. The name did not stick. After a moment of introductory chat while they three stood, something tacit passed between the women, and the friend excused herself, citing a just-remembered, prior commitment.

Alone with him, Merin alternated between disbelief, that she was sitting across from Sidney Beausejour again after twenty years, and a spacy distractedness as she spoke of her life in the interim. Her husband figured most prominently in her narrative. They had met, the future Mr. and Mrs. Capuchin, Sid learned early in the conversation, when she had taken a bus tour of Ho Chi Min City and Vincent had been the guide.

"Have you ever met someone so unaffected and childlike that he strikes you immediately as—I don't know, really—this celestial being?" she said.

"As a matter of fact," he said, letting the corners of his eyes and mouth complete the thought. She didn't appear to catch that he was referring to her, continuing instead with an enraptured description of her husband's charms. She spoke of Vincent, of their time together before they were married, the mystical spell of initial attraction, love's golden, expanding yoke, to which they succumbed, and which continued to bind them happily in thrall to this very day.

Sid suspected that anyone who spoke so uncritically about her spouse was hiding something. No such perfect union existed. He wondered, *Am I being dispassionate or jealous?*

Filling the gap, she told him that she had been working as a poetry book editor when she received a surprise inheritance, with which money she bought a small movie theatre and ran it for a few years until DVDs and the internet put an end to that. She went back to school and got a teacher's degree, taught ESL all over Southeast Asia, met the love of her life, "and the rest, as the saying goes…"

"So, you made it to Asia."

"That I did," she said, sipping her drink, smiling.

"And you came back with Vincent."

"Guilty as charged."

It was supposed to have been his and Merin's trip together. They had planned it, a postgraduation, non-European voyage of discovery. It had been almost all she talked about that summer in Ottawa, until the day they parted to return home. How could she have forgotten that? He wanted to shout it in her face.

She hadn't forgotten; she had merely erased him from the itinerary.

She still looked youthful. A single, neat crease underlined each eye, nothing that would qualify as baggage. Nevertheless, it suggested fatigue. He couldn't remember her having these folds. He did recall kissing her eyelids as a prelude to lovemaking. She would coo while drawing his head to her breasts. Did Vincent Capuchin do that for her? Sid pictured a slim, pretty, hairless, delicately muscled man. Vincent probably knew sex secrets a thousand years old, techniques that made eyelid kissing seem quaint.

He felt it had been a mistake to look her up, a breach of the barricade erected between them in the intervening years. He'd assumed she'd be married or in a long-term relationship; he hadn't expected this level of romantic intensity.

He said again how sorry he was about her mother's death, meaning it less than he felt he should. By now, approaching the bottom of his glass of wine, his condolence had more to do with arresting the flow of happy love-talk emanating from her than it did with genuine sympathy.

"It's sweet of you to say, Sid. She thought the world of you, you know."

"She did?" Sid was certain he had never met the woman.

"Oh, yes. She was always going on about your writing. You were a big reason why she kept reading the newspaper. She didn't always agree with what you were saying, but she held you up as a model. She'd say, 'This is a clear, rational mind at work.'"

"That's flattering to hear," he said, chagrined that he'd felt less than charitable towards Merin, who, he noticed, hadn't said what she thought of his column or whether she read him at all.

"It's true. She never forgave me for letting you get away."

"Now you're pulling my leg. I really don't remember meeting your mother. If I ever had, she wouldn't have been reading me, not yet anyway. I wasn't a journalist then." Her face registered surprise and denial, as though he were contradicting one of her dearest tenets. "Even if she had met me back then, she would have encountered an inexperienced whelp who loved to tell everyone that he was going to be a writer but who had yet to put anything of substance on paper."

"She liked the way your mind worked. That's all I'm saying, Sidney. Gee, don't be so touchy! She followed your progress and grew to admire your work." She rolled her eyes playfully as she downed the last of her drink before catching the waitress's attention. She slipped her credit card into the bill folder before he could extract his wallet from his pocket, and the feeling he had as she propped her purse on the table and made fond, liquid eyes at him, as if he were a foal standing for the first time, was that she was already elsewhere.

A WEEK AFTER they met for coffee, Merin called to invite Sid and his wife over for drinks. The Capuchins lived in the South End not far from Point Pleasant Park. As he and his wife Nancy walked along Young Street, he realized that they must have passed the Capuchins' house dozens of times over the years, all those many visits with their children to the park.

The house was a large, restored Victorian, the gingerbread, filigreed trim updated with violet paint and the front door a solid graphite-and-steel number with window cut-outs in the shape of a crescent moon and stars. Vincent greeted them at the door as if they had known each other all their lives. He was larger and more masculine looking than Sid had imagined he would be, broader in the chest and shoulders but also softer through the midsection. He had an easy, welcoming smile, and he was dressed in a roomy white, collarless shirt, black slacks, and sandals.

"Come in, come in, so wonderful to see you, Sid, hi, and Nancy, hi there—oh my, I just now get it! You must hate it when people pull the Sex Pistols reference out of the vaults."

"We're used to it," said Nancy, looking up at Vincent while waiting for him to return her hand. "True fact: we met at a bar where a Sex Pistols cover-band was playing. My bestie came over to shout in my ear, 'You'll never guess the name of the guy who's standing beside me back there.'"

"Are you as vicious as your namesake?" asked their host as he ushered them along the narrow corridor towards the kitchen, a sleekly appointed galley done up in brushed stainless steel and a dark, close-grained wood, all the cupboards and drawers pressure sprung, not a handle in sight. It looked like a kitchen where food had never actually been prepared. Merin greeted them from where she was standing at a gas stove, one of a pair, stirring a large pot with a long-handled wooden spoon.

"There you are. Hello. Welcome," she said dreamily as if she had just woken up from a nap or had come inside from an afternoon spent lounging in the sun. "Sid is the least vicious person in the world, my love, I can attest to that. He's a pussycat. Isn't that right, Nancy?"

She made Sid take over the stirring of the risotto while she stepped forward to embrace Nancy. He watched the women come together, part slightly and hold each other at arm's length. What sizing up was at play here? What did they think of each other, what did they expect or hope to discover? They could not have been more different physically, Nancy a petite, voluptuous brunette. Though much shorter than Merin, she looked stronger, bigger boned. Her smoothly tanned skin against Merin's paler, freckled face and arms accentuated the taller woman's moles and the blotchiness at her neck: nerves otherwise hidden. Sid had forgotten how much Merin kept buried under a languid demeanour. While he observed them, his one-time girlfriend and his wife, he worked at stirring the glutinous mass. It was like quicksand the way it resisted and pulled on the spoon. He wondered if he'd been chosen to do this to keep him otherwise occupied, less likely to say something awkward or disruptive.

It was warm enough to sit outside to eat, at a round, glass-topped table in the center of a small but private enclosure formed by the back of the house, the wall of the garage, a high plank fence running along the back edge of the patio and the neighbour's cedar hedge. Large, full-leafed poplars leaned into each other above their heads, intertwining, dropping twigs, the occasional brown leaf, seed packets, unidentified organic smut, and dappled shade. All it needed was the sound of trickling water to make it the perfect oasis, Sid thought, adding a grapevine-covered pergola overhead. Dates. Palms. It wasn't quite warm enough for servers in harem pants, abbreviated blouses and veils, ostrich-feather fans cooling the honoured guests of the Capuchins. Almost.

Vincent scrutinized him and Nancy as they chatted, and laughed at their funny stories, although at times his laughter felt forced. He added little to the woven narrative except as a cheerleader of sorts. "Tell me more," he would urge, and "You can't be serious!" Sid wondered how Merin ever got herself hooked up with this lightweight, this one-rung-above-houseboy. He was a good cook, that much was indisputable, the Hu tieu kho as good as anything they'd eaten in the past year or more, and Vincent—Merin called him Vincenzo in intimate moments—was attentive, filling wine glasses, clearing plates without appearing to have gotten up to do so, and returning with coffee and dessert just as magically. *It was ungenerous of me to criticize the man*, he scolded himself, *even to do so secretly.* He could see that Merin loved her Vincenzo with a schoolgirl's intensity. It was touching, really, to witness such devotion in a couple their age. Refreshing. Who cared if the man acted like a domestic servant? They could use a houseboy themselves. Nance would like that, some sweet attentive kid to look at instead of Sid. Somebody to whip up an exotic stir-fry, make the dirty dishes disappear, listen to what she had to say and respond in such a way that she knew he was listening. Wouldn't that be refreshing?

They got talking about their fathers. Merin asked Nancy about hers, a talent agent of some renown.

"He was a royal prick, if you really want to know, a right bastard. A loving, lovable, chauvinistic, sadistic creep."

"Okay," said Merin, "now give us the unexpurgated version."

"Something not many know about my illustrious father: when he was nineteen, he was convicted of armed robbery and served six years in Kingston Pen. Not general knowledge."

"I recall reading something that alluded to that," said Sid, grinning. It had been his first feature article for *Maclean's*.

"You don't want to hear this, do you? Really? It's all so boring." They urged her to continue. "My father never let us forget that he served his time, paid his debt to society, and moved on. He turned his life around. In the very crucible of his captivity, he was transformed. Nothing we did could ever match it for sheer, hard-knock, me-and-my-metamorphosis, self-made-man bullshit. He acted, my father did, as if he were always addressing a documentary film camera for an audience of wayward youth. He was always telling us not to make the same mistake he did. 'Do something with your life, because you'll never get this time back.' And, 'What do you mean it was the last day of classes and your teacher was only reviewing material you already knew, Nancy? Did Mrs. Grenfell have the option of skipping science class? You can bet your sweet bippy she did not, young lady!'"

At nineteen, Nancy's father had fallen in with undesirables, two older men with criminal records for petty theft who convinced the young man to be their driver during a bank robbery. As Nancy told the story, Merin was struck by how smoothly she delivered the details, using language borrowed from old films: cons, heist, getaway, lay low, fuzz, coppers, cooler, heater. The crime was committed in 1952, after all, she expected her to say in her defence. That was the way people spoke. No, she thought, that was the way actors in movies talked. Nancy, a successful talent agent in her own right, now retired, was embellishing, playing up the entertainment angle.

Her father knew better but couldn't help himself, she said. This was the way Sid would have written it. Eldest son of a modest, upstanding family, a good student, fine athlete, he was yet unable to stave off crushing boredom that summer of '52. School was over, finally. He had graduated from grade 12 at Toronto's Central Tech with certification in metalwork, elementary pipe fitting and radio electronics. He had a good job working for his uncle, who ran a scrap-metal business. Hated it. Would have done anything to leave it behind. Nancy's father, not the uncle. The uncle thought scrap metal was gold, every speck of it. Nancy's father knew he couldn't quit the job and still meet his own father's eye, the old man's great expectations for him. Not that he wanted his son to work the rest of his life for his wife's brother. It was a matter of following through on a commitment.

Vincent lit lemon-scented candles that sat in glass holders on the patio stones at the edge of the enclosure, a ring of them. The sun was still high. A cooling ocean breeze raised gooseflesh on their exposed skin, and they moved inside, where they settled on leather couches in a den off the kitchen, and sipped brandy. Vincent was headed back out to extinguish the candles when Merin stopped him: she loved the smell. She wanted the scent to waft through the open window.

Nancy's father was supposed to drive the getaway car when the two other men ran out of the bank. His name was Charles—he wanted them to call him Chuck, but they laughed at that, and they settled on 'Chunk' because he was overweight. Charles had only recently received his driver's license, having twice failed the test, and he was eager to show people that he could drive a car as well as the next man. 'Chunk' it was, then. He borrowed his uncle's car, one that fit the bill: not flashy, far from distinctive, a dark blue that faded into the cityscape and blended well with traffic.

Merin watched Sid watching Nancy tell the story. Though he knew the details intimately, to look at him you would think that this was the first he'd heard them and that it was also the first time he had heard his wife speak, that at this moment he was falling in love. It made her avert her eyes lest he see her intruding on what felt like a private viewing. Unguarded intimacy like this was rare.

You tended to see its uncultured cousin, the public display of what passed for intimacy. Merin no longer blinked at such encounters, which were about as erotic as a butcher's window. She shrugged and moved on, having ignored or missed it completely. Were she to intervene, saying something disapproving, she knew she was as likely to be verbally abused by one partner as the other. That was why this, Sid's adoring gaze for the woman he'd married, was so startling, so unexpected.

"Do you want to know what gave him away?" said Nancy, who was so engaged in bringing her father back to life with her account of his youthful crime that she was unaware of her husband's attention. "He wanted to look tough, so he drove with the window down and his arm hanging out, sleeve rolled up the way he'd seen men do. Except that on that day a woman who worked at the bank and had been across the street on her coffee break at the time of the robbery noticed my father driving by with his bare arm hanging out, dangling against the side of the dark blue sedan, and she thought, 'That fellow will have a filthy arm because of this. Just look at that car. It hasn't been washed since the time of the Flood, it appears.' And also, because the witness's cousin happened to have had his arm ripped off at the elbow in a hay-baling accident on their family farm many years before, she was more sensitive than most, you might say, to that particular danger, and always drove with her windows rolled all the way up regardless of the outside temperature, and certainly never allowed her children to place any part of their body out the window of a moving vehicle.

"Charles 'Chunk' Warburg drove around the block three times, as agreed, not so slowly as to arouse suspicion, changing direction the second time and following a slightly different route on the final circuit, so that he picked up the robbers on the next block over, behind the bank and on the opposite side of the street. He had thought he would drive the rest of the way to wherever they directed him to go; instead, they told him to get out of the car and walk home, their parting words to him, 'For God's sake, don't draw attention to yourself, kid.' They didn't even thank him for doing his part so efficiently. He hit his mark perfectly, pulling up to the curb as they emerged from the alley between the bank and the building next to it. Charles had imagined his role ending with the three of them driving up a lonely lane after dark, arriving at the farmhouse of someone who could be trusted with their secret, hiding the car under hay in a barn, spending the night feeling like and being treated like kings, wealthy ones splitting the take equally three ways, with something generous for the farmer. Instead, he watched the car drive off. He hadn't even asked where and when he would see them again or when he might expect to receive his share and how much that would be. So eager had he been to be part of the caper, to help, to do it right, that he'd forgotten to look after his interest."

"I can't believe he let himself get caught up in such a dangerous, foolish escapade," said Merin.

"That was my father. Even as a little boy, he would decide he was going to do something all on his own, no coercion necessary, certainly not from his parents. And he would quietly carry it out, whatever it was. My grandmother thought the sun rose and set behind her son. I never heard her criticize him, even for taking part in the robbery."

"You haven't told us how he got caught," said Merin. "He walked away, I assume, after his pals fired him as their chauffeur."

"Maybe another day," said Vincent. Vincent the protective. Vincent, perceptive enough to say the equivalent of 'Time for you to go home now. Goodbye,' without it seeming scathingly rude. It was enough, in fact, delivered with gentle but firm, unequivocal humor, to let them all off the hook. They were suddenly strangers again, formal, the thanks and goodbyes at the door more awkward than the hellos. They were aware of what they had committed in reaching back across the years and dragging innocent spouses onto the field, no one quite sure where it was safe to step. It was done, the encounter exhausted now of pretense and best behaviour. They would probably never see each other again, Sid thought, or if they did it would be by chance and burdened by the awareness on both sides of their failure to revive the acquaintance: we didn't call, we've been ultra-busy, Vincent had this thing, Nancy had to go there for that long, so good to run into you again. Was it as impossible as it appeared? The notice of a death, seen by a come-from-away newspaper man who had only recently begun to read obituaries, a random thing (he'd written a few) and then what? Curiosity mostly. Having no recollection of having met Merin's mother, Sid with his condolence announced that he was still thinking about Merin after all those years. It suggested, 'I want you to think well of me and so I send you this message of pretend sorrow over the death of a woman I never knew. I am a selfish man. You wouldn't recognize me now. Let's get together sometime.'

What it didn't answer was the question why. *Why do we expect the intimacy of lifelong friends when really, Sidney, you are a stranger to yourself. A stranger to the twenty-two-year-old you once were, in any case.*

As they walked home, he and Nancy reviewed the evening, opening the smallest, safest parcels first: lovely home; gracious hosts; really liked the taste of that dish, what was its name? It had chopped bok choy, rice-wine vinegar, and something else, something with heat. A patio that size, that's all we'd need. Privacy is key, not necessarily space. He imagined Vincent asking Merin, "How do you think he got caught?" and she replying, "Oh, God, who knows? He was probably so angry he went back into the bank to see if they'd left anything, the double crossers!"

Which, Sid and Nancy knew, was exactly what had happened.

Such a Blunder

The cat scratched to signal to Evan that he wanted the window opened one last time. He figured the animal knew what was up, that the humans were abandoning the old house. It was the only home the big-bellied tabby had known. Mid-October wasn't quite warm enough to leave the window open for more than a few minutes. But then, thought Evan, who would be there to get cold? The new owners weren't taking possession until the first of the month, and the old cat did enjoy watching the leaves take flight. He thought they were moths or birds perhaps, and in anticipation of them he became animated in the windowsill of the little office that looked down over the front porch roof.

He was about to say something to Munster about not leaning too heavily on the window screen, when the cat did just that, pushing the thin aluminum frame out of its housing and leaping out after the screen onto the porch roof.

Evan yelled downstairs, "Can somebody go outside and look for Munster? He's out again." An indoor cat for most of his eleven years, Munster occasionally forgot this fact, tempting speeding cars and urban coyotes only too happy to prey on a docile, eighteen-pound American shorthair.

Evan poked his head out through the window. The screen had slid almost to the edge of the roof, which ran the entire frontage of the house. He would have to climb out to retrieve the screen. Or he could leave it for the new owners to find. The cheapskates, refusing to sign until he and Steph guaranteed they would cover the entire property-tax bill for the year ahead. Demanding not only that there be a full tank of heating oil in place but refusing to let it be added to the agreed-upon selling price of the house. Their son had attended the school the year Evan started as vice-principal. Nobody won battles against people like that. They were always looking for a way to screw you. *Well,* he thought, as he put his right leg out the opening and onto the roof, ducking his head below his shoulders as he squeezed through, *bully for the likes of them!* He'd forgotten to tell them some of the more problematic qualities of the house, which was well built and structurally sound but had water pipes that loved to tryst with frisky tree-roots and which froze in the coldest days of winter if they weren't careful to run an electric heater in the unfinished basement. That and the narrow, crumbling chimney, a functional but poor excuse for a flue. It had been noted by the building inspector, though only the exterior, cosmetic flaws. Structurally the chimney was sound, for the time being. Caveat emptor and all that. When had he turned into his brass-balled father?

He edged closer to the screen, which lay hanging out over the eavestrough. No one, it seemed, had come out to see about Munster. "Hey!" he called. "Anyone down there?"

"What's wrong, Dad?" said Angela. Fourteen, she still reached for his hand whenever they crossed a busy street together. Her sister, Miss Independence, stopped holding his hand when she was six and starting 'real' school, as she had called first grade. Brynne, hyper-attuned to ironic justice, would have been the first to hear her father, the school authoritarian, calling for help from up on the roof of the porch, a perch she and her sister were barred from using.

Steph emerged from under the porch overhang. "Hold on a sec," she said into her phone. She looked up. "What the hell, Evan?"

"Didn't you hear me calling?"

"I'm on the line with the movers. They're running late."

"Munster pushed the screen out. Do you see him down there?"

She held up a hand, palm out. "We would rather not have to hang around waiting for you in the dark." She listened a moment. "Okay, thanks." She hung up. "Morons." Then, to Evan, "He'll come back; he always does."

"He knows we're leaving," said Evan, crouching on the slope to allay the vertigo sweeping over him. "All the signs were there: loss of appetite, accidents outside the litterbox, the days-long disappearances."

"If you ask me, you're more anxious about this move than he is."

"Dad always gets antsy before big life changes." Angie's voice came from somewhere on the porch. He pictured her, suddenly long-legged, clad in her sister's castoff jeans, the overly large hoodie, the asymmetrically cut dark-brown hair, her natural colour after months of a combination of candy-floss pink and shoe-polish black.

"Did anyone look out back?" he asked.

Angie said, "I'll go." He caught only a flash of her as she cantered down the front steps and around the side of the house. When he stood, he felt the wave of dizziness grip him again and he turned towards the window of his study. Falling forward into the slope of the roof, he put out his hands. He misjudged the distance and landed hard on his chin and the heel of one hand. Immediately he began to slide on his stomach, backwards in the direction of the eavestrough. This is not too embarrassing, he thought, as he gained momentum. He was moving too quickly to gain any sort of traction on the slick shingles. The gutter came away in his hands after he had hung from it for an instant, and he was down, landing hard on one foot, which he felt turn over before he tumbled onto his side. The first slash of pain in his foot and ankle subsided into a burning ache.

He saw that he had been lucky not to have landed on the front steps leading up to the porch but beside them in the relatively soft dirt of the flower bed. The window's screen lay under him, its aluminum frame bent along a vertical edge.

Stephanie told him to lie back and not move. "I'm calling EMS."

"No ambulance," he insisted as he tried to stand. Brynne was there on the other side, crouching attentively like her mother but not knowing how to help. Her father had always seemed to her another species, attractively exotic, often annoyingly obtuse, not entirely fathomable. Evan had not prepared her well for the posture-filled world of men, especially when they presented this way, stubbornly suffering, silent or aiming for silence despite the noises coming from them that betrayed discomfort. When she was a little girl, she thought her father indomitable and wise; now, sprawled like this in the dirt, he seemed as immature as a grownup could be. The urge in her to comfort him fought the contradictory urge to scold.

He was saying, "Brynne, if you can hold steady. I'm going to … try leaning my weight on—that's good. Okay. Now lift slowly with your legs. Good girl." She hoped no one she knew was watching. At the same time, she felt proud to be her father's crutch. He rested an arm heavily across her shoulders. He used to carry her on his shoulders. She was slim, as was he—they had each excelled at track and field and cross-country running—and he never appeared to gain weight, much to Stephanie's annoyance. Nevertheless, as Brynne braced to support him, he was heavier than she expected him to be.

A pre-teen rode his bicycle across the sidewalk and onto the lawn, letting his ten-speed fall as he dismounted. "What's wrong with Dad?" he said.

"He fell off the roof. Where have you been all day?" Brynne demanded. Her question bristled with accusation.

"I went riding. How long was I gone for?"

"We could've used the help."

"You said I was getting in the way and was going to break stuff."

Evan stood leaning his weight on Brynne, his injured foot held off the ground. "Trev, do us a favour, please. Tell your mother not to call the paramedics. Or, if she has—"

"Too late," said Stephanie, stepping out of the front door and onto the porch, and peering down at him, her hands resting on her hips.

"It's just a sprain, I'm sure of it."

"And when did you receive your medical degree?"

"Please call them back."

"You can't cancel an ambulance, Evan."

"I'm pretty sure you can," said Brynne, not knowing one way or the other but unable to stop herself. Lately she had been contradicting her mother at every opportunity. Some days she felt that if she did not get away from these aliens soon, she was going to end up strangling them in their sleep.

Angela approached from the opposite side of the house, stepping from the paved driveway onto the front lawn. She had Munster trapped in her arms; her cheek pressed against his barely tolerant head. She held him high, at shoulder level. There was nothing triumphant about the way she re-entered the scene. As if she had become Teutonic in more than the pronunciation of her given name, Angela felt only the animal's distress, at being held against its will, at being outside and vulnerable, at being the only sane being in a family of loud, unpredictable creatures, at being captive in a meaningless universe and knowing in his marrow that he was ageing almost a decade now for every one of his captors' years.

"What were you doing on the roof, Dad? That's so random."

"Trevor, not now," said his mother, unmoved by her husband's request. The phone, as much an extension of her as any article of clothing, was inert in her hand. She had only to catch her youngest daughter's eye to make Angie take Munster into the house. "And could you shut your father's office window, please?"

Uncomfortable as a prop for her father, Brynne found the smell wafting off him enough to make her hold her breath. Why did he wear that same shirt every day? It was a flannel-lined work shirt with double breast pockets that had buttoned down flaps, big enough for everything—pens, wallet, small notebook, reading glasses—and it rarely made it into the laundry basket. It was paint splattered, stained, and funky with stale body odour. She tried turning her face away, but that made him think she wanted him to turn his body with hers. They were facing the house. She made a move to direct them up the stairs and inside the house; he had other ideas.

"The way I see it, there are two people here besides me who can drive. I'm—shit! Ow! Ow!" He lifted the afflicted foot off the ground. "Brynne?" he said, leaving out an entire unvoiced thought, the one that said that her mother, the cruel fitness instructor, wanted him to suffer the indignity of being seen, by their soon to be former neighbours, being loaded into the back of an emergency vehicle and driven with urgent speed at who knew how many hundred bucks an hour into the city for examination and treatment. And say, wasn't this apt retribution for wrenching them once again out of their comfortable life, one that had taken them five years at least to get used to? Get thee to a physician, Principal Mountcastle. Take your rightful medicine.

"Can I ride with Dad?"

"What do you think, Trev?" said his mother.

"Yes?"

"Evan, the movers."

He wasn't sure why she had chosen to mention them then. Had she meant that to fall off the roof of the porch and wreck his foot, at this of all possible moments, was not only a stupendously stupid and preventable thing to have done, but that it contained the seeds of subversion? He was about to say that this was not the result of plotting on his part, when they heard the siren approaching from the north, growing in volume and pitch.

BECAUSE STEPHANIE HAD TO WAIT at the house to meet the moving van, she sent Brynne in her, Stephanie's, car to follow the ambulance. It was everything he deserved, the humiliation of the ride while he lay strapped to a gurney, the wait, later, in dismal chairs made all the more depressing by the people filling them. He was sure that these were perfectly happy, normal folk turned repugnant by their presence in the hospital's ER. When they reappeared, he noticed, those who did come back after being attended to and treated, their entire countenance had changed. They might not be smiling yet, but they were, almost to a person, more relaxed and confident. Those sporting casts, bandages, splints, and slings had irrefutable evidence that their affliction was real and legitimate. These were the ones who seemed most pleased with themselves in their relief to be going home. See, they seem to want to say, I wasn't faking.

Brynne spent most of the five-hour wait texting her friends. From time to time she would sigh, stand, go to the washroom, return, buy something to eat from the vending machine, say something derogatory about the triage system, particularly its lack of fairness, pointing out that people who had arrived after her father were being taken inside to the examination area before he was. They talked about the selection of magazines available in the waiting room: too few, too old, too Boomer oriented. Evan had been given a bag filled with ice cubes to hold against his ankle, and he was able to prop his foot on a pillow placed beside him on the bench. When the ice began to melt and leak, Brynne emptied the plastic bag in the washroom sink. They didn't ask for another. He could have used something pharmaceutical for the pain, which returned once his ankle warmed up. The nurse who responded to his request said that she couldn't administer drugs until after Evan had seen a doctor.

"Do you have anything?" he asked Brynne.

"Why would I have anything, Dad?"

"I don't know. For when you have your period? Your mom usually carries that sort of thing in her purse."

"No, I'm sorry, I don't. And thanks a bunch, Dad. Why don't you speak louder? I don't think those people sitting on the other side of the room could hear you."

"I'm sorry, Brynne."

"Yeah, me too. Why aren't you next? This is totally four-oh-four."

She loved him, but this was turning out to be a disaster of a day. How could he have been so careless as to fall off the roof and why wasn't anyone coming to call his name and how could a perfectly competent man, a school administrator—headmaster they'd call him in the U.K., which was how far away she wished they were moving—how could a man who was going to be boss of everybody commit such a blunder?

The first hour in the waiting room passed more slowly than the next two together. He daydreamed through the fourth, hardly noticing its passing. Was it the ache in his ankle that made him focus elsewhere, as far away from this congregation of the woeful and woe begotten as possible? He was barely aware of Brynne's comings and goings. Despite some early expressions of impatience, she was being stoic about it all. It beat waiting for the moving van at the house, one he imagined she didn't care for all that much, given its exposure on the busy main street, where everybody she knew or cared about could drive slowly past and see what she was up to. Brynne was the most private of the five of them. She fretted intensely about the way others perceived her and would rather no one see her at all than one person catching her in a bad light. No doubt she would have expressed the thought in a different way. He wished she could be as unconscious as her sister was about such matters. Dreamy, inwardly focussed Angie, her ego muffled in layers and levels, the subterranean chambers of her fantasy world.

Evan was beginning to worry about his ankle, which, despite being freed of its running shoe and propped on a pillow and a seat situated perpendicular to his, was throbbing so much that it felt as if it would burst its skin casement at any moment. A nurse approached. Where was Brynne? He was sure his name would be called now, finally. He had lost track of the length of time he had been sitting in wait. He did know that he was the person who had been sitting in that grubby space the longest. He tried to sit taller and to catch her eye. He grinned, closed-lipped, somewhat grimly, to show his forbearance and great willingness to follow orders. Yes, here I am; it has not been all that long a wait, not when compared with a lifetime, the span of a civilization or the age of the planet.

The nurse called someone else. Nobody stirred. Evan looked around, then over his shoulder. This was the limit! His ankle was the only part of his body he could feel now. If a doctor were to come along now and offer to amputate the foot, Evan thought he might consider it. The nurse called the name again. "Mr. Mantolini? Paolo Mantolini?" From the far reaches of the room, behind Evan and in an area that included vending machines, washrooms, and children's play corner, came an indistinct voice followed by another. "Here. He is here," a weak, reedy, elderly woman's voice. The man and woman were as short as children, bent over, appearing motionless. It took them most of a minute to reach the spot where the nurse stood. The man pushed an upright walker that had big spongy fabric taped over the handles. The woman, his wife, Evan assumed, leaned heavily on a metal cane, pharmacy-issue and height adjustable, with a thick rubber tip and ergonomic grip. She wore dress shoes, pumps with collapsed heels, and her ankles and lower legs were so bloated that Evan assumed the shoes were on there for good. Mr. Mantolini had his right hand pressed to his abdomen but in an apparently unconscious gesture, as though he didn't know what else to do with the appendage. By the way the old man minced each step, Evan guessed he was suffering the effects of a rupture. Hernia, perhaps. He thought, why am I even waiting? I'll never be seen or if I finally am they'll think I'm soft, a pussy. Steph used that word, the jock in her seeping out. Don't be a pussy. Man up. Bite the bullet. Suck it up, buttercup.

The Commons

Lionel stood with Evan watching the throng of skaters move counterclockwise around the Commons oval. Brynne skated with her mother; Angela, with her uncle Lester, hand in hand.

Evan said, "You don't have to stand here with me. Go rent a pair of your own."

"I'd rather watch," said Lionel. "My goodness, your girls, they're so…"

"Yeah, I know."

"And the new job? Principal Mountcastle. I suppose I've got to show due deference now."

"It's been fine. A little bumpy the first month or two. I like the school. Strong community support. If you've got that you've got more than half the battle won." He looked down at his foot and ankle in their cast. "And, of course, there was the sympathy vote."

"It's taking, isn't it, a long time, you know, to heal."

"This is my second cast. The bone didn't set right, and they had to—"

"It's all right, you don't have to—"

"—break it again. Reset it."

"—tell me."

"Sorry! They did. It's fine."

Angie called from the center of the ice, "Dad! Watch!" and executed a wobbly spin, her arms bent at the elbow and held tight against the front of her, hands tucked under her chin. She accomplished four rotations, in appreciation of which the men clapped and whistled.

Lionel's eye was caught by a little girl who was being held up by her parents, one to each side. She was wearing a pair of double-bladed skates strapped to her boots. She was not moving her feet, not having fun. He felt his arms being stretched high with hers, the tearing ache underneath, in the armpits, the blood draining from his hands. He predicted she would give this torture one rotation of the ice surface and that would be it.

After skating they gathered at a nearby restaurant. At the next table over was the little girl Lionel had seen, the one learning to skate. She moved from lap to adult lap. It was an old man's turn to hold her. Lionel saw a resemblance in the man to their father, had their father lived another twenty-five years. The grandfather pretended to be put out. She fiddled with his eyebrows, pushing them up and squealing delightedly when he made them dance. *Secretly Grandpa is in love with her*, Lionel mused. *He wants her all to himself. He is glad she's a girl: she doesn't have to live up to inflated expectations. I would have made a good father,* he thought, as the old man sent the tot around the corner of the table and into the arms of a woman who looked like a fashion model. She had large hoop earrings and a smile of perfectly aligned teeth.

The food began to arrive. When Evan shifted his feet under the table, he kicked Steph's skates. She looked down, shifted them under her chair, and went back to whatever she was saying to Brynne. Lionel was talking with Angela, asking her about the music she was listening to, what she liked. Lester was distracted by the people sitting at the table beside them. Lionel broke his brother's reverie when the waiter passed him his plate of eggs. Evan had chosen the restaurant, a breakfast chain he liked, with its bottomless cup of coffee and the artistic way the fruit came arranged on the plate. His daughters weren't so crazy about the greasy eggs and fried meat.

"What time is your appointment?" he asked Lionel.

"In about an hour."

"You got time to make it?"

"Yes, Evan, I have time. It's only three blocks from here. Are you trying to get rid of me?"

"You didn't skate," said Evan. "I assumed you were still under the weather or in a hurry."

"Don't worry about me," said Lionel. "I will make my appointment on time. Worry about your own life."

Brynne looked over at them from the far end of the table. Beside her, Angie was texting on the sly, her phone held just below the edge of the table. Trevor was still at a friend's house after a sleepover.

"What is it you're after, Lionel? What do you want out of life? Lionel, my brother, do you still feel the pain?"

"Dad," said Brynne, "cool it."

"My daughter thinks I'm exceeding the bounds of decorum. She would rather we talked about the food and the weather, or maybe about money. Don't worry, this isn't really me talking, it's the painkillers. No undesirable feelings or felt desires allowed."

"If I thought you cared…" said Lionel.

"When you sit down with your shrink, tell her hi from me, the middle son, monkey in the middle. Peg-leg Pete. Add a howdy-do from our big brother, of course, who I suspect is only here to maintain order, make sure family relations don't spiral out of control. Would you say that's an accurate accounting, Lester? Thank you, by the way, for taking time out of your busy schedule. You know, with fillings. Nothing more than fillings."

"Lester, tell us what's happening with the church," said Stephanie.

"He sold it. Thirty pieces of silver. God's gonna smite him but good."

"Evan, stop. For Christ sake," she said.

"No, for Mammon's."

"Just ignore him."

"Back to my question. What does our illustrious entrepreneur and art dealer want out of life? Now that Pop isn't here to ask, I feel it my duty to."

"If you must know, I'm selling the shop." Lionel removed his glasses and polished them on his napkin. The waitress returned with a carafe of coffee. She gave everyone a refill whether they wanted it or not. "I'd been thinking about it for a while. I guess getting sick kind of sealed it for me."

"Huh. I never pegged you for a quitter, Lionel," said Evan.

"Dad. That's just mean," said Brynne.

"Girls," said their mother, "is there anything you want to see downtown?"

"She doesn't want us to hear the good stuff," said Angie.

Stephanie dug in her purse and extracted some twenties. "Go. Check out Park Lane. Give us another half hour. Forty minutes. Meet you back here."

"Dad, do we have to?"

Evan wanted to leave. Let them stay and gab. He wanted to chew his foot off and vamoose.

"Nobody's calling you a quitter, Lionel," said Lester after Brynne and Angela had left. "Right, Evan?"

Evan looked at Stephanie and said, "I'm done. Let's catch up to them."

"He doesn't mean it, Lionel. You're doing what's right for you. He understands that."

"I can speak for myself," said Evan.

"Yeah, well, you always have," said Lionel as he stood and slung his messenger bag over one shoulder. "Thanks for breakfast. I would offer to treat next time, but the thought of a next time with you, Evan, makes me…"

"Makes you what?"

"Oh, use your imagination, Principal Mountcastle. Or have you abandoned that, too?"

When he was far enough away and out of earshot on the far side of the Commons, Lionel let out a loud, prolonged, angry cry that got lost in the snow and didn't return. It felt draining but liberating to scream like that. He didn't care who might have heard.

Walking on, he thought about his therapist, a young psychologist who reminded him of the kid who used to sit with his dog on the sidewalk in front of the shop and pretend he was homeless. The therapist didn't have a lot of experience, but he listened intently and remembered everything, even things Lionel had forgotten he'd said.

After the session, he had a date to meet Laurel for lunch. He decided he was going to ask her if she was happy in her marriage, and, if she wasn't, which he had suspected for several years now, he was going to offer a suggestion, one that would require a significant change in her situation. He was prepared for her to say no. It wouldn't be the end of the world if she did. They were, after all, each other's oldest friend and would continue to be so. Still, something told him she wasn't happy being the Missus Doctor Gaudry, and that, free of that title, she might join him, Lionel Mountcastle, in a midlife adventure the details of which had yet to coalesce in his mind. If nothing else, it might make her a little less annoying.

Author's Acknowledgements

Heartfelt thanks to the following, without whom this book would not exist: Great Plains Publications, in particular Catharina de Bakker, for her percipient editorial eye and gentle scalpel; Liz Cumyn, for letting me raid her master's thesis for neuroscience terminology; Vivien and Andrew Hamilton, for reminding me that teaching is the highest calling; and Sharon Murphy, for her love and unwavering support.